Permanent Resident at the Purse Table

Permanent Resident at the Purse Table

Keisha Bass

URBAN CHRISTIAN

www.urbanchristianonline.com

Urban Books, LLC
97 N18th Street
Wyandanch, NY 11798

Permanent Resident at the Purse Table Copyright © 2014
Keisha Bass

ISBN 13: 978-1-60162-712-4
ISBN 10: 1-60162-712-2

First Printing February 2014
Printed in the United States of America

10 9 8 7 6 5 4 3 2 1

This is a work of fiction. Any references or similarities to actual events, real people, living or dead, or to real locales are intended to give the novel a sense of reality. Any similarity in other names, characters, places, and incidents is entirely coincidental.

Distributed by Kensington Corp.
Submit Wholesale Orders to:
Kensington Publishing Corp.
C/O Penguin Group (USA) Inc.
Attention: Order Processing
405 Murray Hill Parkway
East Rutherford, NJ 07073-2316
Phone: 1-800-526-0275
Fax: 1-800-227-9604

Permanent Resident at the Purse Table

by

Keisha Bass

*To the women of the world who
see themselves as "less than":
know you are fearfully and wonderfully
made, and perfect in God's eyes.*

The only eyes that matter . . .

For the Lord does not see as man sees; for man looks at the outward appearance, but the Lord looks at the heart.
—I Samuel 16:7

Acknowledgments

Thank You, Lord, for turning my dream into a reality. Someone once said our talent is God's gift to us, and what we do with that talent is our gift to Him. Lord, I hope I am making you proud and giving you the best gift I possibly can. Thank You for using me to glorify who You are.

To my family, Daddy (Art), Linda, A.J., Angel, Chaundra, and Jeff, thank you for all of your unconditional love and support. I thank all my nieces and nephews as well for the laughs and cute memories they give me daily. Special thanks to Angel for reading the entire manuscript in one week and sharing your enthusiasm for my characters with me. And to Chaunie, thanks for helping me find the right words when I couldn't put my finger on exactly what I was trying to say in a unique way and for your assistance with the story's timeline. And to my extended family in Houston, I appreciate all of your encouraging words, especially Aunt Edie who always believed in me and this story, and told me I could when I thought I couldn't. Thank you to all my girlfriends for giving me inspiration to pull from.

To my editor, Joylynn M. Jossel-Ross, thank you for believing in my project from the beginning and understanding exactly what message I wanted to convey. Also, thank you for all your hard work to make my debut novel the best it could be. And to the entire Urban Christian team, I truly appreciate you taking a chance on a first-time author and working to make this book top notch, inside and out. For researching the legal part of this story, I'd like to thank Brittany Gabrielson and Jade Mens. I appreciate your time and effort.

Acknowledgments

Thank you to all the members of North Texas Christian Writers (where I first learned about critique groups) and American Christian Fiction Writers (where I grew in my critique group) for all of your guidance and cheers along the way. Especially to my local chapter, the DFW Ready Writers and the Brainknockers crit group: Janice, Michelle, Lynne, Kellie, Jane, Lyndie, Dana, Jackie, Marilyn, Patty C., Patty G., and Marji. Thank you for working on the "bad teeth," and helping me to grow as a writer. Michelle, your advice has been invaluable. I am grateful for your help every step of way on this journey. And thank you to Cheryl Dawson who's always said she saw this happening all along. Thanks for being my own personal publicist.

To my Word of Truth family, I love being a part of such a genuine church. You are a fun group of people who show their love for God every day. Thanks Pastor Eben and Pastor Sara for leading us in our walk with Christ, and thank you to the entire leadership team who pray for us on a regular basis. It has been a pure joy to fellowship with my WOTFC peeps. Shot out to the Jones True group. You are a special group of women. Thank you for your love, laughs, and prayers.

Thank you to my Crowley ISD friends, especially my H.F. Stevens crew. My students and the faculty and staff have been my personal cheering section and I appreciate your sincere interest in my project.

And finally, I'd like to give a BIG thank you to anyone who purchases this book. I appreciate you giving your time to read the words the Lord put in my heart. I hope this novel challenges your thinking in some way and you enjoy the journey the main characters go on. May you always love who you are in Christ and live out your purpose!

Love and Blessings,
Keisha Bass

Chapter 1

Ava sat next to the waterhole that posed as a lake. Flicking the cool, murky water with her toes, she contemplated her next move. An old Nike shoebox rested across her lap.

Gripping Xavier's sunglasses, she shook her head. "Humph, cheap."

She threw the shades back in the box and picked up the CD of slow songs he'd made for her after an argument. Snapping the CD in two, she tossed the pieces in the shoebox and considered throwing the box, and her memories of him, in the water.

Toni, one of her closest girlfriends, planted the idea in her brain. Toni's words echoed in Ava's mind *Girl, when you see his stuff float away, a calm feeling will overcome you and you'll get closure.*

Ava giggled at her friend's dramatic suggestion and the visual therapy it could provide, but she didn't want to pass her problems on to Mother Nature. The sign that read DON'T MESS WITH TEXAS along with the $500 littering fine also aided in her decision. She walked by a garbage Dumpster on the way to the lake and knew that location would work. *Maybe even better.* Imagining his personal belongings getting crushed at the landfill with the rest of the trash would give her peace.

"Lord, why did I put myself through this again? Last time my heart broke, I said I'd wait on you to bring the right one. Then Xavier showed up, and I jumped into a relationship and into bed with another fool."

She jerked her feet from the water and slid them into her weatherworn sandals. "Okay, Lord. I will listen to your voice. I will wait on you to bring that special man." Ava stood and picked up the box. "In fact, I declare celibacy right here and now. I pray for the man you have picked out for me. And Lord, while I'm praying for stuff, can you help me lose about fifty pounds?" She chuckled. "You know, so I can feel comfortable in my own skin when the right man does show up. Thank you for everything you do. In Jesus' name."

God had to be listening and He'd answer her prayers, but she knew He moved in His timing. Ava just wanted to know when that would be. She tucked the box under her arm as tears began to race down each side of her face. Wiping her tears with her free hand, she turned her back on the lake idea.

The Dumpster loomed about twenty yards ahead of her, but the stench hit her nose before she could take another step. As she got closer, the purpose of her actions became more real. *I will not rush into anything next time. I will follow God's leading.* When she arrived at the Dumpster, she turned the box upside down and shook out the contents. She chucked the box on top of the trash, slapped her hands clean, and walked away. Ava could admit to herself she would miss Xavier, but knew she wouldn't be missing much.

Ava heard footsteps coming up the stairs that led to her apartment. She hurried to the door because she knew if Toni and Rene were alone for any amount of time, a conflict might arise. With a tired grin and glass of red wine, she pulled the door open.

Toni, gasping for air, leaned against the doorframe. The department store dress bag hung off the edge of her arm, ready to fall to the ground. "Girl, why don't you move to the first floor? This is a mess."

Rene giggled.

"What are you hee-heeing about?" Toni rested her hand on her scrawny hip.

"If you would do some cardio like I keep suggesting you do, these stairs wouldn't be such a problem." Climbing the three flights of stairs to Ava's third-floor apartment hadn't been a problem for Rene.

"And like I keep suggesting to you, you know where you and your suggestions can go." Toni found enough breath to laugh.

Ava dropped her head. *Here we go.*

Toni hugged Ava and sashayed into the living room. "Plus, I don't need to work out. I look good."

"Well, you didn't look so good coming up those stairs. I didn't know if I needed to help you up the steps or find the nearest oxygen mask." Rene passed by Toni, touching her shoulder. "And anyway, it's not about looking good, Toni. It's about how you feel. Being healthy. As a model, you should know that."

Ava folded her arms across her plump body. *I wonder what she thinks of me.*

"I hear you, Rene. I'll get my workout on one day. But I really don't need to." Her hands traveled down her silhouette. Smiling, she said, "I was born with all this fineness and I feel just fine. Thank you very much."

Ava, sporting black Capri pants and a burgundy blouse that had trouble keeping her cleavage hidden, followed Toni to the mauve-colored couch and plopped down. "I can't believe I finally let you two talk me into going out. I guess nagging does work."

Toni took a deep breath. "Girl, please. It's ladies' night. Which equals us gettin' in free and beaucoup of men lined up to get in like they were handing out free Super Bowl tickets. You need to forget about Xavier and we're going to help you."

"And the best part: two-dollar margaritas 'til ten o'clock. You know they try to get us faded so they can talk us into giving up our good stuff." Rene looked at her watch. "And we only got a little over an hour until ten, so I hope you're ready, Ava."

"Me? I'm as ready as I'm going to get." Ava had worked for an hour to put herself together enough to look halfway hip. She pointed at Toni. "What about her?"

Toni lifted the department store plastic off her dress. "It'll just take me a minute."

"We've heard that before." Rene strolled into the kitchen and poured herself a glass of wine.

"I'm serious. I don't have to do my hair 'cause it's already done. Just give me five minutes." She grinned. "Ten at the most."

Ava ran the tips of her fingers through Toni's hair. Toni was perfect from head to toe. "Your hair is cute. Did you get it cut?"

"Just got my ends trimmed," Toni said.

Returning to the living area, Rene waved her hand at Ava. "Hey, don't talk to her. You'll stop her progress."

"You're right." Ava turned toward Rene. "So you're here on time? What gives?"

"Ha, ha, ha. I can barely hold in my laughter." Rene moved over to the loveseat across from Ava.

"Just saying, that's just so out of character." Ava enjoyed calling her friend out.

"I rode with Toni. She was nice enough to pick me up."

Ava widened her eyes. "Well, I guess we are all doing things out of character tonight."

"Leave me out of it." Toni fumbled with the dress tags.

Ava tried to cross her legs like Rene but gave up. The stress pulling on her thighs was too much. Maybe one day she'd win the battle, but for now, she'd have to sit like a boy. She chose comfort over appearance. "Why did Toni need to pick you up?"

"Don't ask." Rene leaned back.

"Too late. I already did." Ava knew Ishmael, Rene's fiancé, had to be involved some kind of way, but she didn't want to speculate out loud.

Toni pulled her shirt over her head and slipped on the black form-fitting dress. Ava tried not to stare enviously. She sucked in her stomach. Glanced down. No change. She'd never have Toni's abs and it wasn't fair. She did sit-ups every night. Well, every other night when she remembered, but still no results.

Jumping in before Rene could answer, Toni said, "Girl, you know she let Ishmael use her car to handle his *business.*" She bent her index finger and middle finger on both hands to symbolize sarcastic quotation marks.

"So, not that it's any of your *business.*" Rene returned the same gesture. "He went to see his son."

Raising her eyebrows, Toni scowled. "You let your man of what, not even six months, take *your* car to go see his baby's momma at *her* house?"

"His baby, not his baby's momma. And it's been nine months. We've been engaged for six, Ms. Know-it-all. Plus, he had Shanice drop Isaiah off at his mom's house."

"Do you really think he'd go through all that movin' around when he can just slide on over there and kill two birds with one stone?" Toni slipped on her heels as she seemed to enjoy pushing the subject further.

Tapping her foot on the plush carpet, Rene glared at Toni. "Those are the words that came from his mouth."

"And you believed him?" Toni looked in the mirror over Ava's barstools to fix any out of place hair.

"His car is in the shop." Rene folded her arms. "Why shouldn't I believe him?"

"I'll leave that alone." Toni scurried into Ava's bedroom.

"Good." Rene turned to Ava. "So, what's up with Xavier? Is he still bugging you?"

Ava was glad the hassle between her friends finally came to an end. "Not since I hung up on him earlier. He actually wanted to make Valentine's plans."

"No, he didn't." Rene rolled her neck. "What'd you say?"

"I said I hung up on him, didn't I? I guess he doesn't believe I'm for real this time. I thought he was the one, too. Well, I wanted him to be. But I finally realized if he really loved me like he said he did, he wouldn't make me feel bad about myself all the time." Ava set her glass on the coffee table. The wine wasn't helping her relax like she'd hoped.

Rene reached over and patted Ava's leg. "Good for you for kicking him to the curb."

"And it didn't help that phone numbers popped up in his pants, jacket, gym bag. Basically, if it had a pocket, he hid a number in it." Ava puffed out air, vibrating her lips. "I want a husband, but dang, is it that hard to find everything I want in a man I can trust?"

"To me it looks like he wanted to get caught. There is this new thing called a cell phone. He didn't think to put the numbers in his phone?" Rene frowned.

"The bad part is he had two phones. Playa move if I ever saw one. I guess he thought since I used his phone sometimes to get on the Internet, he'd better play it safe. But instead of safe, I see he was just sorry."

Ava pictured Toni in her full-length mirror, checking out how her new dress draped over her slim frame. Toni yelled from behind the door, "I really don't know what to tell you guys, except all men are dogs and you can't trust any of them. Get the good stuff when you need it and expect nothing more. Now that might not be a pretty answer, but it's the truth."

"Not all men are dogs, Toni," Rene defended the opposite sex. "I found a good one."

Toni stuck her head around the partially open door of Ava's bedroom. "Woof, woof!"

Ava bit her lip, but soon busted at the seams in laughter. Ishmael, at times, did resemble a pit bull.

Rene raised her voice. "There are some good men out there, Ava. Toni's just upset with Eric. You know he called her today, too."

"He did? What did he have to say?" Ava picked up her glass from the coffee table and walked into the kitchen to set it on the counter.

"Not a dern thang." Toni strutted out of the bedroom as if she were on the catwalk. "He wanted to come by and see me. Talk things over before I filed for divorce."

"And your answer was?" Ava hoped for a no.

"Heck naw! All I can think about is him and that girl in my bed. I don't think I'll ever get that image out of my mind. Can't trust him. So what's the use?" Toni primped in front of the mirror. Again. "I needed this time apart to get my thoughts together and financial affairs in order before I filed."

"I can understand that." Ava straightened her clothes. Glad for the elastic in the waist, but the pants seemed to have shrunk in the legs and backside. *Did I wash these in hot water?* "Let me know if he ever decides to pop up over your house again without calling. We got your back."

"Yeah, I know." Toni offered an uncertain giggle.

"Sounds like he was singing the same song Xavier was. What is it with men? They don't know they want to be with you until after they've messed up? Can't they figure that out before?"

Toni folded the clothes she came in wearing and packed them in her bag. "You know the saying: you don't truly love something 'til it's gone. Something like that."

Ava eyed Toni's dress, then Rene's outfit, and decided she looked more like their mother. She should stay home. But they would be upset with her if she backed out now. *Skinny wenches.* They would never understand what it felt like to sit and watch the party going on, and not be a part of it. Men skimmed over Ava like bad fruit in the produce section. While Rene and Toni, ripe for the picking, were asked to dance, Ava kept an eye on their purses. Which was ironic, since Ava never carried a purse herself.

Rene's size-six frame fit into any piece of clothing she chose to wear. She dressed cool and sophisticated, and her confidence led her everywhere—from top of her class in high school to passing the bar exam the first time to becoming a state prosecuting attorney. And in between, men not only threw themselves at her feet, but kissed them while they were down there.

Ever since Toni was a little girl, people told her she should model. With her size-two build, she posed for countless print magazines and glided down runways all over the country. No word could express the amount of self-confidence and poise that ran through Toni's body. She commanded attention. And got it.

Ava, on the other hand, just wanted to get through the day without a stranger looking at her sideways. She saw Toni and Rene as movers and shakers while she viewed herself as someone who had a lot that moved and shook.

Ava silently hated on Toni's look, but offered a compliment. "Toni, lookin' good, chick. Whatcha tryin' to do? Catch one of those so-called 'dogs' you were just talking about?"

"No. I'm just doing me. I'm not looking to catch but can't help it if I do."

Rene swallowed her last sip. "She talks a big game, but she knows she can't wait to get a hold of another man's good stuff now that she's done with Eric."

"Why y'all keep saying 'good stuff'?" Ava lowered her brow.

"That's Toni's new phrase for some exceptionally decent loving."

"Go ahead, Toni, give me the full explanation."

"Glad to." Toni smiled. "It's code for relations with a man so good to you, the first taste you get you think you're in love."

"I don't know about all that now." Ava shook her head. "It just doesn't get that good."

"You know, the good stuff." Toni nodded as her eyes fluttered. "Loving so perfectly amazing, it has you doing stuff you normally wouldn't do."

Ava's curiosity stepped in. "Oh yeah, stuff like what?"

Toni, wearing a mischievous grin, fixed her eyes on Rene. "Like letting your man use your car to go to his baby's momma's house!"

After Ava and Toni saw Rene thought the punch line was funny, their smirks grew into booming laughter. Toni always found a way to get her point across. And usually, some humor was involved.

Rene's light caramel-colored skin transformed into a flushed red. "His stuff is good. I give up, Toni. You win."

When the laughter died down, Toni and Rene grabbed their purses. Ava watched her friends put their purse straps over their shoulders. *Guess I'll be babysitting you both at the table a little later.* She stuffed her house key and ID in her pants pocket, and secured her cash in her size forty double Ds, and they paraded out the door.

As Toni drove down Loop 610, Ava couldn't help herself. "So I guess Eric had the good stuff and then some? 'Cause I gotta tell you, Toni, you were trippin' behind that fool."

Toni spoke with assurance. "Man, please, I was not trippin'."

"Not trippin'?" Ava and Rene questioned simultaneously.

"How about the time you called me at four in the morning, might I add, on a work night?" Ava put her right hand
up to her ear, using the pinky and thumb to simulate a
phone. "Yelling, 'this no-good-for-nothing poor excuse
of a man hasn't made it home yet, Ava! He better be glad
too, 'cause if he were here, I'd kill him!' Had me on the
other end of the phone trying to calm you down." She
turned her attention to Rene. "I wish you could've heard
her, Rene."

"I remember the story," Rene proclaimed from the
back seat. "And I remember she lost fifty cool points
behind all that mess, too. Come to find out he'd passed
out drunk at his sister's house."

"Okay, okay, you got me." Toni raised her hands in
surrender. "That's a perfect example of what I mean by
good stuff. But shoot, you would've done the same thing
if you thought your man was laying up with some female.
Who would have known a few months later it would take
place in my own house? Isn't it ironic?" She hummed a
familiar tune. "Don't you think?"

Hating she'd brought it up, Ava touched Toni's shoulder. "You okay?"

"Yep, I'm cool." Toni poked out her lips. "I just wish I'd
read the extremely bright signs. Especially the fact that
he became very jealous, which he never was before. He
was so concerned with my whereabouts and who I was
with when he was the one off doing dirt."

Ava nodded. "That's usually how it happens."

"I'm going to go ahead and file for the divorce Monday
morning." Toni sighed. "I can't stand the sight of him."

Rene leaned forward and stuck her head between Ava
and Toni's seats. "Let me know if you want my homegirl
to handle it for you. She'll get him for everything he
owns."

Ava tilted her head toward Toni. "You sure you wanna go out?"

"I'm driving, ain't I? You couldn't pay me to stay home tonight." She ran her fingers through her hair. "You just beware of that good stuff that'll get thrown your way, Ava, because we don't need you trippin'.'"

The corners of Ava's lips turned down. They weren't putting that on her. "I don't think it gets that serious. And earlier today I had a revelation. If I stop dealing with fools, I might find what I'm looking for. Or better yet, it might find me. So I decided to be celibate."

"What?" This time Toni and Rene questioned her simultaneously.

"Y'all heard right, and don't make fun of me either. I'm for real. I'm tired of falling for the same type of guys. The hit it and quit it brothas. I've fallen for them before, thinking I can change them. They end up changing me. Plus, you're supposed to wait until you're married. I'm going to wait for the right man." Ava glanced out the window. "And I'd be willing to bet he's not at Club Jams. Clubs are always filled with men who think they are God's gift to women. So, I'm not looking for any good stuff. Just good music, good friends, and good drinks."

"Okay, Ms. Thang. You just watch. You haven't been given any of that stuff that can make you go way left." Rene sat back in her seat. "I remember when I first slept with Ishmael. I was up the next morning making him breakfast. Ready to help him find another job and everything so he could move on our side of town."

They all giggled.

Toni stuck her finger out at Ava. "And when you do get some of that good stuff, you'll be callin' *me* at four in the morning."

Ava's neck moved with every word. She was the strongest of the three women. At least when it came to cutting a man off. "The devil is a lie. I don't see myself acting crazy over any man."

"Oh yeah? It happened to me." Toni pointed her thumb backward. "It's happening to Rene. And you know how we like to do things together."

"Nope. Not this chick." Didn't they know her track record? Ava was stronger than her friends.

"Never say what you won't do." Rene validated their point with a cliché.

"Sure enough, I didn't think I'd be up before dawn investigating Eric's whereabouts, looking like the spokes-woman from hell the next morning. Bags all under my eyes. I called in sick and almost missed out on getting paid." Toni pulled into the crowded parking lot. "Lucky for me, they were willing to reschedule. That was not my finest hour and I pray we don't see drama like that again."

Ava winked at Toni. "Amen to that."

In her heart, Ava believed every word that shot out of her mouth. Being the fool behind a man wasn't her style. She longed for the man of her dreams and desired to wait on him. And she trusted she would do just that.

But couldn't be certain.

Chapter 2

Ava studied the intricate braided leather straps on Toni's purse. *I'm ready to go.*

She looked at her watch, then at Toni with her fourth partner on the dance floor. If Toni had a dance card, she'd be well on her way to having it completely filled. Ava tried not to feel jealous, but she didn't need a full card to be thrilled. One dern dance would've made her night.

Several men had asked Rene to step out on the floor, but she turned them down. Her focus was still on Ishmael. Ava watched her friend leave the table, phone in hand, and head to the restroom. No doubt phoning the man. Why couldn't she leave that sucka alone and enjoy hanging out with her girls? Rene could move on just like Ava did.

Sitting at the table alone, she had to be the picture of pathetic, but doubted that anyone even noticed her. Ava ordered another drink from the waitress parading by every couple of minutes. Her plan was to replace her insecurity with alcohol. Margarita and piña colada wouldn't judge.

Her groove thang longed to do some shaking, yet every man who approached her vicinity showed interest in another woman, simultaneously stealing a fragment of her self-esteem. What was wrong with her? Sure she was a little overweight, but she was a good person. And with such a pretty face. At least that's what her mom always said.

There Toni was all hugged up with Mr. Somebody's palms nestled on the lower part of her back. She stood close to him, thin and perfect, grooving to the beat. How nice that must've felt. The touch of his strong hands and warm embrace, the answer to security. Ava longed for strength, security, and serenity in the men she dated. But what she got was sarcasm, secrecy, and stupidity. She could use another drink.

Rene marched back to the table and reclaimed her seat. "You ready to go home?"

Are you kidding? About two hours ago! "Girl, I've been ready."

"You want me to go get Toni so we can bounce?"

Ava sipped her drink and glanced at Toni's radiant smile. With the divorce looming, she wouldn't have much of a chance to enjoy herself like this for a while. "No, I don't want to rush her if she's having a good time."

Rene rummaged through her purse, pulling her lipstick out to refresh her lips.

Toni walked up with her partner right on her heels. "What y'all doing?"

Watching you dance. Oh yeah, and taking great care of your purse. "Nothing," Ava replied.

"Well, good then, I'm not interrupting. I have someone I want you guys to meet." Toni rubbed the arm of the handsome gentleman. "This is Roderick."

Ava and Rene shook Roderick's hand. His captivating light brown eyes drew Ava in. The broad shoulders and trimmed goatee against his mahogany skin didn't hurt one bit. In a way, he reminded her of Eric. But she would never share that with Toni.

An equally handsome man sauntered up behind Roderick. Both men could've graced the runways all over the world for years to come. "Hi, ladies, I'm Jason."

The trio of ladies smiled. Jason nodded in Ava's direction, but rested his attention on Rene. This was nothing new. In fact, it was getting old. Maybe she needed to get some uglier friends. She recalled the day Xavier approached her in the frozen food section of the grocery store. It was just her and her grocery list. Yep, to receive a man's attention, Toni and Rene needed to be MIA.

"It's nice to meet you both." Roderick placed his hand on Toni's back. "You all are a bunch of lovely women. Can my boy and I buy you ladies a drink?"

Toni gazed into Roderick's eyes. "No, thank you. I'm the designated driver tonight. But I could show you another move or two on the dance floor."

"Sounds like a plan to me." Leading her to an opening in the crowd, Roderick cupped Toni's hand in his. They already resembled a couple.

Jason scooted close to Rene. "How 'bout you? Would you like to dance?"

"No, I'm good." Rene pulled out her phone.

He didn't budge and acted as if he was interested in the happenings in the club, yet his eyes frequently traveled back to Rene.

I'm sitting here too, fool! The temptation to tell the joka off mounted, but all that came out was, "You want to walk around a bit, Rene? My behind hurts."

Rene closed her cell phone. "Sure."

They hopped down out of the tall chairs, pushing away from the pub-style table. Jason attempted to help Rene down, but she raised a hand. He backed away; then as Ava and Rene strolled around the club, he stuck to her friend like a leech on unclothed skin.

Ava kept her eyes focused on the floor. If she did happen to lock eyes with a man, it was for a millisecond. This was just one of the things she didn't like about herself. She knew men were attracted to confident women, but she was more at ease staring downward.

If a man looked at her and didn't smile—or, even worse, laughed—she didn't know if her cracked ego could take it. The floor wouldn't do that to her. The hardwood proved stable, consistent, and nonjudgmental. Xavier had chipped away at her self-image enough the past few months. She may have not looked confident, but the floor didn't care about her being overweight.

Toni leaned into Roderick as the rhythm slowed, loving the smell of his spicy cologne tickling her nose. Attraction resonated between them and he seemed nice enough, but how much could she really tell about him by a couple of dances? She put her lips to his ear. "So what do you do for living, Roderick?"

"I'm a production assistant for a local TV station. And you?"

At least he has a good job. "I'm a model."

"I didn't ask you what you looked like." He chuckled. "I was asking, what is your line of work?"

She smirked at him. "Very smooth. But I am a model. Mostly print work in some fashion magazines. And I have a few runway shows under my belt."

"Sounds exciting."

"It is." She readjusted her grip around his neck and snuggled her cheek close to his shoulder. How comforting and natural. Almost familiar. If she didn't know any better, she'd think Eric had slipped in Roderick's position when she blinked. "But what I really want to do is design my own line of clothing."

"Why don't you?"

"I'm working on it. I've taken some courses at the Fashion Institute and am finishing up a business course online. Hopefully, I'll be putting my stamp on the fashion industry sooner rather than later."

"Beauty and brains. I guess you have all the fellas knocking at your door."

You can knock on my door anytime. She smiled. "Maybe a few here and there."

"Yeah, right, a few. I guess you got all the game, huh?"

"Not all of it. Just enough." Toni winked at him.

He moved closer to her and whispered in her ear, "What other games do you like to play?"

She leaned back, tapped her index finger on her chin and said, "Mmm, let's see. Spades, dominoes, and on occasion, Monopoly."

They shared a laugh as the music stopped. Roderick slipped his arm around her waist and guided her off the dance floor. Toni wondered if this would be the last she'd see of him, or if he would pursue her. She hoped the latter. Roderick was one she would like to know better. Who knew, he could be the one to take Eric's place.

Ava, Rene, and Jason returned to find their previous spot occupied so they chose a different booth. Ava moved her watch around her wrist to view the time.

Toni bounced into the booth. "Hey, Ava, you 'bout ready?"

"Yep," Ava replied. *I was ready to go five minutes after we got here. I could be at the house, chillin' with a bowl of ice cream and a movie.*

"I'm ready to roll too." Rene fumbled with her phone.

Roderick covered Toni's hand with his. "Why don't we all go to breakfast? My treat."

Ava hoped Toni's answer was a polite no. She didn't want to have to take a cab home, but she was not about to sit and watch the two men flirt with her friends, making her feel less than desirable. Even if a free breakfast was involved.

Toni lowered her eyes. "I don't know. It's almost two in the morning and I have to work tomorrow."

"You have to work on a Sunday?" He stepped back.

"Well, I fly out to Miami tomorrow. That's a model's life. Go when and where the money is. But I had a nice time. We must do this again."

"Okay. I understand. I had a nice time as well. How about you give me your number, so I can call you and we *can* do this again?"

"Why, of course." Toni batted her eyelashes.

Ava could've thrown up right there on the table. His words, enticing and suave, seemed to send Toni back to her giddy schoolgirl days. Ava just hoped she would wait awhile before testing the waters. Toni wasn't divorced yet.

Roderick took his phone out of the inside pocket of his blazer.

Toni snatched it, dialed her number, and pushed the green lit button. "Now you have my number. Don't lose it. Use it."

Roderick displayed his pearly whites. "You know I will."

Ava handed Toni her purse and only received a thank-you in return. No payment or anything. Even young teenagers made five dollars an hour for their babysitting jobs.

They all exited the club. As soon as they were out the doors, Rene flipped her phone back and stepped away, making another call. *Will she ever give up on Ishmael? She should let him and all of his issues go.* Ava knew Rene could do much better.

Feeling someone behind her, Ava turned and got a dose of Jason's Jack Daniel breath. He must've finally given up on Rene, and decided to switch his efforts in another direction: her. "So, Ava, what are your plans for the rest of the night? Or should I say morning?"

"Excuse me?" Disgust filled Ava. *Is this fool serious?*

"What? Just wanted to know if you felt like having some company." He lowered his chin and looked up at her under expressive eyebrows. The sultry expression reminded her of some cartoon, but she didn't feel much like laughing.

"Oh, I see. Since Rene isn't interested, you want to try to bring your game my way?" He could think again. Ava wasn't about to have leftovers or last-ditch efforts.

Jason pleaded his case with a devilish smile and a smooth response. "No, it's not like that. I just wanted to know if you wanted to have a little fun. Maybe I can tuck you in?"

Anger rose in her belly. "Are you kidding me? You barely talked to me all night and all of a sudden I'm who you want to go home with?"

"We're both adults. I don't see anything wrong with hanging out. And if we happen to engage in a little physical activity"—he shrugged his shoulders—"so be it."

"You don't even try to hide the fact that all you want is sex. I don't get it. But what you ain't getting is this." She pointed both index fingers at her body. "You can move around and go tuck yourself in." At that point, Ava wished she did carry a purse, so she could have something to knock him over the head with.

She shuffled her steps to catch up with Rene, who was yelling into her phone. Ava couldn't remember the last time she suffered so much humiliation. Oh, yeah. There was Xavier and all of his sadistic splendor.

When they reached the car, Toni hit the unlock button on her key chain. As she drifted a bit past the car with Roderick, Ava and Rene settled into their seats.

After Rene hung up the phone, Ava turned to her. "Everything okay?"

Rene nodded her head, but looked out the window.

Watching Toni and Roderick share an extended hug, Ava longed for that alluring embrace.

Toni hopped into the car and slowly drove her Cadillac through the parking lot. "What'd y'all think of Roderick? He seems cool, right?"

Ava shook her head. "He seems cool, but his friend is a straight-up sucka."

Rene backed up Ava's claim. "Sure was. I kept telling him I was engaged and even showed him the ring. He didn't seem to care. What was he talking to you about, Ava?"

"Can you believe he actually had the audacity to try to 'tuck me in tonight' as he put it?"

"Are you serious? Well, he seems nothing like Roderick." Toni sat quiet for a moment. "I hope he's nothing like his friend."

"I hope so too. For your sake." Ava moved the air vent toward her, trying her best to cool her temper and the sweat beading down the sides of her face from the walk to the car. "You plan on seeing him again?"

"I might. Especially since I feel like I can't trust Eric anymore. He's the only man I've been with since high school. I need to explore and see what else is out there."

Ava hoped Toni wasn't moving too fast. A breakup took time to heal, especially a broken marriage.

"I say go for it." Rene fidgeted with her cell phone, her look troubled. "He may have the good stuff you're looking for. And who knows, Ava, Jason may've had it too."

"Well, I won't be the one to find out. But even if he does have the good stuff, ain't no telling how many chicks he's shared it with." Ava didn't want to ask, but she couldn't hold the question back. "And will y'all please tell me, is it me?"

Toni exited the freeway to Ava's apartment. "What are you talking about?"

"After Rene turned him down, what made Jason immediately want to come to me and see if he could get into my pants? I mean, maybe it's me. Why do I attract these types of guys?"

"It's not you, Ava. Don't even think that. You are worth more and deserve more. He's just one jerk. There are some good ones out there." Rene's assurance wasn't working.

"I told you all men are dogs. And they stay in heat." Toni smirked. "No, Ava, I'm only joking. Don't let that one fool get you down. He ain't nobody! Remember, you're waiting for the right one. And obviously he's not it."

"I know y'all are right, but it just runs me hot. I finally get approached by a man tonight and all he wants is sex." She smacked her lips. How could her friends relate when they didn't have the same problem? "Do I have a sign on my head that reads OPEN FOR BUSINESS?"

Toni squinted her eyes toward Ava's forehead. "I don't see anything. But I can't be sure. I need to keep my eyes on the road. You may want to have Rene take a look. You know she's the avid reader."

Everyone laughed as Toni pulled in front of Ava's apartment. Ava got out of the car, and said good-bye to her friends. As they drove off, she wondered if there was something wrong with her. Why did men seem to pick her out for the wrong reason?

Still upset with Jason's poor choice of pickup lines, Ava was proud of how easily she turned him down. A few weeks ago she might have allowed him to keep talking until she gave in to his plea just to feel close to someone, but not tonight.

As she changed out of her club attire and into her granny gown, she thought about her prayer earlier by the lake and couldn't believe how soon the enemy tried to cancel her promise to God. He was working all the time, but he couldn't even wait a full twenty-four hours to try to throw her off of her celibacy game.

She could mull over her situation better with a package of Oreos and a big glass of ice-cold milk. After getting her snacks and retreating to her bedroom, she turned on the TV and flipped through the channels. Alone again. Did she really do the right thing? Jason was a good-looking man. *Wait. Of course I did. Focus.*

Even though her body may have welcomed an advance from an attractive man like Jason, she did know she was worth more. And not only did she deserve more, she wanted more. She also hoped if she stood strong in her convictions, the perfect man for her would eventually cross her path. If he truly was out there, she didn't mind waiting a little longer for God to help him find his way to her.

Chapter 3

Ava stared at the ceiling from her warm bed. Church started in an hour, but her thousand-thread count sheets invited her to stay longer. Her mother's words bounced around in her head. *If you can stay out all night, you can definitely have your behind in a church pew somewhere on Sunday morning.* She imagined her mother's facial expression and finger pointing. Sneering at the thought, she released a deep breath, and then popped out of bed and got dressed.

As she drove to the House of the Lord Baptist church, many reasons to turn around and jump back under the covers ran through her mind. She continued in spite of her thoughts. About ten minutes later, as folks from all walks of life filed into the sanctuary doors, Ava wore guilt on her face, along with a stylish purple hat. She could still smell the club smoke in her hair, and wanted the hat to do its job of hiding the unpleasant odor. Several hugs and hellos were passed out, and then she took her seat toward the back.

After the choir belted out a few powerful numbers, and the collection plate had been passed around, Pastor Monroe traveled to his place in the pulpit. His wife, Sandra, gazed at him from the front row.

"Today, I'd like to talk to you about being a lukewarm Christian."

A couple of amens and hallelujahs were shouted toward the front. Ava's backside and shoulders descended into her seat.

Pastor Monroe cleared his throat. "The scripture reads in Revelation 3:15–16, 'I know your deeds that you are neither cold nor hot. I wish you were either one or the other. So, because you are lukewarm, neither hot nor cold, I am about to spit you out of my mouth.' That's from the New International Version." He wiped his brow with his starched handkerchief. "Congregation, God is asking you to choose Him, or choose the world. Living a double life does not please Him. He can't use you to move His Kingdom forward."

In order to fit in with the rest of the congregation, Ava shook her head and raised her hand at every other phrase. Pastor Monroe's eyes came her way on occasion. She wanted him to look somewhere else. Anywhere else. Thoughts of who else needed to hear this message comforted her.

Maybe I'll get the CD of this sermon for Rene and Toni. She brainstormed a couple of more names and completed a mental grocery list, then realized the service was coming to a close. An associate pastor led an altar call for those who desired to get saved. Ava picked up her Bible and straightened the strap on her sandal.

When the doors of the church opened, she hustled through the lobby, past the floral arrangements and crowd of folks congregating in the lobby. Her feet moved faster than they did when she arrived. She didn't need anyone asking her how things were going. Especially since things weren't going anywhere.

As she turned on the air in her car and adjusted her seat belt, her cell phone's buzz startled her. Rene's photo appeared on the screen.

"Hey, Ava. What's going on?"

"Not much, girl. Just leaving church." The pride inside rose in her chest. Among her close group of girlfriends, Ava was the one who attended church on a somewhat regular basis. She had Rene and Toni beat in that area at least.

"How was the service?"

Ava pulled out of the parking lot. "Good. It was one of those messages where you feel like the preacher's talking directly to you."

"Yeah, I know exactly what you mean. But it probably just felt like that. I should've had my backside in the seat next to you."

"Well, maybe in the seat next to the seat next to me. You know I'm saving one for my future husband."

Rene giggled.

"So what's up?" Ava believed there was more to Rene's phone call. She could hear it in her voice.

Rene's laughing ceased. "Ishmael's got me going through some things."

"Anything I can help you with?" Ava turned the volume up on her cell. What had he done now?

"Well." Rene paused. "I need a ride to this towing yard over off 59. I need to get my car."

"Get your car? Didn't Ishmael have it last night? Where was he that he got your car towed?"

Rene's deep sigh spoke volumes. "At some apartment complex. He says he didn't see the signs about visitor parking."

"At some apartment complex?" Ava rolled her eyes. An apartment complex and his mother's house were two different spots. With Ishmael, plans constantly changed. Would Rene ever get tired of that? "I thought he was at his mom's house."

"As did I. I don't know, girl. I just want to get my car. Can you take me?" Rene sucked her teeth. "Ishmael's car is still in the shop."

"Of course. I'll be there shortly." Ava double-checked that she hit the end button on her phone before she spoke.

"I can't believe this. What is his problem?" Tension built up in her as she made a U-turn. "Lord, if Ishmael is not the man for Rene, please remove him from her life. She seems to have more bad days than good ones with him. Your will be done. Amen."

Right when Ava was her loneliest, God had a way of sending her a gentle reminder of what she could be going through if she'd still been attached to Xavier. She might have missed the companionship, but she didn't miss the drama.

When Ava arrived at Rene's house, her stomach growled at her. She should've stopped off on the way and got something to eat. Rene leaned back on the wooden bench on her front porch, sporting thick black sunglasses. Walking with determined steps, she opened the car door, slid in, and looked at Ava as if she wanted to bring the phrase "cuss like a sailor" to life.

Ava backed out of the driveway, not sure if she should say anything; but something in her needed more details. "So what does Ishmael have to say about your car?"

"He said something about meeting one of his club-promoting homeboys to pick up some flyers for a concert next week."

"Mm-hmm."

"Yeah, I know. I'm an idiot." Rene rubbed her fingertips back and forth over her pant leg.

"You're not an idiot. You trust him to do what he says he's gonna do." *Even though he never does it.*

Rene's shoulders elevated. "I guess. I'm just getting tired of plans changing. It's always something. If it's not baby momma issues, it's the club promoting thing, or his janky car breaking down. Not to mention his momma. She's a nice lady, but she stays in his business. I just don't know if this is something I want to be married to for the rest of my life."

Recalling her prayer for Rene just twenty minutes earlier, Ava gave God an internal smile. "Well, do you know how much it will cost to get your car out?"

"Not sure. But he said he'd pay me back. With interest."

"I'm sure he will." *Yeah, right.* When had Ishmael ever paid her back for anything? He'd picked up the bill on frustration and aggravation many times over, but paying in cash was not his forte.

Rene put her hand on top of Ava's. "Please don't say anything to Toni. I can't take her right now. That's why I didn't say anything last night."

"Last night?" Ava frowned in confusion.

"Yes. I called him last night when we were leaving the club, and he told me." Rene looked down at her fidgeting hands. "I was hot, but didn't want to hear Toni's mouth."

"I know you and Toni get into it every once in a while. But really, I think she's just looking out for you." Ava felt like a counselor. "Be it in her own outspoken, opinionated way, but she means well."

"Whatever your name for it is, she can work my nerves." Rene used a roll of her neck to emphasize the important words. "And if she would've made one of her comments, I think I would've just snapped."

Maybe Ava was more like a referee. "I understand, but I really do think it comes from a good place."

Rene sighed. "I'm sure it does. But in that 'good place' you're talking about, there's also judgment. And she has no room to talk with the mess her own marriage is in."

Ava's eyebrows jumped as she tucked her chin. "Okay. Let's change the subject."

"I'll leave it alone, but I just would like to note that you and I were fine back in college and you just had to bring her into our group."

"Well, Ms. Law School, you were always studying, so I had to have somebody to kick it with. Plus, like I said, she means well. She just needs to work on her delivery."

"Yes, that's true. She needs to deliver her opinions to someone else."

"All righty then." Ava cleared her throat. "I'm starving. You up for a bite to eat after we get your car?"

"Sure, why not?"

The rest of the ride was in "I'm here for you, girl" silence. Ava didn't want to press any more buttons. Rene's fingers tapped her forehead as she looked to the sky, seemingly searching for answers. Ava knew if Rene wanted to talk she would. Rene was never short on words. The lawyer in her could always find something to say. But with gloom resting all over her face, words were scarce.

After fifteen more minutes, Ava exited where the GPS told her to and followed its directions to the All City Towing Yard. She pulled inside the rusty gates and stopped in front of the small shack of an office. A black and gray sign dangling on its last hinge read OPEN 24 HRS.

Ava would accompany her friend inside if she wanted her to.

Rene opened the car door. "I'll be back."

Guess not. The situation was probably embarrassing enough without Ava getting a front-row seat.

Rene's steps quickened as she got closer to the office. She yanked the screen door open and marched in.

A heavyset, middle-aged man with a white beard sat behind a shabby wooden desk. Switching his cigar to the other side of his mouth, he asked, "May I help you?"

"Um, yes. I'm here to pick up a silver BMW. It was brought in sometime last night or early this morning. My name is Rene Jacobs."

He sifted through some papers on a clipboard. "Ah, yes. We have that beauty parked right up front a few rows over. I'll need to see your proof of insurance and ID, get payment, and you can be on your way."

Tapping her toe on the floor, she unzipped her purse and pulled out her insurance and license. "How much will it cost to get it out?"

"Let me see here." He looked through the bottom of his glasses. "Three hundred and seven dollars."

"What?"

"I'm sorry, ma'am." He removed the cigar and placed it in an ashtray. "But along with our fees, the apartments have fees, plus mileage and all. The signs were clear in the parking lot."

Rene caught herself. She didn't want to get an attitude with him. It wasn't his fault. *Just get the car.* "I know, sir. I'm just angry with the person who didn't see the signs." She smiled. "By the way, can you give me the address where my car was towed from?"

"Certainly." He flipped the top sheet over and studied the following page. "That would be 525 East County Road, Houston, Texas. It says here, right in front of building 3200."

"Thank you. I appreciate it." She handed him her credit card and thought about who Ishmael knew on the east side of town. Whoever it was, she had never been there with him.

Ishmael would pay her every penny of the fees back, too. And he would never get the keys to her car again. If his piece of crap car broke down, he'd have to ask a homeboy or his mother to borrow theirs.

After she signed the receipt, he handed her a copy. She scribbled the address he'd just given her on the back of her receipt.

"Again, Ms. Jacobs, about three or four rows over, right up front." He pointed toward the back exit of the office. "You can go through this back door to the lot and when you pull up to the gate, I'll let you out." He saluted her with two fingers and a grin minus a few teeth, and reinserted the cigar to its rightful place.

She forced a smile and then traveled through the short hallway to the back door.

The smoldering sun glared down on all of the vehicles in the lot. Some cars were intact while others had damages ranging from minor bumps and bruises to more severe dents that made them almost unrecognizable.

Rene spotted her car parked at the front of the fourth row. She strolled around each side of the car and inspected every inch of metal. When everything looked in place, she hit the unlock button on her key chain and got reacquainted with the interior.

She drove to the front of the lot while looking over the seats and in the console for remnants of Ishmael's previous night. A large cardboard box full of advertisements for the club took up most of the back seat. The same flyers he supposedly needed to pick up from Mike's house. Ishmael had a great deal of explaining to do.

When the gate opened, Ava looked up from checking her text messages. Rene motioned for Ava to follow her. All seemed well, but Rene drove faster than usual down the busy street. Ava suspected the heavy foot of anger leaned on the gas pedal. She followed Rene into the parking lot of the Westland Hills Mall and parked in front of the food court.

Ava stepped out of her car and walked around to Rene's door. "What's the verdict, counselor? How much was it?"

Rene sat back in her seat. "Three hundred and seven dollars! Can you believe that?"

"Dang. I'm sorry, girl."

"Ish is the sorry one."

Don't say a word, Ava. Holding her mouth shut was like closing a stuffed suitcase. But she managed.

Rene locked her car. "I figured we could do some shopping after lunch. I'm not ready to go home anytime soon."

"Whatever you want to do. I have a training tomorrow that starts at ten o'clock so I can hang all day if you like."

"Good."

They entered through the automatic sliding doors. Ava asked, "What do you have a taste for?"

"I don't know if I'm really that hungry. You pick the place." Rene looked up and read the sign above the first store. Her eyes lit up. "Ooh, there's that store 5-7-9. I thought they went out of business. Wanna go in there for a minute?"

Ava smacked her lips. Was she serious? "Girl, please. I ain't five, seven, or nine! I'm more like five plus seven plus nine! What I'ma do in there? Get a bracelet?"

Rene laughed. "Ava, you are too funny. But yes, they have jewelry and other accessories. You may see something you like."

"No, you go ahead." Ava smiled. "I'll run down to the big girls' shop."

"Okay. I'll meet you back in the food court in twenty?"

"Sounds good. I feel like Chinese, so I'll meet you over at Chinatown Grill."

Ava turned and walked down the row of specialty stores until she reached her destination. Full-figured women calmly searched through racks and tables of clothes. Ava scanned the entrance to see how many people walking by noticed her going in the big girl store.

"Hi. Welcome to Avenue." A smiling clerk greeted her. "Everything's half off today. Looking for anything in particular?"

"No, just looking." Ava joined the other shoppers in their search for the perfect outfit. Well, forget perfect. Something that fit would do.

Last time she tried on clothing she was a size twenty-two. The same size or a miraculously smaller size would please her. She picked up a pair of black slacks with plaid buttons, and then grabbed a plain navy V-neck top.

Ava took a deep breath, looking at the sales associate. "I guess I'll try these on."

"Sure. Here you go, ma'am. Let me know if you need anything."

Ava placed her wallet on the bench, hung the outfit on the clothing hook, and removed her clothes. She took a minute to look over her body in the full-length mirror and poked out her lips. As she stepped into the pants, one leg at a time, she could tell that these were not the pants for her.

She gave them a good tug over her belly, and attempted to button them up, but was unsuccessful. Holding in her breath, she tried again. This time, victory. But the button held on for dear life. For fear the pants would burst open, she unfastened them.

After she removed the pants, she threw the V-neck over her head. Ava viewed the shirt straight on and then turned around to see the back view. The roll that hung over her bra was not what she wanted everyone to see when she walked away from them. Next, she fumbled with the sleeves that looked glued to her arms. *This is ridiculous. I gotta do better.*

"Ava? You in here somewhere?"

What was Rene doing in here? Could she not find anything in the itty-bitty store? "Yes, I'm in the last dressing room."

"I decided to come find you. I need my girl right now. Want me to find you a cute outfit?"

Not really. "Sure, girl. Go crazy."

Moments later, Rene handed Ava a white and hot pink top with horizontal stripes, and some too-little jeans. She didn't want to hurt her friend's feelings, but Rene could've left those garments on the rack. Ava changed back into her clothes and toddled out of the fitting room.

The associate stood outside the dressing room, grinning. "How'd everything look?"

"None of it worked for me." Ava handed her the clothes. She probably would've had more success with the bracelet idea or other accessories in 5-7-9.

"Okay, ma'am. Would you like to try another style or size?"

"No, thank you."

The sales associate returned the clothes to their racks. "Well, have a nice day."

Yeah, whatever. "Thanks, you too."

Ava trudged toward the exit, Rene following her. Next time, they should just go straight to the food court.

Chapter 4

Ava and Rene ordered their favorite dishes from Chinatown Grill. After sitting down with the chic food court trays, it only took Ava a few minutes to make a good-sized dent in her chow mein noodles. She chewed the delectable bitter-salty combination as she watched a couple flirting with each other a table over. Craving that closeness, she mentally removed the female from the scene and pictured herself feeding the man and cleaning his chin with a napkin.

Rene's cell phone went off. She blew out a heavy breath of air.

Ava looked up from her plate. "What's the matter?"

"Ishmael keeps texting me saying he wants to start the making up process." She twisted her fork in her fried rice.

"Are you up to it? I mean, do you want to see him?" Ava hoped Rene's answer would be a definite no.

"Yeah, I guess. He's said sorry a thousand times and I know people make mistakes." She put her fork down and tapped her fingers on the table. "Part of me misses him, but I'm getting tired of every time I turn around there's some drama waiting for me."

Ava wiped her mouth with her napkin. *What would be the best advice to offer without sounding like a hater?* "Don't see him until you're ready. There's no rush. He ain't going anywhere. "

"I don't know if my mind is ready." Rene smiled. "But my body is."

"No, you didn't, girl." Ava lowered her eyes. "I knew you two had slipped up before, but I thought you guys were putting it on hold until the wedding night."

"I know, Ava. But I'm not as strong as you. I need to have him next to me. In more ways than one. He definitely has the good stuff with some to spare."

"Please *spare* me the details." Did Rene not think Ava would've loved a man next to her too? But that feeling only lasted so long. And after the comfort of a man's affections went away, the woman would be left with his clothes on the floor, him being more concerned with impressing his homies than keeping things on the up and up with her, and gas coming out of every part of his body. If Ava was to put up with all that and more, she'd want it to be from someone she liked and not just lusted for.

"No, I'm just saying. He is the best I've ever had. So gentle and sweet, but at the same time he takes care of his business. And don't even get me started on his equipment."

"Okay! TMI. I don't want you to get started on that or anything else." Was Rene trying to sabotage Ava's newfound celibacy?

"I'm sorry." Rene snickered. "And I know premarital sex is wrong, but anything that feels that good can't be wrong. Am I right?"

"Well, since you keep talking about it; what about how you feel when it's over? I want the day when I can enjoy sex with my husband and not feel guilty afterward." She looked around to see if any bystanders were listening. Rene asked for candidness and Ava was going to deliver. "Sex is a beautiful thing in a marriage. And you know I'm no saint, but I want to take a shot at doing things the right way. 'Cause obviously what I've been doing ain't working. Then I feel my relationship will truly be blessed."

"I know all that, Ava, but it's hard to say no to those muscles, that smile, and those captivating green eyes."

Ava's brow rose as she stared over Rene's shoulder. "Shh. Speak of the devil."

Rene turned around to look behind her. "Ishmael?"

"Surprise." His six foot one inch frame stood next to Rene. As he bent over to kiss her, he had to hold his belt buckle so his pants wouldn't hit the floor.

Just because he halfway did the club promoting thing didn't mean he had to walk around like he was the next big thing to hit the rap scene, baggy pants and all. What did Rene see in this wannabe thug?

"I'm sorry, babe. I had to see you," Ishmael said.

"Now?" Rene rubbed her forehead, seemingly conflicted and embarrassed.

"I couldn't wait any longer." He extended his hand toward Ava for a handshake. "Hey, Ava. How are you?"

Shaking his hand was the last thing she wanted to do. "Just fine, Ishmael."

"And you're looking fine too." He winked at Ava. "Don't mean to bust up your girlfriend time, but I really needed to talk to Rene. And I needed to start working off those towing fees she had to pay. I plan to pay her back with some one of a kind interest." He grinned. "If you know what I mean."

Ava rolled her eyes. "I wish I didn't." Snapping her fingers and disappearing like a genie was the super power she needed at that moment. "I'm going to leave you two alone, so you can talk."

"You don't have to go, Ava." Rene stuck out her hand.

"No, it's okay. I need to go home and plan the menu for an event I'm catering in a few weeks." Ava rubbed her hands together. "It's the first time I get to plan the menu from scratch."

"Be sure to put your famous chicken and dumplings on that menu. They're the bomb." Ishmael seemed happy to see her go so he could work his magic on Rene.

"Will do." She gave them a two-finger salute.

"Are you sure, Ava?" Rene's eyes saddened. "Please stay."

Ignoring Rene's plea, Ava didn't want to be the third person on a two-person bicycle. "No, I'm good. Y'all go 'head." She threw her napkins on her plate, and picked up her tray. "Hope it all works out." *Yeah, right. Please, Lord, forgive me for that lie.*

Ishmael confidently grinned. "Oh, it will. Thanks."

"I'll call you later, girl." Rene half smiled and added an awkward giggle.

"You do that." Ava nodded and scurried through the tables and into the mall traffic. It was just like Rene to kick her to the curb for Ishmael. He had a hold over her that Ava didn't understand. Could his stuff really be that good? They'd probably make up two seconds after Ava left. More power to them. Ava could find something to do. She could go home, grab a good book, and jump into a bubble bath. Maybe roll by the Krispy Kreme drive-through first.

Rene sat still with her eyes following every motion Ishmael made toward her. He scooted his chair closer. She leaned back and awaited his explanation.

"I'm sorry, Rene. I know I should've paid more attention to where I parked your car, but my plan was to run in and run out." He rubbed the side of his low-cut fro with a dollar sign trimmed into it. Ironic, since he never seemed to have any money. "But you know when me and my homeboy Mike get together, a five-minute confab turns into twenty or thirty minutes."

"Yeah, I know that. And since you do too, you should have paid more attention. And I wouldn't have had to pay over three hundred dollars to get my car out."

"My bad, baby. And I can't believe it took over three hundred dollars to get your car. Crooks. I will pay you back every penny." He tickled her side. "And of course there's that special interest I was talking about. We can take care of that tonight, if you'll stop being mad at me."

Rene pushed his hand away. He wasn't getting off that easy. "Don't play. I'm upset. I don't even spend that kind of money on myself. And yes, you will surely pay me back all three hundred and seven dollars. About that interest you keep talking about, I'm not *interested*."

He put both hands around her waist. "Come on, baby. Don't be like that. It was an honest mistake. That won't happen again."

"Oh, I know it won't happen again. 'Cause you won't be driving my car anymore. Speaking of which, how'd you get up here?"

"My moms let me borrow her car."

Of course. Either that or she would've driven him up there herself. *Momma's boy if I ever saw one.* "Isn't that sweet of her?"

"Yes, it is. I'm blessed with two of the sweetest women in the world in my corner. So let's say you follow me to my mom's, we drop off her car, and go to your place and chill. I'll cook for you, and we can relax and talk."

"Just talk?" Rene didn't believe that for a second.

Ishmael raised his hands in the air as if to surrender. "Yes, I promise. Just talk. And then maybe after you've calmed down, I can interest you in my interest." His wink sent a subtle chill down her spine.

She shook her head and stood. Why couldn't she resist his charm? The inner battle ceased. Rene wanted her man back. "Come on, let's go. Maybe your momma can talk some sense to both of us. I don't know which one of us needs a talking to more."

He rose and tagged alongside her out of the shopping mall like a hungry stray puppy.

Chapter 5

Ava, almost home, wondered how Rene and Ishmael's conversation had gone. He probably begged until Rene gave into him. She hoped Rene could stand her ground at least a little while, so he'd remember this and not let history repeat itself. But she knew by the way Rene talked before he showed up, his job of getting her to forgive him would be an easy one.

Replaying Rene's description of Ishmael's good stuff in her head, Ava imagined more than she would ever admit to. He was definitely an attractive man, but she didn't need to hear the details.

Kids playing football in the parking lot of her apartment complex acted as if they didn't see her driving their way. *I guess I get dissed by men of all ages.* She gently honked on the horn for an unsolicited timeout in their game, then drove to her designated covered parking spot. A white truck sat across the lot in the visitor's section that resembled Xavier's ride. *I know this fool is not here.*

As Ava approached the staircase, she could see Xavier standing on the top step in front of her apartment. He looked down and waved. What could he possibly want? She'd already said all she needed to say to him. And he couldn't have picked a worse time. With Rene sharing how well Ishmael performed in the bedroom, her flesh screamed for a man's touch. *Lord, give me strength.*

By the time she reached the bottom of the last flight of stairs, he had taken a seat and was now sitting with open arms. She glared into his eyes. "What are you doing here?"

"I came by to talk. Hope you'd let me take you to dinner tomorrow night for Valentine's Day."

"We have nothing left to talk about. And you never wanted to take me out before. I'm uh, how'd you put it? 'Borderline fat.'" She folded her arms. "That sound about right?"

"I said I was sorry. Sometimes you tick me off and I lose control. But I do think we have something to talk about. I love you, Ava, and I can't let this go."

"You don't have a choice in the matter." She came up the rest of the steps and maneuvered around him. *I should kick him while he's down.*

He grabbed her hand. "After almost a year together, you can't stop your feelings for me like that."

She jerked her hand back. "This was a long time coming. I just wanted a man and was too selfish to end it."

Ava's pride and self-centered side could have made it another month or two with Xavier. Even though they didn't go out much, when they did she felt lucky to have him by her side. His build, muscular and solid, looked nice against her stout frame. The strong outline of his jaw told more of his story. He was put together and exuded swag with every step he took.

Xavier sauntered over to her. She could hear the overly starched crease in his jeans as he moved. "Why does this have to end?"

"Because I want more."

He placed his hand on her shoulder. "Let me be that more for you."

"You've tried. And I tried, but I can't do it any longer. I'm tired of the smart comments about my weight." She backed away from him.

"I thought I was helping you."

"Helping me?"

"Yeah. Like motivating you to want to work out. I don't know. I sincerely apologize." His eyes reminded her of a lost puppy's.

"Thanks, but that was only part of it. All the phone conversations you mysteriously had to take in another room and phone numbers in your pockets." She had several issues with him. These two were just at the top of the list.

"I told you I was holding those numbers for my cousin."

"Then he's cheating on his wife?" Ava double pumped her neck. He must've mistaken her for a naive teenage girl.

"That's his business. I was lookin' out for him. That's my boy."

She lifted her right eyebrow and grinned. "Well, birds of a feather, right? Plus, I want a man who can lead me in the things of God. Not someone I have to drag."

He took hold of her hand. "I can be that, Ava. Please give me another chance."

"Xavier, I'm out of them."

He leaned in and kissed her lips. She used both hands to push him back. *Nice try.* He went in again, this time running his hand through her hair, then resting his hand on her cheek. *Shoot!* She lingered in this lip lock a bit longer. Ava's neighbor stepped out to throw away a bag of trash.

The interruption startled her and she jumped back. "Xavier, stop."

"There's still passion between us, baby. Give me five minutes to plead my case. And if your answer is still no, I'll leave you alone."

She put up the peace sign. "Two minutes." Ava pushed the door back and held it open enough for him to slither in. When he brushed past her, his cologne left a trail, sending a shock wave through her body. *Dang.* He knew what scent to put on before he trekked over to her place. In the past, that fragrance had proven to be irresistible to Ava's womanhood. She dropped her keys and wallet on the breakfast bar, and turned toward him with her hands on her thick hips. "So go ahead. Plead."

"I know I have my faults, like anyone else, but you make me want to be a better person. In fact, I am a better person when I'm with you."

"Well, I'm not. I'm a hot mess. Always worried about what you might say when I put on my clothes. Or when I take them off. Constantly thinking you'll leave me when you find someone smaller. I just—"

"Ava. You're beautiful just the way you are."

"I don't feel beautiful with you." She didn't want him to see her cry, but one tear escaped and traveled down to her chin.

He glided over to her. "I can show you better than I can tell you."

His hands pulled her body up against his and caressed everywhere they could reach. Their kiss was now mutual as she threw both arms around his neck. A warm, tingling sensation shot down her spine to the tips of her toes and jolted her even closer into his body.

Two minutes had come and gone. The familiarity, among other things, felt good. Then when his fingers ran over the plumpness that overlapped her bra strap, Ava caught herself. *This is how he got you back the last time. This is lust, not love.* She moved her arms between them and shoved him back.

"What's wrong?" he asked with a look of confusion on his face.

Ava kept her hands up. The barricade of arm's length away was the only thing that could stop her from taking the unwelcome affection too far. "Everything. I need you to leave."

"Leave?" His voice elevated to a higher pitch. "What are you doing? Trying to tease me?"

"No. I don't want this and I let it go too far already. I can't do this with you again, X."

"Then who you gon' do it with?" His face scrunched in anger.

"It's not about anybody else. I don't want to be with you anymore. I'm done."

"You didn't seem done a few seconds ago."

She moved toward the door. "I know. I didn't mean for that to happen."

"It happened because you still love me."

"No, I don't. Please leave." Opening the door, she knew this good-bye was the true end of their relationship.

He looked out the door but didn't move. Ava didn't want a scene, but had no problem calling the police if he didn't leave her apartment. As a juvenile probation officer, she possessed a service pistol. The .22-caliber gun tucked away in her nightstand was only twenty feet away. She had no problem using it if he needed help getting out the door.

"Xavier, you need to go."

"Dang it, Ava! I'm tired of you playing games."

"I'm not playing games. Now good-bye." She gripped the door handle.

He stepped toward the door. "Okay, see if you get anybody who looks as good as me again. And who's willing to put up with your big butt. Ain't nobody gon' want you."

A few choice words were on the tip of her tongue. It took an act of God to hold her mouth mute.

"Well, maybe if you lose fifty pounds," he scoffed.

No, he did not. She squeezed the doorknob. "Are you finished?"

"Yeah, I'm finished. Finished with your two-ton behind." He turned to look in her eyes. "Glad it's over!"

"Not as glad as I am." She shut the door hard enough to rattle the wall. "Ahh! Why didn't you let me cuss him out, Lord?" He was truly crazy. Five minutes before she was beautiful just the way she was, then when he didn't hear what he wanted to hear, he flipped the script.

She stormed down the hall to the guest bathroom, yanked a few tissues out of the box, and threw the box against the wall. Wiping her tears, she marched into the kitchen. Enough was enough. Why did she put up with his crap for so long?

The cabinet above the sink stored wine glasses and corkscrews. She snatched one of each and slammed the door closed. After placing the glass and corkscrew on the counter, she grabbed a bottle of Chardonnay out of the fridge. Tears and mumbling flowed as she forced the wine bottle open and poured herself a hefty glass. She would never say two words to him the rest of her years on this earth. Nor spit on him if he was on fire.

Raising her glass to the ceiling, she mocked, "Well, I'm fat and that's that! Here's a toast to me and my big butt."

She gulped down the first glass, took a deep breath, and then poured herself another.

Chapter 6

Rene pulled up behind Ishmael into his mother's driveway. She and Momma Carter got along well, but Rene harbored feelings that she was an enabler. He was a proud momma's boy and his mother was definitely a proud momma.

Ishmael opened the front door wide. "I'm back, Momma. And I have your future daughter-in-law with me."

Heavy footsteps rushed out from the kitchen. "Hey, son." His mother gave him a hug and a kiss on the cheek and then turned to hug Rene. "Hey, pretty girl, it's great to see you."

"Hello, Ms. Carter, it's great to see you too," Rene replied.

"How are the wedding plans coming along?"

"Everything is coming together real well. June third is less than four months away, so just about everything is done." She followed her into the kitchen. "I need to finalize the photographer and make a decision about our cakes. You know my best friend Ava is going to do them for us."

"If you need any help with anything, let me know."

"Thank you. I'll hold you to that."

By now, Ishmael already had a bite of his mom's German chocolate cake in his mouth. Rene strolled over and cut herself a small piece. No matter how much of a health-conscious eater she claimed to be, she had a weakness when it came to Momma Carter's cakes: moist, flavorful, all-around mouthwatering goodness.

Rene could bake and throw together a decent meal, but she was nowhere close to Ishmael's mother in the cooking department. He would have to learn to make do with her average skills in the kitchen once they were married.

He swallowed a piece of his cake, dropping crumbs on the front of his shirt. "All this talk about cake has me on this here."

"Go 'head, baby. Have all you want." Momma Carter disappeared into the hallway that led to her bedroom.

Ishmael cut a small bite of his cake and fed it to Rene. She first refused, and then opened her mouth just wide enough to take the piece he offered.

As she chewed, he ran his fingers over her hand. "I'm really sorry, Rene. I know you put up with a lot from me. But I am going to do better. I can't have you mad at me."

Yep, he knew how to weave his way back into her good graces. "I'm not mad anymore. And I do appreciate all the apologies."

"I love you and don't know what I'd do without you in my life. I cannot wait for you to be Mrs. Ishmael Carter."

"I love you too, but I was thinking more like you'd be Mr. Rene Jacobs." She chuckled.

He leaned into her body. "Whatever. Give me some sugar."

She obliged. They had their share of arguments, but the making up was affectionately easy. Rene knew this was due in part to her letting him slide on a few things every once in a while. He frequently borrowed money and paid it back later than he said he would. Ishmael had several late arrivals with no phone call when she was expecting him. He'd cancel plans altogether when something suddenly came up with his club promoting project. But she did love him and that meant loving all of him. Including his faults.

Momma Carter returned to the kitchen and cleared her throat. "I guess I'm interrupting the lovebirds. Excuse me."

"Momma, we're in your house." He smiled. "So, excuse us."

Rene adored the little ways he showed his mother respect.

"No, baby, I'm just teasing. I love to see you two happy. That was me and your father when we were about to head down that aisle. He would never kiss me in my father's house though."

Rene asked, "Was he shy?'

"No, not shy. Scared is a better word for it. Scared of my daddy's shotgun that hung over the fireplace in the living room."

Ishmael sat back in his chair. "Granddaddy had a gun in the family room?"

"Yep. He said it was a reminder to your Aunt Teresa's and my gentleman callers. He proudly had the gun hanging in there, so our courters knew he had one and knew how to use it." She laughed with a look on her face like she was reminiscing on the good ol' days.

"Daaang! He was no joke, huh?" Ishmael threw his last piece of cake in his mouth.

"Nope. But he loved us and protected us best he could. And we loved him right back. He just 'bout scared your daddy off. But he had his eye on this prize." She struck a pose. "So he wasn't going nowhere."

"Momma, we don't want to hear about you and Daddy. Please."

"What?" She tapped the back of his shoulder with her index finger. "How you think you got here?"

Ishmael, seemingly embarrassed, shook his head and looked down. Rene rubbed the back of his neck and said, "I think it's cute."

"Surprise, surprise. You takin' my momma's side." He grabbed Rene's hand. "Come on, let's go before you two start ganging up on me."

Momma Carter started wrapping up two big slices of cake in some tinfoil. "So soon?"

"Yeah, Momma. We got some thangs to do." He lifted his eyebrows.

"Well, here, take this cake." His mother handed her the wrapped-up dessert. "You can't leave it here. I'll eat it up and that's too much sugar for one person."

"Thank you, Ms. Carter." Rene stood up and gave her a hug. Ishmael's mother was as sweet as her cakes.

"You're very welcome. I want you and Ish to come by this weekend and have dinner. Think you can make it?"

"I don't see why not."

Momma Carter searched the refrigerator for leftovers to wrap up for them. Her sending them out the door with food had become a part of her farewell routine.

Ishmael grabbed Rene's hand and kissed it. "Let me run upstairs to my old room real quick. I need to get a load of laundry my moms did for me."

"Okay, you momma's boy."

"You got that right." He smiled.

"I'll be here." Every time they came to visit, he had to load up. If it wasn't laundry, it was food. If it wasn't food, it was movies or some new clothes, or a new book she wanted him to read. Sometimes even money. When he joined Rene in holy matrimony, would Momma Carter really turn him loose? Would Ishmael be able to be turned loose? Did he want to be loosed?

His mother stepped from behind the refrigerator door with a casserole dish, placed it on the counter, and added more tinfoil to the top of the dish. "Oh yeah, Ishmael, Shay dropped some mail off for you the other day. I put it in the basket on the table by the front door."

Rene knew that Momma Carter called Shanice "Shay," but didn't know why she'd be dropping mail off for him. He'd moved out from her place almost two years ago. She'd be sure to ask him when they got in the car. "He went upstairs. I'll grab it for him."

"Thank you, sweetie."

Walking over to the oval-shaped table in the foyer, a sick feeling emerged in the pit of Rene's stomach. She snatched the mail with his name on it and looked at the address, which read 525 East County Rd. Apt. #3214, Houston, TX 77803. That street sounded familiar. Rene opened her purse to throw in the mail. *Where do I know that address from?* Pausing, she studied the front of the top envelope. *Can't be.*

She placed the cake on the table, and hunted in her purse for the green receipt from the All City Towing Yard. Once she found the receipt, she flipped it over where she had written the address her car was towed from that the towing yard attendant recited to her. She saw the addresses matched number for number and word for word. Her body heat rose to 99.9 degrees.

Rene dropped her purse to the ground and fumbled through the rest of his mail. On every bill and piece of junk mail she read the same address affixed under Ishmael's name. He must've mistaken her for a fool. All those apologies were a product of him blowing smoke. His words, not worth a dime, had to be dealt with immediately.

After a few more seconds passed and Rene allowed this newfound information to sink in, Ishmael came hopping down the steps carrying a bulky laundry bag. He reached the bottom, and looked at Rene holding the mail with her eyes firing into his. "What's the matter, babe?"

Rene pushed the front of one of the envelopes in his face. "So you were at Mike's house, huh?"

Ishmael lifted his hands in the air. "Wait, let me explain."

She yelled, "Explain what? You were at Shanice's house and got my car towed. And you lied about it. That about sum it up?"

"I didn't want you to be upset."

"Well, you missed the mark on that one. I guess that's why the flyers were still in my car." Attorney Jacobs was now present.

"Yes, I picked up the flyers from Mike. Then Shanice called and said she couldn't drop off Isaiah, so I went to pick him up. Nothing happened."

"If nothing happened, why couldn't you just tell me? I'm about to be your wife."

"I know how you feel about Shanice. So I skipped over that part. Thought it'd be best."

Rene needed him to stop thinking and just be honest. "Missed the mark again!"

Ishmael's mother made her way into the foyer. "What's going on?"

He put his hand in the air. "I got it, Momma."

"Got what? I don't understand. You two were fine five minutes ago."

"Sorry, Ms. Carter. That was before I caught your son in a lie."

Momma Carter walked over to Ishmael. "Boy, are you lying to this young lady?"

He turned his mother around and gently led her back to the kitchen. "I said I got it."

When he returned to the foyer, Rene threw the rest of the mail at him. She hoped they hurt, too. Maybe there were some credit card offers in the mix that could pop him in the head. Or better yet, an offer for collectors of heavy commemorative coins with some free samples.

"Hey, baby, calm down." He knelt down to pick up the scattered envelopes. "Now what was I saying?"

"Um, let's see. You were probably about to lie about your lying. But what I'm saying is the wedding's on hold!" Her uncertainties were abruptly front and center.

"What?" He let the mail fall back down to the ground. "Rene, don't overreact." He reached out to put his hand on her shoulder.

"Overreact? You smooth lied in my face!" Dipping her shoulder before he could touch her, she picked up her purse. "I need some time to gather my thoughts. I don't feel good about being in a relationship with someone who can lie that easily. Makes me wonder what else have you lied about."

He shook his head as his eyes saddened. "Baby, please."

She shook her index finger. "Nope. That 'baby' crap is on hold too. I don't know if I can trust you." Time apart would be a good thing. The last couple of weeks were filled with doubts and second-guessing her choices.

As she headed for the front door, he grabbed her forearm. "Rene, just tell me this."

"What, Ishmael?" She jerked her arm out of his grasp. Nothing he said could save his case.

"I understand you need some time. But putting the wedding on hold?" He resembled a sad child who wasn't getting his way. "For how long?"

She cut her eyes at him. "Let's go with the same thing you told me when I asked you when you'd be getting your car out the shop."

Confusion settled on his face. "Which was?"

"Until further notice." Rene walked out of the house and slammed the door behind her.

Chapter 7

With Valentine's Day less than twenty-four hours away, Toni was overjoyed to be in Miami. Thoughts of Eric and the trip they took to the Florida Keys last summer pounded her brain since she'd arrived. Her emotions were all over the place. She missed Eric, but was determined not to call him. Being a few states over made it easier for her to stick to that decision.

Toni had given her heart to Eric a long time ago in high school and he still had a hold of it. But as deep as that love ran, the hurt caused by his infidelity ran even deeper.

She stood on the balcony of her ocean-view room of the luxurious, resort-style hotel, taking the postcard photo in. The bright sun kissed the bluer-than-blue water, as the fresh breeze hit her face with the right amount of serenity to calm her nerves. She could stay in that spot all day.

If it were not for the four-thirty wake-up call in the morning, she'd order the hotel's most expensive wine and relax with nature's beauty and her thoughts until she fell asleep. Her creative director for the shoot, however, would have something to say if she showed up a sluggish, tired mess. So she chose a good night's rest over an alcohol-induced one.

She opened the mini fridge and took out a bottle of water, remembering the good times she and Eric shared. A knock at the door broke her concentration.

"Who is it?"

"Concierge, ma'am."

She opened the door.

"Good evening. This was dropped off for you at the front desk." A thin kid in the full getup complete with a bellman's hat handed her a manila envelope.

"Thank you." She turned to grab her purse.

When she returned with his tip, he reached out for it. "Thank you, ma'am. Please let us know if you need anything."

"You're welcome. I will."

Toni sat down on the plush bedspread and pulled her itinerary out of the envelope. The hair and makeup team expected her in their trailer by five in the morning. Her bedtime would have to be eight o'clock. It was seven o'clock Houston time, but eight in Miami.

She was a little hungry but decided against ordering room service and chose an apple from the complimentary fruit basket in her room. A heavy meal wouldn't do her any good anyway. Doing a shoot in summer wear usually included a bathing suit or two. As she bit a huge chunk out of the apple, her cell phone's ringtone played a smooth R & B rhythm.

Who would be calling her now? Maybe Ava was checking to see if she'd made it okay. She dug it out of her purse, but didn't recognize the number. It was a Houston area code though, so she spit the apple into a tissue and answered it.

"Hello, Toni. It's Roderick from the other night. How are you?"

She smiled. "Yes, I'm doing good. How are you?"

"Fine now that I'm talking to you. Are you busy?"

"Nope, just sitting here in my hotel room relaxing." She lay back on the bed. His call was a nice surprise.

"So you made it there all right. Good. How was your trip?"

Besides the thoughts of Eric? "It was great. What are you up to today?"

"Not much of anything. Rode my motorcycle and enjoyed this perfect day. I wanted to see when you'd be back in town, so we could go out. Maybe dinner and a movie?"

She nodded her head with every word to convince herself to go. "Yes, I'd like that. I'll be back Tuesday morning." A diversion from Eric could prove to be what she needed.

"I know Valentine's Day is tomorrow, but we can celebrate just as well on Tuesday evening."

"Celebrate what?" Why did he mention Valentine's Day? She hadn't known him a full day yet.

"Hopefully, a new friendship that can turn into something more."

"Okay." *He fixed that mistake quick.*

"We can have a nice dinner, a little conversation. Get to know each other better."

"Sounds good."

"Wonderful. I'll set everything up and plan to pick you up about seven?"

She grimaced. "How about we meet at seven?" He seemed to be moving at a jackrabbit's pace.

"Okay, no problem. I'll call you Tuesday afternoon sometime, and let you know where to meet me."

She hung up the phone and went back to the apple. As she ate, she replayed the night on the dance floor and conversation she and Roderick had. He seemed cool, but she was nowhere near letting her guard down with him. She looked forward to the dinner date, but honestly wished it would be Eric sitting across the table from her.

Searching her phone contacts for Ava's name, she couldn't wait to tell her about her date. Ava's phone rang a couple of times and then went to voicemail.

After she heard the beep, Toni left Ava a message.
"Hey, girl, it's me. I made it to Miami safely and now
sitting here, relaxing in this beautiful room, or trying to
anyway. I miss Eric. I know I shouldn't, but I do. Plus,
just made a date with Roderick. The guy from the club.
I don't know what I'm doing, but maybe he'll be a good
distraction. Call me back when you get the chance. Love
you."

She placed her cell phone on the nightstand, finished
the apple, and retreated to the bathroom to complete her
nightly routine: wash face, brush teeth, floss, and apply
anti-aging cream and moisturizer. The king-sized bed,
complete with five pillows and a soft comforter, called her
name. She looked forward to climbing in for a pampered
night's sleep. Plugging in her phone charger, she noticed
a text message. The message read: Couldn't wait 'til
tomorrow to tell u I luv u. Miss u so much, Toni. Hope all
is well. Always thinkn of u. Luv Eric.

Eric had her on his mind as much as she had him on
hers. And even though she had the divorce papers drafted
and sitting on her desk at home in an envelope ready to
be signed, she couldn't bring herself to even open them.
Toni loved him in spite of all of his mistakes and was still
unsure that divorce was the road she wanted to travel
down. Their connection, although blemished, was strong.
She read the message two more times, cheesing from
one ear to the other, then turned her phone on silent and
went to sleep.

Chapter 8

Ava, now on her third glass of Chardonnay, moved from the kitchen table to a soothing bathtub full of bubbles surrounded by candlelight. The Japanese cherry blossom aroma amused her nose and assisted in relaxing her muscles. Toni called earlier, but she let her voicemail do the work. Toni must've made it to Miami in one piece, but Ava wasn't in the mood to divulge her and Xavier's demeaning argument details and near-sex experience. Her friend would definitely have a thing or two to say about that. Ava would be sure to call her tomorrow.

As she reached for her glass, her cell phone went off again. *What is this? The party line?* Her mother's picture appeared on the screen, and since two weeks had gone by without Ava talking to her, she answered it.

"Hey, Ava. Hadn't talk to you in a while."

"I've been busy, Momma. I was going to call you tomorrow and wish you a happy Valentine's Day. How've you and Daddy been?"

"We're blessed and highly favored. How are things with Xavier?"

Ava's head fell. She had a choice to make: lie and tell her everything was great and have a peaceful chat; or tell her the truth, and deal with her mother putting in her two cents. Who was she kidding? More like twenty-two cents. Ava had consumed enough wine to handle the conversation. "I guess he's fine, Ma. I broke it off with him."

"You did? Why?"

"I don't want to go into specifics right now. He's just not good for me." Couldn't she trust her daughter's judgment just once?

"He loved you, didn't he?"

"I don't think I'd call it love."

"Well, what happened?"

Ava rolled her eyes so hard they hurt. "He's just not for me."

"What you gon' do now?"

"I was fine before him and I'll be fine after him." Was she helpless? Did she need her name added to the "sick and shut-in" list at church?

"Yeah, but I ain't gettin' any younger. Am I ever going to see you get married?"

"Really, Momma?"

"I'm serious. Your brother's been married for almost two years, he just got a promotion at his job, and he and Elaine are now trying to have a baby." She smacked her lips. "I was hoping to at least see my other child get married before I died."

"Well, I guess it just ain't my time yet."

"Ava, you too picky. A girl your size can't be all that high and mighty."

If you weren't my mother, I'd be hanging up now. "How about somebody who treats me right, Momma? Is that being too picky?"

"He couldn't have done anything that terrible. Every time I seen him, he treated you fine."

Wishing she had never answered the phone, her euphoric feeling from the wine started to wear off. "Momma, I gotta go."

"Don't get off now, Ava. I'm trying to help you. You have such a pretty face, but no one can see that. If you lost some weight, then you'd have a whole sea of fish to choose from."

What was God's punishment for cussing your momma out? There was that scripture about honoring your father and mother. "I really need to get off the phone. Now. Tell Daddy I said hi, and y'all have a good night."

"Okay, Ava. I love you and just want what's best for you."

"Love you too."

Ava tossed her cell phone into a pile of dirty clothes that lay on her bathroom floor. She lifted the bottle of wine off the ground and refilled her glass. After taking a lengthy sip, she set the glass on the edge of the tub and turned on the hot water. The noise of the water raging out of the faucet could drown out her mother's opinionated words.

Immersing her body farther into the water, she tried to see how long she could hold her breath. *I should just drown myself right now.* It was no wonder Ava thought the way she did. As far back as she could remember that was her mother's MO. Break her down, break her down, break her down. Would there ever be a time when she'd build her up?

She spent a few more minutes in her pity pool party, then climbed out of the tub and put on her bathrobe. Blowing out each candle, she managed to brush her hair into a ponytail. A booming knock at the front door swallowed up the space in her apartment. Ava almost jumped out of her robe. It was eleven o'clock at night. She was expecting to crawl into bed, not have visitors.

"Ava!" a man's muffled voice called from the other side of the door.

For Xavier's sake, it better not be him.

"Ava! Open up. It's me, Ishmael."

What was he doing at her place at this time of night? "Just a minute." She looked through the peephole, secured the knot in the robe straps across her waist, and cracked the door open.

"I'm sorry, Ava, but have you seen Rene?"

"What?"

"Have you seen or talked to Rene?"

"No, I haven't." Hopefully, she finally decided to kick him to the curb. "But you can't come up here yelling like that. I have neighbors."

"I'm sorry. Can I come in for a minute? I don't know where else to go to try to find her."

She reluctantly allowed him to enter her apartment. "Wait a minute. Let me get decent." Ishmael took a seat on the couch as Ava disappeared into her room. It was too late to be playing counselor for the struggling couple. She would do her best to help him and send him on his way. Her day had been stressful enough without adding Ishmael and Rene's issues.

When she returned in shorts and a T-shirt, he stood up. "Thank you for letting me in. I've been to her house, her office, and her parents' home. I even went to 24 Hour Fitness. You know she likes to work out when she gets upset. I've called her I don't know how many times and she won't answer." He seemed on the verge of tears. Or maybe an angry breakdown. Ava couldn't be sure which way he was headed.

She put her hand up. "Start from the beginning. What did you do?"

"We got into it earlier over her car being towed."

"Y'all were making up when I left you at the mall."

"Yeah, well, everything was cool then, but when we went to my mom's house to drop her car back off, Rene found some mail with Shanice's address."

"And let me guess. That's where you were when her car got towed?" *Idiot.*

He looked down at his feet. "I went to pick up Li'l Man, and I didn't want to tell Rene because I knew she'd get upset."

"How'd that work out for you?"

"Dang, Ava. I know, but you don't have to be so cold."

"Sorry, that's the wine talking. Would you like some?"

"No, thanks. I'm good."

"Let me get my phone and try to call her." Leaving him in the living room, she searched among the pile of her unmentionables. After she found her phone, Ava picked up the glass of wine and returned to Ishmael, who was staring at his phone.

"Crap! She will not pick up." He threw his cell on the couch along with his red and blue Houston Texans hat. "Ava, did you call yet?"

"Yep, same thing. It goes straight to voicemail."

"I mean, doesn't she know how I feel about her? I can't control what Shanice does or doesn't do. It's all about Li'l Man for me."

"She's hurt right now. Give her time. You sure you wouldn't you like something to drink? Wine, water, coffee?"

"No, I'm fine."

Ava moved into the kitchen to put her glass in the sink. As she stepped from the carpet to the tile, the glass slipped out of her hand, shattering on the floor. "Dat gum it!"

Ishmael rushed to the doorway. "You all right?"

"Yeah, I'm okay. I've obviously had too much to drink."

"Let me help you." He stepped over the mess and grabbed the broom from the corner of the kitchen. As he swept the broken pieces of glass, Ava took the paper towel roll off the metal holder and soaked up the wine.

She looked up at him. He was so quick to run to her aid. "I wish I had somebody to chase after me."

"What about X?"

"He's not what I want. He puts me down every chance he gets."

Ishmael raised the dustpan off the floor. "Puts you down? For what?"

"Depends on the day." She sighed. "But mostly my weight."

"Ava, you are beautiful inside and out. Don't ever believe anything different. I know guys like him. They don't amount to much. I'm surprised you don't have a line of men at your door."

She laughed. "Thanks, but I'd need to lose fifty pounds first." *Maybe more.*

"No, you don't. Quit putting yourself down." He smiled and emptied the glass out of the dustpan into the trash. "Believe me, if I wasn't with Rene, I'd try to holla."

Ava smiled and tossed the wet paper towels in the wastebasket he held out for her. After putting everything back in its place, they made room at the sink for one another to wash their hands. Reaching for the dish towel at the same time, Ishmael pulled it closer to him. Ava pulled it back her way, dried her hands, and tossed the towel to him.

He placed the towel back on its hook and took hold of her hand. "Listen, Ava. You are special, and sooner rather than later, the right guy will come along and sweep you off your beautiful feet."

"I'll let you tell it." *If only that were true.* She shrugged her shoulders and walked away.

Ishmael grabbed hold of her arm and turned her back to face him. He ran his finger down her arm and caressed the inside of her palm. "No, I'm serious." He stepped to Ava and kissed her on the lips.

Wait, what? "Ishmael, what are you doing?"

"I want to show you how special you are." His kisses moved to her neck. Strong traces of his cologne heightened the temptation. The warmth of his touch soothed every fiber in her body one by one. Ava felt secure and sexy, and more like a woman than she had in months. He wanted her.

The three glasses of wine, Ishmael's debonair looks, and Rene's description of his "good stuff" in the bedroom added up to the curious tension that took over Ava's motions. As she returned the affectionate gestures, she felt like a queen sitting on a pedestal. He led her down the hall to her bedroom, leading her down the wrong path in more ways than one, and closed the door behind them.

Chapter 9

The morning sunlight wove in and out of the blinds. Ava lifted her head to look at her alarm clock. Before her eyes could focus on the numbers, the bell sound of her cell phone acted as an alarm. The upbeat ring didn't match her slothful disposition. She reached for the phone, and realized how much her head hurt. *I ain't drinking no mo'.* The text message read: Happy Valentine's Day, baby girl! Love you, Daddy

She set her cell down and turned over to look on the other side of the bed. Ishmael was nowhere in sight. A piece of paper rested in his vacant spot. Ava picked up the scrap paper and read it aloud. "Please don't tell Rene. I want to make things right with her. Act like nothing happened. Thanks." She crushed the note and threw the ball of paper across the room. *This fool here. How could I sleep with Ishmael?*

After all of her puffed-up talk about how much she wished Rene would leave him alone, Ava tested the waters and fell in. The deep end. That act of sin was wrong on so many levels. Striking herself in the head, she repeated, "What have I done?"

When she stopped beating herself up, her stomach sounded like a bulldozer riding over gravel. A bolder moved up her chest and into her throat. She dry heaved, covered her mouth, and then sprinted to the bathroom. As Ava knelt in front of the shiny, white throne, the ice-cold floor cooled her skin. This would be a Valentine's

Day she would never forget. How did this happen? One minute, she was chillin' in the tub alone with her thoughts and her wine, and the next, she was engaged in relations with Ishmael.

In between trips to the bathroom, she called in sick to work. She didn't want to look bad missing her first day of training for her new supervisor's position, but there was no way she could go in the office an emotional wreck with a hangover. Drinking the entire bottle of water from her nightstand, she paused. Returning Toni's call was the only thing she could think to do.

Toni's voicemail answered. Ava spoke with instability in her voice. "Hey, girl, sorry I missed your call last night. Wish I hadn't. I messed up, Toni. I messed up big time. Please give me a call as soon as you can."

After replaying last night's scene in her head, she yanked the sheets and pillowcases from her bed. The pile of bedding covered her entire upper body as she blindly walked to the laundry room, and dropped the guilt-stained sheets in the washer. Cleaning up behind her mistake drained all of her energy.

Ava slumped into the couch and sat bewildered. Had Ishmael seen Rene yet? Ava knew sex outside of marriage was wrong, but she'd have been better off sleeping with Xavier. At least she wouldn't have hurt anyone but herself. This would destroy Rene when and if she found out. Ava needed to tell Rene herself, but had no desire to disclose the hurtful information.

The knock on her front door was like a hammer to her skull. When she looked out the peephole, she made out Rene's image. Ava's heart catapulted into her throat. Did Rene already know about the catastrophic indiscretion?

Ava wasn't prepared for this surprise visit whether Rene knew or not. *Get it together*. Taking a deep breath, she opened the door.

"Hey, girl." Rene handed her a cup of coffee. "I know you said you didn't have to be at work until ten, so I brought coffee and doughnuts."

"What time is it?"

"Almost nine."

"I'm not going in today." Ava cleared her throat. "I called in sick."

"I thought you didn't look too good." Rene sat across from Ava. "What's the matter?"

You really don't want to know the answer to that question. "I have a headache and my stomach is messed up, but I'll be fine."

Rene scooped up the Texans hat on the arm of the couch. "Who's is this?"

A nervous heat ran through Ava's body. "Oh, that was Xavier's."

"Ishmael has one just like it."

Ava swiped the hat from Rene's hand. "Yeah, he must've left it over here yesterday when he came by." *Just lying. Lord, forgive me. For everything.*

"He came at you again? I guess he's not the giving up type." Crossing her legs, Rene took a sip of coffee. "Anyway, girl, I had to tell you what I went through last night."

Ava's ears perked up as heat flared around her neck. "Mmh?"

"You know after you left Ish and me at the mall, I followed him to his mom's house to drop off her car. Well, I saw some mail that Shanice had left over there for him."

"Yeah?" This would be the second time Ava heard this story.

"Do you know it was the same address he got my car towed from? Can you believe that?"

"Really, girl?" Ava did her best to sound and act surprised.

"I mean he lied straight to my face. And more than once." Rene blew the top of her coffee cup.

"So what'd you do?"

"I told him things are on hold for now. You know I can't feel good about marrying someone who can lie like that."

Just wait 'til you hear what I have to tell you. "And what did he say?"

"He couldn't say much. He got caught and I really wasn't trying to hear anything he had to say anyway. I told him to stay at his momma's house until further notice." Rene bounced her fist off her thigh. "My mom told me not to let him move in. She always said shackin' up leads to no good. Why didn't I listen to her?"

"Well, y'all are supposed to get married in a few months. His lease was up so you probably figured why not."

"I figured wrong. Guess what else I did last night?"

Ava's imagination and nerves scampered wild. "What?"

"I went to Shanice's apartment, and we had a little talk."

"You did?"

"Yep. Ish kept blowing up my phone, but I was on a mission to get some answers. She turned out to be cooler than I thought. Even offered me a drink."

Ava was taken back. "Offered you a drink?"

"Sure did. And I took it, too. I needed something to calm me down."

"What'd she have to say?"

Rene took a deep breath. "She basically said all their conversations are about Isaiah. And Ishmael did get a change of address, but he still receives mail there every once in a while. Old creditors and stuff like that. I guess he was telling the truth about their relationship, but why couldn't he just be upfront with me? No need for all the secrecy."

Ava got to what she really wanted to know. "Have you spoken to him since then?"

"Nope. And don't plan to. Suffering a little will hopefully make him understand we're supposed to be in this together and to quit hiding stuff from me. I'll talk to him soon enough. And call the wedding back on too. I just want him to think about some things for a bit." She brushed her hair back. "He hasn't called me at all today. I guess he's getting the hint."

Ava half-smiled. "Mmh."

Rene's ringtone pierced Ava's ears. After Rene viewed the screen, she said, "Speak of the devil."

Ava looked into Rene's eyes. "And he shall appear."

"I'm going to take it. You mind?"

Yes, I do. "No, I don't mind." Hoping Rene didn't say anything about being at her place, Ava's ears strained to hear any bits of the conversation.

This was not the time to say anything to Rene about the night before. She'd pray about it first, and ask God to make crooked places straight. Would He really listen to her though after her actions? If He didn't want to make the situation better or want her to literally lie in the bed she'd made, then He could at least give her the courage to do the right thing and tell Rene herself. Ava just needed to wait until the time was right. A public setting would be best, or at least have Toni present. But now was definitely not the time.

Rene closed her cell phone and gathered her belongings. "I'm going to take off, girl. He has a lot of explaining to do, so I guess I can let him get to it."

"But you just said—"

"I know what I said, but I might as well hear him out." Rene grabbed Ava by the arm and ushered her toward the bedroom. "But before I leave, I'm going to put some chicken soup in the crock pot. That way, it'll be there warm when you're ready."

Ava zoomed past Rene to her bedroom. *Which way did I throw Ishmael's note?* If Rene came in her room for any reason, Ava did not need her finding that balled-up piece of paper. She dashed over to her TV stand and peeked underneath the piece of furniture and behind the stereo speakers. Nothing. Fumbling through a basket of clothes, the sounds of Rene opening soup cans and banging the cabinets closed fueled her fear. Her heart pounded the inside of her chest.

A piece of paper rested by her desk. Her hopes fell when she opened the folded paper and read the work schedule she printed out the day before. The room could use some tidying up.

She spotted the balled-up paper in the corner by the window. Rene's footsteps approached as Ava hustled to conceal the evidence. She kicked the paper underneath the heavy cherry wood dresser and hit her big toe on the thick standing leg. "Dang it!"

"What's the matter?" Rene called out from the doorway.

"I stubbed my toe." Ava wanted to cry for many different reasons, but fought back the tears.

"I told you to get in bed. What are you doing?"

She swallowed. "Nothing. Just looking for something."

Rene turned to Ava's bed. "Where are your sheets?"

"What?" Guilt tore at Ava's heart.

"Where are your sheets?"

Think. Faster. "Oh, I got sick on them earlier."

"Want me to help you put some more on?"

Ava assertively shook her head. "It's fine." She jumped in bed and pulled up the comforter reeking of Ishmael's cologne.

"Well, I put two cans of chicken soup in the crock pot. It's nothing like your homemade stuff, but it should do the trick. Need anything else?"

"No, you've done too much already. I appreciate it."

Rene bent down to hug Ava. "I'm going to leave you to rest. Call me if you need me."

Did she smell her fiancé's scent? "Thank you." Ava couldn't feel any worse.

"I'll show myself out, love. I'll pray you feel better soon."

Ava cringed. Here Rene was taking care of her, and she in return took care of Rene's man. She was not the friend Rene deserved.

After her friend had made sure she was set for the day, she rushed off to Ishmael's explanation and apology. Ava now knew what the pull he had on her was all about. His good stuff was great. He had reminded Ava how much of a woman she was. She gave Rene grief about putting up with his wretched ways, and now she was in no position to judge.

Lord, I wish I could rewind the clock. I'm going to lose my best friend over this crap.

Tears filled her eyes while thoughts twisted in her head. What was Ishmael going to tell Rene? What would people say when they found out? When she heard the front door close, she slumped out of bed and bent down to lie in front of the dresser to retrieve the piece of paper.

Was Ishmael thinking about their encounter? Was he really attracted to her? She extended her arm, exerting the little strength she had left. *I shouldn't be in this position.* Nausea set in. Again. Ava had only a few seconds before she'd need to make a break for the restroom. She snagged the proof of their encounter and tore it to shreds and flushed it down the toilet.

How would Rene react? Her best friend would probably never speak to her again. Would Ishmael try to weasel his way back into Rene's good graces? *Or into my bed again?*

Her head exploded. Ava slogged out of the bathroom and closed the blinds, then gulped down two Tylenol PM and crept back into bed.

Chapter 10

Ava sat in her car, rubbing her sweaty palms together, as she waited in the fifteen-minute pickup lane outside of Toni's terminal at the airport. Revealing her serious slip-up to Toni would surely get her read the riot act, but she needed to tell someone. How could she even explain acting on her poor judgment?

When Toni walked through the sliding doors, Ava popped her trunk and got out of the car. "Glad you made it back safely." She held on to her tears like a mother holding a newborn.

"Me too."

After they made their way into their seats, Ava lowered the keys into her lap and stared downward.

"Sorry, I didn't you call back yesterday. We shot all day, and then the photographer's assistant threw him a little birthday celebration afterward." Toni breathed a concerned sigh. "You sounded distressed on your message. What's going on?"

"I don't know where to begin."

"Just say it. You know we can get through anything."

"I . . . I . . ." Ava cleared her throat and burst into tears. "I slept with Ishmael."

"You what!" Toni's stunned eyes widened.

"I know. I can't believe it either." Her voice cracked as she went on. "I don't know exactly how it happened. One minute I was helping him look for Rene, and the next we were kissing in the kitchen."

"Kissing in the kitchen?"

"Yeah." That sounded like a bad song. "I dropped my wine glass on the floor and he helped me clean it up."

"So you were drunk?"

"No. Maybe. I don't know." The trio probably all needed to put the alcohol down. Their past proved they couldn't handle having a drink or two.

Toni massaged her temples. "You had to be drunk to sleep with that fool! How could you do this to Rene? How could you do this to yourself?"

"I wasn't in my right mind. Xavier popped up over there earlier and we ended up getting into it. My mom ticked me off with her usual comments. And I did have quite a bit of wine." Ava grabbed a Kleenex from the glove compartment. "Plus, Ishmael kept telling me how special and beautiful I was. It was all bad timing."

"Bad timing?" Toni's face puckered. "Ava, going to the bank and it getting robbed while you're there is bad timing. This goes way beyond bad timing."

"I know, Toni. But I don't know how else to explain it." What had her life boiled down to? The few flattering comments Ishmael made overrode her morals and loyalties to Rene. Was Ava really that simple of a woman?

"Well, you better think of some way to explain it to Rene. You are going to tell her, aren't you? I mean, you can't let her marry that poor excuse for a man."

"Yes, of course I'm going to tell her. I just need some time."

"I knew he was a dog. But dang, Ava, did you have to be the one to prove it?" Toni couldn't seem to stop shaking her head.

"I can't believe I did this." Ava sniffled. "I'm going straight to hell, aren't I?"

"I don't know about all that but you need to sit down and talk with Rene. I'll be there if you want me to."

"I think I will take you up on that. She's going to want to kick my tail."

Toni nodded. "As well she should. But I'll be there to help you talk through it."

Ava would go to the Lord in prayer that Rene wouldn't resort to violent behavior, but it'd be good planning to have Toni present as a backup just in case.

Having dropped the bomb on Toni and making it out with only minor bumps and bruises, Ava put the car in drive and journeyed on to Toni's house. How many major bumps and bruises would she have to try to make it out with when she divulged the news to Rene? What a mess. She and Rene were like sisters. In fact, they were closer than Ava was with her own family. How could Ava, under the influence or not, make that act of intimacy with her friend's man okay in her head? It was going to take a lot of prayer. After Ava did tell her, she'd give Rene her space and hope for the best.

Toni unhooked her seat belt as Ava pulled into the driveway. Struggling to be finished with the conversation, her lips tightened. She had much more to say to her friend on the Ishmael subject, but didn't want to step on her while she was down. "Well, just so you know, I'm going to dinner with Roderick this evening."

Ava's eyes read confusion.

"The guy from the club the other night."

"Oh, yeah. With the jacked-up friend." Ava giggled nervously. "Who am I to be talking, right?"

Toni's lips pulled at the corners.

"Be careful." Ava waved. "Text me if you want me to call you with a sudden emergency."

"I will and you hang in there. Isn't there some saying church folks use like this too shall be passed?"

"You mean this too shall pass?" She giggled. "We're not talking about kidney stones."

Mmh. Oh, now Ava wanted to correct her but couldn't correct herself before she decided to slip under the covers with Ishmael. What holier-than-thou saying did she have for that?

Toni removed her bag from the trunk and trekked into her house. *How could Ava let this happen?* Did she not see what Toni was going through having been cheated on by Eric? Ava had a front-row seat to Toni's pain. And now Ava, the other woman, had made sure Rene was the star of the show. Ava had her set of issues, like everyone else, but the way she dealt with them in the past had never been this crucial.

By the time Toni dropped her bags in her bedroom, she was ready to call Roderick and cancel. However, she needed a distraction from her thoughts of Eric as well as Ava's unfortunate situation. As she plopped down on the bed, her cell phone buzzed. The text message read: Hope u had a safe trip. See u tonite at A Taste of Italy off Gessner at 7. Lookin forward to it. Rod

If Eric knew that Toni was dating again, how would he react? She'd only been in a relationship with him and he was her first and only. He'd always possessed a certain pride about that fact. Making him jealous would be a good way to get him back for his indiscretions, but what was the point? What would stepping down to his level really accomplish? And using an innocent guy like Roderick to do it would be against what she stood for. It'd almost make her no better than Ava. Almost. Toni loved Eric and wasn't interested in hurting him. She just wanted him to know how much his actions hurt her.

She napped until about four, and then ascended out of bed and chose the right outfit for her first date with Roderick. Everything needed to be perfect. Toni wanted to make sure if she wanted a second date, he would too. She showered and perfected her makeup, crafting her look to resemble one of her modeling photos.

When she cruised into the valet parking lane, Roderick stood outside of the entrance of the restaurant. Still as handsome as he was the first night they'd met, he strolled over to her as she handed her keys to the parking attendant.

He opened his arms. "I've been waiting to see you all day."

"I've looked forward to this as well." She smiled.

Roderick opened the door, and escorted her into the restaurant. The hostess scrolled down the list and found their reservation. She motioned for the waitress to guide them to their table. Roderick and Toni followed the bubbly waitress through the dimly lit eatery.

The décor was high class. Tables were adorned with crimson roses, fine china, burgundy cloth napkins, and full place settings including a bunch of pearl-handled silverware Toni was never sure about. One fork for this. Another for that. What was wrong with cleaning one fork off with the napkin and carrying on with the meal? Smells of steak and fresh seafood tugged at Toni's stomach.

Roderick pulled out Toni's chair, the gentleman Eric had forgotten to be. He ordered a bottle of wine. "Their signature Merlot is like they have a vineyard right in their backyard. Can I interest you in a glass of red wine?"

She nodded, then recalled Ava's fiasco that involved wine. Toni should probably turn the offer down. "Maybe just a glass."

"How was your trip back?"

"It was good. A little turbulence here and there but nothing too scary."

"I appreciate you meeting me for dinner."

"No problem. I don't have to work tomorrow so I'm good." *But I'd rather be at the house chillin'.* Toni's attitude was stank. Could she put aside her thoughts of Eric and disappointment in Ava to enjoy a meal with a potential companion?

Small talk continued until their entrees made it to the table. Toni revealed more about her clothing design projects and dreams, while Roderick shared he was up for a promotion soon if he could produce his next two commercials without any hiccups. She had always been attracted to professional brothas, so he already had a check in the plus column.

He ate the last bite of his medium-rare steak and put his fork down. "Hey, I have an idea."

Toni wiped her mouth with her napkin. "Yeah, what's that?"

"Why don't you come down to the station tomorrow since you're off? I can fit you into a test shoot. We'll be shooting tomorrow afternoon. And if all goes well, I may be able to get you in a commercial or two."

She shook her head. Was he trying to run a line on her? "I don't know. I've mostly done print work, but no commercials."

"You can do it. Just be yourself and be beautiful. I know you won't have any trouble with the latter." Roderick winked at her.

"Thank you. But are you sure?"

"Absolutely. Of course, I'll need to take a headshot or something in with me in the morning. We have narrowed it down to two actresses and a model for this new campaign. You could even the playing field for the models. I could let you know by lunch."

"Really?" Commercials did sound appealing and would be a nice change in her hectic travel schedule.

"Yeah, why not? Do you have a photo or your portfolio with you?"

"No, I left everything in my suitcases at the house."

He leaned back in his chair. "It's not a problem. We could get it before the night is over."

"Mmm. I'm not sure about that. I don't know you all that well to have you coming to my house on a first date."

"It's no biggie. I understand. But I will need to show my boss something. I can't have you come in sight unseen on our final callbacks."

"Well, I guess it wouldn't hurt this once. This is business, right?"

He grinned. "That's right."

The waitress brought the check, and he paid in cash. They rose out of their chairs and headed out of the restaurant. Roderick followed Toni to her house in his black Range Rover. He had a good job, nice car, was attractive, and could possibly help her get to the next level in her career. Happier by the minute that she decided to go on the date, Toni periodically checked her appearance in the rearview mirror, and even freshened her lipstick at a stoplight.

When she got out of the car, he rolled down his window. "You want me to wait here?"

"I appreciate that, but you can come in. I'll get my portfolio and you can decide what photo will be best to take with you." His offer to wait outside made her more comfortable with the situation.

Roderick hopped out of the car and trailed behind her. She offered him a seat and went in her bedroom to locate her leather briefcase. Her modeling portfolio was stacked on top of everything else. She grabbed it and bounced to the front of the house.

He opened the folder and turned page after page. "This is beautiful, Toni. Yep, I could definitely get you a test shoot, so keep your afternoon free."

"Thanks, Roderick. I will."

He moved closer. "I'll take this photo here of you on the beach in the swimsuit, and this one in the clothing store. We'll show range."

They shared a laugh.

"Okay, I'll be right back." Toni drifted into her office and searched among her files of photographs from different modeling jobs. She located the two photos he requested, put them in an envelope, and returned to the living room.

Roderick's suit jacket lay across the back of the loveseat. She turned the corner to see him standing with every button on his shirt undone. "What are you doing?"

"What does it look like?" He unfastened his belt.

"It looks like you need to put your clothes back on." *Who does this fool think he is?*

"Oh, no, Ms. Lady, we're just getting started."

She snatched his jacket from the loveseat and hurled it at him. "We ain't getting nothin' started."

"Are you telling me you let me in to get some pictures and nothing else?"

"That's exactly right. And you can leave my pictures here, and just get out."

"I ain't going nowhere." Roderick thundered over to her and wrapped his hands firmly around her arms.

"Are you crazy? Get your hands off me!"

"You know you want this. All that talk about not letting anybody in here on a first date. Well, this is a first date, and I'm here."

"That was about business. And now I see you were just trying to work your way in my house. Now let go of me and get out!" She was an idiot for trusting this joka. All his talk, fueling the idea in her head that she could be a spokesmodel or that he could help to push her career in another direction. Toni had to be more careful in the future.

He pulled her blouse out of her skirt and his hand traveled underneath her clothing. She grabbed his hands to push them off her, but she proved too weak for his burly strength. "Did you not hear me? I'm telling you to get out."

"I'm not interested in what you have to say. I'm interested in what you can do." His hand squeezed tighter on her arm.

She pushed her hands into his chest, but he stood his ground. *Lord, please get me out of this. I won't ever be this stupid again. Please.*

"Stop fighting me, Toni. You're making this harder than it has to be."

"Leave me alone." She hiked her knee, grazing his groin area and ran for the door.

He roared at her, causing a lamp to crash into her glass coffee table. Pieces of glass smashed everywhere. "Come here, trick!" Roderick pulled the back of her hair, turning her around by the fierce grasp. Using his left hand to rip the front of her blouse open, his fingers intruded under her bra. Toni exerted all her strength to wrestle his hands away from her. When that didn't work, she poked him in the eyes with a quick two-finger motion.

"Ahh!" He readjusted his grip on her hair and slapped her across the face.

She screamed as the left side of her face was on fire.

He collared his hand around her neck and yelled, "I told you not to make this hard. It's going to happen whether you want it to or not!"

The door vibrated. A male voice was on the other side of the door. "The heck it is! Ain't nothing going to happen but me kicking your tail. Open the door!"

"Eric? Hurry! He's attacking me." She repeatedly pushed his hands off of her.

Roderick relaxed his grip on her neck. "Who's Eric?"

"Someone who's about to whoop you." She backed away from him. Just then, the door burst open. Eric stood there. He stormed at Roderick, taking hold of his collar, fighting him to the ground. Then Eric repeatedly introduced the backside of his fist to Roderick's face.

Toni rushed to retrieve her cell phone out of her purse to call 911, hoping it was charged enough to make the call, since she never did get that landline her mother told her she might need for emergencies. She never figured she'd have this type of emergency.

Describing the events to the dispatch operator made her more neurotic, only able to spit out a few words in between hurried breaths. The operator assured her someone was on their way before she hung up. Once Eric was physically tired, he got up off the ground and backed away from Roderick who lay on the floor unconscious.

Sitting crouched in a ball in the corner of the living room, Toni exhaled. Eric road in on his white horse and transformed into her knight in an Air Jordan sweat suit. He'd shown up at her house many times before, but this time she was overjoyed. He knelt down beside her. Turning her body toward him, he held her in a tight embrace. As her heart pounded, she buried her head into his chest while her tears fell into the creases of his shirt.

When the police arrived, they arrested Roderick and placed him in the back of one of the two squad cars. After Toni and Eric gave their statements, Toni thanked the officer and closed the door. How could she show Eric how grateful she was? With showing up at the right moment, he had come a long way in a short time. A knock pounded the front door.

Toni looked at Eric. "Who is it?"

"Officer Walker."

She unlocked the door and opened it to let him in.

The officer scratched the back of his head. "Um. I hate to do this, but Roderick is pressing charges against Eric." He moved over toward Eric and began placing handcuffs on him while he read him his Miranda rights.

Toni was in disbelief. "Are you kidding me? If it wasn't for him, I could've gotten raped."

"Yes, ma'am, I understand. But he did beat him up pretty good. Some might say it was overkill."

"Overkill? Boy, this is the justice system at its finest."

Eric gazed into Toni's eyes. "Don't worry. I'll be fine."

The officer guided Eric out of the house. "It probably won't take much to get this all cleared up. If he posts bail tonight, he'll be out by morning."

She followed them onto the porch. "I'll be right behind you, Eric. And I'll give Rene a call, too," Toni yelled toward the officer. "My lawyer."

Eric turned his head as best he could in her direction. "I'm just glad you're okay."

She smiled and wiped her tears. "Thanks to you. I'm grateful you were here."

Eric tensed his body, so the officer couldn't push his head into the car just yet, and raised his voice. "I'll always be here for you, Toni."

The officer put Eric in the back seat of the second patrol car. After she watched the car pull off through her window, she changed out of her torn clothes and into a more comfortable outfit of sweats and a T-shirt, and then cleaned the makeup off her face.

Replaying the scene over in her head, Toni drove in silence to the police station. That was the Eric she knew and fell in love with. In the past few months, he'd called numerous times and shown up at her house unexpectedly to apologize, and try to fix the disorder he'd caused in their marriage. She didn't want to listen to anything he had to say. But after tonight, she could at least hear him out. When Toni arrived at the station, she paid Eric's bail, and waited for him to be released.

Chapter 11

Ava had never gone more than three days without talking to her best friend. Rene might've suspected something was up. The good thing was that Rene, who had recently told Ishmael the wedding was back on, was busy with wedding plans, her current court cases, and now handling Eric's case, would hopefully not notice the lack of conversation between them.

All during her lunch break at work, Ava dreaded heading home. Friday was the best day of the week, but chatting with Rene on the weekends was inevitable. And Ava needed to tell Rene the truth about her and Ishmael's betrayal sooner rather than later. Rene would be finalizing wedding plans in the days to come, and Ava didn't want her to continue making those plans until she knew everything. Not that she would move forward in the planning once she found out, but paying deposits she couldn't get back would add to the jankyness of the situation.

After lunch, she went to the county jail to visit two of her juvenile inmates. As she strolled down the row of cells, she heard comments like "Dang, she's bad built," and "Look how her shoes slump over," along with other ridicule and laughter. Ava acted as if she were deaf, but the cruel comments cut straight to her heart. *That's okay, 'cause while y'all are in here locked up, I'll be enjoying a cheeseburger and fries.*

Her visits went well as she discussed release dates and the definition of good behavior with the adolescents. One of her kids, a thirteen-year-old boy named Tommy, asked to speak with her in a private meeting room.

They traveled to a nearby room with a guard.

Tommy nervously rubbed his hands together. "Miss Alexander?"

"Yes, Tommy. What's the matter?"

He hesitated, looking downward. "I need some help, but I can't say anything or I'll get into trouble."

Ava scooted her chair closer. "What do you mean?"

Although he said nothing, she read fear in his eyes. Hoping this wasn't a ploy to play on her emotions, she took the bait. "You need to tell me or I can't help you."

Tommy's stone face barely opened his mouth to speak. "It's about gangs."

"You aren't getting mixed up in that mess, are you? You have one month left until you get out."

"I know, but it's hard in here." His eyes filled with water. "I don't want to but then I'll be left out."

"Tommy, what you're talking about is peer pressure. You have to be your own person. Forget about what everyone else thinks." Wishing she could do the same, she went on. "The folks trying to get you to join their gang will still be locked up when you're on the outside getting a fresh start in the right direction. And you need to stay out of trouble in here to be released out there."

Tommy shook his head with a partial smile. He was a good kid. Just picked the wrong friends to hang out with at the wrong time, and got caught in the driver's seat of a stolen car. Ever since his father left, he'd been trying to find approval from many different sources. Nothing worked in his favor yet. But Ava was determined to get him back on the right track.

"Listen, I want you to do your daily duties and stay away from kids who are going to pull you down. Concentrate on who you are and who you want to be. And what you're going to do when you get out of here. Like check back into school, handle your business in the classroom, and get involved in some extracurricular activities."

"Yes, ma'am." His grin grew larger by the second.

"Hey, you like running in races; we can have you join the track team." Ava stood.

He laughed and gave her a hug. "Thank you, Miss Alexander. I'll see you soon. And I'm going to be good. I promise."

"That's what I want to hear."

On the way home, she rolled through the drive-through and ordered her favorite combo with a milkshake. The remarks made to her a couple hours before didn't sting so much as she savored every bite of delicious melted American cheese on each inch of the hamburger patty. The fries had just the right amount of salt, and the sweet coldness of the shake sent it over the top. Once the meal had disappeared, her anxiety about the hurtful comments did too.

Instead of eating away her problems, Ava needed to take her own advice that she bequeathed to Tommy: not to worry about what others thought. But her brain had been trained for so long. It'd be a struggle to change now. Mulling it over in her mind tired her out. She soon fell into a deep sleep on the couch.

Her cell phone went off Saturday morning early, waking her. Seeing Rene's picture on the screen, she set the phone on the coffee table. Saturdays consisted of trying new recipes for her catering ventures, washing loads of laundry, and catching up on her favorite recorded shows on the DVR. All of this kept her busy and her mind off of the situation at hand. For the most part. Ava hated avoiding her friend.

Sitting on the edge of her bed, she closed her eyes. "Lord, I pray for your guidance. Please forgive me and help me to forgive myself. Right now, I need your strength. I know my mistake will damage my relationship with Rene, if not end it all together. I truly do care about her and did not intend to hurt her in any way." She slipped underneath the covers. "I need to get hold of this self-esteem, self-image, whatever my problem is 'cause now it's leaking into other areas of my life. Please help me, Lord."

Ava clamored out of bed the next morning to get dressed for church. Looking forward to pouring every-thing out at the altar, she planned to take the courage she needed away with her when she left the House of the Lord church. God knew what she was feeling and what she needed, but Ava didn't have the slightest idea for moving forward in her situation. In fact, she was in the negative range now. She had backslid and backtracked so fast, she didn't know what moving forward felt like anymore.

As churchgoers filled the sanctuary, she headed for her designated seat in the back. She found her row and crossed over a handful of people to reach her seat.

Rene sat there with a welcoming smile. "Hey, Ava."

Ava halted in her footsteps. Her swallow hurt going down. "You didn't tell me you were coming this morning."

"Well, I called you yesterday, but you didn't call me back." Rene put her arm around Ava as she sat down. "I missed my best friend."

"I missed you too." Ava, stunned in her seat, was glad the service started.

During the worship portion of the service, Ava's thoughts scattered all over the place like a child's spilt marbles on the floor. What would they do after the service? Would she be able to unveil her wrongdoings?

After the offering was collected, Pastor Monroe stood behind the podium. "Good morning, church."

The crowd flooded the pulpit with greetings. Ava looked down at her church bulletin for fear Pastor would be talking directly to her again, and with Rene sitting an inch away.

"It's a blessing to be in God's presence this morning. Today's message comes from the book of Matthew. Please turn there with me."

Everyone with their Bible flipped through pages, while others with their electronics utilized their touch screens. "I want you to stop in Matthew 10:26." He paused to look up at the congregation. "When you have it, say amen."

"Amen," the congregation answered in unison.

"I want to focus on the second part of that verse. In the NIV Bible the verse reads, 'There is nothing concealed that will not be disclosed, or hidden that will not be made known.'"

Someone called out, "Say that, say that!"

"Church, can I be real with you?"

While others encouraged him in their own way, a man on Ava's row shouted, "Please do, Pastor!"

Ava's heart drummed inside her chest. *Not too real, Pastor.*

"You may be going on in your everyday life, thinking you can get away with certain actions and behaviors. Hoping what you do behind closed doors will never become public knowledge." He wiped his brow. "But God's people, let me set you straight. First of all, the Lord knows all and sees all. He sees what sins are committed and your part in them. And guess what? He loves you anyway."

A "glory" and a "preach, Pastor" went forth. "Secondly, it's just a matter of time before the people around you find out what you think you have kept hidden."

Really, Lord? Ava looked to the ceiling and fidgeted in her seat.

"I can remember when I was in college some twenty-five, twenty-six years ago. I came home for a visit and called myself going to smoke my reefah, that's what we called it back then. I hid around the back of my parents' garage." He smirked. "Raise your hand if you know I got caught."

Several folks in the church raised their hands and a few laughed.

"And by my momma, too. Here she thought I was her perfect li'l angel. And from then on out she saw her li'l angel as a reefah cheefah." Chuckles flooded to the front. "Let me tell you something, church. A guilt-free conscience is the way to live your life. All secrets come out. It's just a matter of when. Let the truth set you free today."

Did Ava want to be set free this soon? A nervous heat shot through her body. Her bulletin turned into an old-school church fan. The rapid waving back and forth almost caused her to lose her grip on the pamphlet of church info. Or, it could've been the temptation to go into a nervous panic. Either way, Ava needed to calm down and cool down.

Pastor Monroe continued, "You may think it's only an external problem, but the torment of what you are doing or have done is definitely an inside job, tearing you up internally. Free yourself by coming clean, asking for forgiveness, and repenting. Turn away from those sins that hold you back from moving forward in what God has for you."

Ava was sure her face read every ugly detail she and Ishmael shared. She looked everywhere in the church except Rene's direction. What would be the best way to start off the conversation with Rene? Ava left her seat to go up for prayer at the close of the service.

Rene gave Ava a consoling embrace when she returned to her seat. "Feeling better, Miss Ava?" They walked out of the sanctuary arm in arm.

"Yes, I do." *I am lying in church.*

"Well, you wanna go grab a bite to eat?"

"How about I whip up something at my place? I'll call Toni and we can make it a wonderful Sunday dinner for the three of us." With Toni in the room, Ava could conjure up enough courage to tell Rene about her betrayal of their friendship. Ava prayed that, hopefully, Toni could drop what she was doing and beeline it over to Ava's. Having her there could prove to be a good buffer, conversationally and physically.

"That sounds good. I need to talk to her about Eric's case anyway."

"Good news I hope."

"Yep, that punk Roderick ended up dropping the charges. He came to the conclusion his own attempted rape was enough. And the charges against Eric only put his own violence against Toni in the spotlight even more. I have some technicalities to go over with her and some documents for Eric to get notarized."

"Awesome work, counselor." Ava grinned, but it didn't take long for her focus to revert to her own spiritual crime she had committed against her best friend.

After she and Rene separated to find their cars in the parking lot, Ava sent Toni a text: Get to my house asap. The stuff is about to hit the fan.

Chapter 12

While Ava threw together a Sunday meal, she and Rene caught up. Her fingers seemed to move faster than her brain. Tossing the lettuce with her shaking hands landed half of it on the floor.

"You okay, Ava?"

"Yep, I'm good." She rushed, picking up the spilt salad.

She set the bowl of the remaining clean lettuce on the counter too close to the stovetop and the chicken grease popped out of the pan, stinging her skin. She grabbed her wrist. "Dang it!"

Rene hustled over with a concerned frown. "Are you sure you're all right? Do you need any help?"

Ava shook her head. What she needed to do was settle down. "No, I got it."

Scooping some butter, Rene rubbed a lump on Ava's skin. She welcomed the help Rene gave for her physical pain, but knew sharing her and Ishmael's bad deed with her friend would cause Rene great emotional pain. And more than likely sever their friendship. What would Ava do without Rene in her life? They were best friends since middle school. Which brought up the question, how could Ava sleep with her best friend's significant other? Did she really value their friendship at all?

After setting the crispy fried chicken aside to cool, she continued with the macaroni and cheese, green beans, and homemade biscuits, hoping this comfort food would live up to its name and comfort her for the task ahead.

Ava glanced between her wristwatch and the front door like she was watching a tennis match. She did her best to gauge when Toni would walk through the doorway.

As Ava finished food preparations, she continued to pray for what to say. The Holy Spirit would have to fill her mouth with words because she had come up with zilch. Both cooking and praying were the perfect calming agents she used frequently. Going back to that night of weakness, the first correction would have been to not answer the door when Ishmael came knocking. And after she did let him in, Ava should've gone to the Lord in prayer. One bad decision led to the next, and now she was about to hit Rene with a Mack truck of disloyalty.

"Do you want something to drink, Rene?"

"I'll have some sweet tea." Rene glided into the kitchen. "I can get it. You go 'head and do your thing on those burners over there. Gotta love the aroma of all this home-cooked food." She patted Ava's shoulder as she scooted by to get to the fridge. "Reminds me of growing up. When Momma was throwin' down in the kitchen, you knew everything was all right."

Ava may have been creating a feast of nostalgia, but everything was definitely not all right. And now things with Rene and Ishmael would never be all right. Surely, Rene longed to have that warm, safe feeling of comfort she saw in her parents' relationship growing up. They all desired that with their future husbands, but now Rene's dream would be pushed back because of Ava and Ishmael's despicable action. Ava lost her appetite.

The front door swung open. Toni breezed in, still wearing sunglasses. "Mmm. Fried chicken."

Whew! She made it. Ava looked up from her mixing. "How are you doing, Toni?"

Giving Toni a hug, Rene said, "Yeah, girl, how are you?"

"I'm good. When everything happened with Roderick, I was a bit shook up. But I'm okay now."

"Look at your face." Ava touched Toni's chin and moved her face to get a good view of the damage. "What are you putting on it?"

"Ice and vitamin E. After Eric finally got released, we returned to my house and he put a slab of steak on my face. He had me looking a hot mess, but I guess it made it a little better." Toni caressed her cheek. "I'm not accepting any modeling jobs for about two weeks. Hopefully, it'll heal completely by then. Or at least I'll be able to hide it with makeup."

Rene leaned back on the counter, grinning. "So, Eric showing up unannounced this time was a good surprise, huh?"

"Yes, it was. And he has called every day since then to check on me." Toni pulled on the end of her hair with a dreamy expression. "He's really been there for me this week."

Ava smirked as she heard the obvious change in Toni's voice as she talked about Eric. From revenge to respect. "That sounds promising."

"Too early to tell. I miss the old him. And I've seen glimpses of the guy I married, so we'll see." Toni would never admit her true feelings concerning Eric stepping in and saving her, but her body language, all smiles and giddiness, revealed everything.

Rene took her glass and sat down at the kitchen table. "Well, I'm happy for you, Toni. Maybe one day you'll be able to forgive and forget, and get back together."

"I don't know about all that." Toni tossed her hair out of her face. "I am glad to have his friendship back, at least for the time being. Speaking of forgive and forget, Ava, how are things with you?"

Heffa, please! How did Toni know she was ready to spill the extremely large beans? Toni could've at least pulled her to the side and asked her privately first. "I've been better."

"Really? What's the matter, Ava?" Rene sauntered over to the kitchen counter.

Courage needed to take over because Ava wasn't prepared to say anything just yet. "I haven't been myself lately. I have something to tell you, Rene."

"What is it?"

Toni marched into the kitchen and affixed herself between her two friends as they both leaned again the kitchen counters across from one another.

Ava stared at the floor. "I've been really down about my weight and Xavier, and been feeling sorry for myself. Basically, having a pity party with me the only one there."

Rene put her hand on Ava's shoulder. "Why didn't you call me?"

"The night I was extremely down in the dumps, you and Ishmael had got into it over your car being towed."

"So? You know I would've dropped whatever I was doing and been there for you, Ava."

"Well, Ishmael came over here looking for you. I had like three or four glasses of wine. I tried to help him find you, but you didn't answer either of our calls."

"Yeah, I told you I was at ol' girl's house. Shanice."

"Yes, I know, but that night when you didn't pick up, Ishmael kept complimenting me, and then one thing led to another." Why was she telling Rene this? "And we . . ."

Rene leaned her head forward as if to guide the words out of Ava's mouth. "You what?"

Stepping backward, Ava prepared for the backlash that was sure to come next once she uttered the devastating words. Could she utter the devastating words? "We . . ."

"We what?" Rene raised her voice as she placed her hand on her hip.

Toni put her arm in between them. "Just say it, Ava."

"We slept together."

A fire grew in Rene's eyes. "Excuse me!"

"I'm sorry. I didn't mean for this to happen. I told you what I was going through, plus the wine. I wish you would've answered your phone."

"So, because I didn't answer my phone, you slept with my fiancé?" Rene removed her hoop earrings and threw them on the counter.

"That's not what I meant. I'm sorry. I just—"

Charging at Ava, Rene pushed Toni out of the way, knocking the chicken and salad on the floor. Rene used both hands to shove Ava into the pantry door, peering into her eyes.

Toni regained her footing and reinserted herself into the battle, hands up in the air. "Rene, stop!"

"Leave me alone, Toni. This is between me and Ava."

"I know it's between you guys and Ava is wrong, no doubt, but you don't want to hit her."

"Oh, yes, I do." Rene swung around Toni's head, but missed.

The fierce wind from her fist brushed Ava's skin. "It's okay, Toni. Let her hit me. I deserve it." She didn't know if getting hit would make Rene feel any better. But she was willing to take that chance. Anything she could do to make things better between them. Even take her friend's right hook in the face.

"And you're supposed to be my best friend. I see why you haven't called me all week. Too busy wallowing in your guilt."

Ava remained silent. The right words to say at this point would never come out. How could they? The right words didn't exist. There was nothing right about any part of the situation. The only words that came to Ava's mind were betrayal, sin, and unforgivable.

"And that hat you said was Xavier's." Rene bent her head and stepped closer. "It was Ishmael's, wasn't it?

"Yes."

Rene's head bounced back and forth. "Your lying behind could've fessed up then."

"I don't know what to say, Rene. I know I made all those excuses, but none of that makes it right." Ava shook her head. "Ishmael asked me not to say anything, but I couldn't let you go on with this wedding not knowing everything."

"Go on with this wedding? There is no wedding. I'm not marrying that fool! And there is no friendship between us either. I don't have a groom, or a maid of honor. More like a maid of dishonor." Rene's eyes seem to shoot flames into Ava. "You better be glad Toni's here, or I'd beat your tail into the ground."

Ava burst into tears. "I'm sorry, Rene. He made me feel special. I didn't mean to hurt you."

"Are you that insecure? Can't find a man of your own to do that for you? And after all we've been through." Rene seemed on the brink of tears. "How could you do me like this?"

"I'll make it up to you, Rene. I promise. Please find it in your heart to forgive me."

"Don't hold your breath." Rene grabbed her keys. "In fact, do hold your breath. 'Cause I couldn't give a hot darn what you do. I don't know who I grew up with, but you ain't her. Good-bye and good luck. Trick!" She slammed the front door.

Toni followed Rene out of the apartment while Ava fell to the floor. She'd brought all of this on herself and couldn't do anything about it. As much as she wanted to make Rene understand her side of the story, she couldn't control Rene's actions or feelings and had to deal with the chaos she created.

When Toni returned, she knelt down to pick up the food that lay scattered all over the kitchen floor. "I tried to calm Rene down before she got behind the wheel, but there was no use."

"Just leave it. I can clean up later." The mess on the floor represented her life. She'd brood there a bit longer.

"No, it's okay. I don't mind."

"No, really. I'm a terrible friend, Toni. You better get away from me before I end up hurting you too."

Putting the cleaning on pause, Toni put her arm on Ava's knee. "Don't say that. You can't let this mistake cancel out all the good you and Rene have shared. I told you Rene's going to need some time. This cuts deep; believe me, I know." She stood and snatched a dish rag off the sink. "And Rene may or may not be able to forgive you or come to terms with this, but know you did the right thing by telling her."

"Well, if I did the right thing, why don't I feel any better? I didn't get to say everything I wanted about how sorry I truly am."

"I know. But you just need to give her space. Hopefully, she'll come around when she's ready to."

"No problem there. I'm so embarrassed I don't think I'll ever leave my apartment." Ava calculated the food, bottled water, and tissue she'd need to stock up on like people did in natural disasters. She planned to take cover and never walk outside her four walls.

"Stop it, Ava. People make mistakes. It happens. You apologized and I believe it was sincere. Just be there when Rene is ready to talk. That's all you can do." Toni lifted Ava's face. "And don't give Ishmael another thought. If he comes by or calls, steer clear of him. I don't care what he says."

Ava didn't care either. Except, part of her wanted to know how Ishmael would explain what happened to Rene. Phrases like "It meant nothing" were sure to be in use. Ava wouldn't be able to defend herself and she was positive he'd make her out to be the bad guy. "I don't think he'll show up around here anytime soon. I'm sure he'll blame me for Rene calling off the wedding, but he's just as responsible as I am."

"You got that right. And don't let anyone, including him, tell you otherwise." Toni helped Ava stand. "Now, come on, girl. Let's clean up this mess."

Chapter 13

Rene left Ava's apartment and drove straight home. What just happened? Ava had her insecurities and Ishmael had his issues, but never in this lifetime did Rene think that their demons would cross paths. Having a lead foot was an understatement as she weaved in and out of traffic. Asking Ishmael what the heck he was thinking resided at the top of her list, but Rene had a few items to gather at home first.

Everything that resembled Ishmael's property landed in two large boxes. She snatched the picture frame that held a photo of them in happier times and chucked the frame in the box. The glass shattered upon impact as she moved on to the next object. Rene yanked his game system from under the TV, tearing the cords out and smashing the box the cords were plugged into.

As she threw the game next to the picture frame, the teddy bear he'd given her for Valentine's Day laughed at her from the couch. Grabbing the bear, she headed to the kitchen and retrieved a pair of scissors out of the junk drawer. That dang'on bear wasn't going to be grinning much longer. Cutting the curved red felt strip smile off its face proved to be therapeutic.

She hacked off an ear, since Ishmael never listened to her anyway. After setting the shears down, she strained to pull the head off. When cotton stuffing poured out of its neck, her soul was satisfied and she tossed the bear in the box. Once she was confident she had boxed up everything

Ishmael owned or anything that reminded her of their relationship, she carried each box to the car.

Adrenaline guided her to Ishmael's mother's house. As she kept an eye out for cops alongside the roads, her foot remained heavy on the gas. A speeding ticket wasn't what she needed right now, but her emotions were driving the car.

When she pulled onto the driveway, she put her BMW in park and jumped out. She dragged the boxes out of the back seat, shredding the corners of each box, and left them in Ms. Carter's front lawn.

She shouted, "Ishmael! Come out here now," then ran to the front porch and beat her fist on the edge of the screen door.

His mother looked through the screen. "Rene, is that you? Why you out here yelling?" She tilted her head to look behind Rene. "And what are those boxes for?"

"Sorry, Ms. Carter, but I need to talk to Ishmael."

Crinkling her face, she asked, "What's the matter?"

Rene wasn't interested in small talk. "I just need to talk to Ishmael."

"Okay, I'll get him for you, dear." Momma Carter turned halfway around and hollered, "Ishmael, get down here!"

Not sure what she would do when she saw Ishmael, Rene paced in front of the door. He came shuffling down the stairs. "Sorry, Momma, I was in the restroom. You got my neck bones on the stove?"

"Yes, I do, but you got more to worry about than them neck bones. Rene's here and she's upset."

He reached the foyer and opened the screen door to let Rene in. "Ah, hey, baby, what's up?"

"What's up? I dropped your crap out there in the grass. The wedding is off."

"Off?" He frowned. "What are you talking about?"

"Oh, no." His mother covered her mouth.

"Yes, off. Isn't there something you forgot to tell me? Oh, wait. You didn't forget. You were just never going to tell me at all. In fact, you wanted Ava to keep it a secret."

Ishmael's light-skinned face turned fire-truck red.

"I guess you have nothing to say."

"Baby, that was a big mistake." He rubbed both of his hands over his face. "I went there looking for you."

"And when you didn't find me, you decided sleeping with Ava was the best way for us to work things out?" *He must think I'm the dumbest broad on the planet.*

"Boy, you what?" Momma Carter slapped him in the back of the head.

He shrugged back. "Ouch! Dang, Momma."

"Yep, Ms. Carter. He sure did. So, it was nice to have known you, but I'm done. There will be no wedding. No marriage. No me." Rene turned around and waved goodbye, and walked to her car. "You two take care."

Ishmael hustled behind Rene. "Babe, please stop. I love you and I'm sorry. I know I don't deserve it, but please listen to me a minute."

"There is absolutely nothing you can say. Let me save you time and energy. Leave me alone. Forever!"

"Don't say that, Rene. After all we've shared in this relationship?"

"Well, that doesn't really mean anything anymore, now does it? Especially, since you're sharing it with other people. And my best friend at that!" It took everything in Rene not to swing at Ishmael's face.

He turned away, pounding his fist into the palm of his other hand. His mother flung the screen door open, carrying a silver stew pot.

"Momma, what are you doing?"

She placed the pot next to the two large boxes. "You need to call one of your friends to come and get you 'cause you can't stay here."

Rene watched the scene play out from her car.

"Why not? I've been staying here."

"I know, but that's when I thought you'd only be here a week. I've babied you too long and that's why you act the way you do. You are a grown man."

"Momma, are you serious?"

"As a heart attack." Ms. Carter rolled her neck.

Ishmael scratched his head. "You not even gon' let me finish cooking my neck bones?"

"Naw, you can take them with you. If I let you finish them at my house then you'll just talk your way back into staying here, and you gotta go. But I would never deny my child food."

"Mm-hmm. Just a place to stay."

"Don't get smart with me, boy. I've done enough. It's time for you to help yourself. Now, I love you, but now is a perfect time for some tough love." She left him standing in the yard.

"Ah, you got a pot, but no window!" Rene laughed as she put her car in reverse, backed out of the driveway, and sped off down the street.

Ishmael wouldn't get another minute of her time. This would be the last of her worrying behind his actions. Maybe gray hairs would stop appearing at random, and she could save money on getting her hair dyed every few weeks. Or better yet, she could put the extra dollars toward counseling. For Ava.

Chapter 14

Here it was springtime and the Houston humidity still had Ava sweating as soon as her feet hit the pavement. She changed clothes to go to her parents' house for dinner, searching for something cool but that would also make her look smaller. Her mother's critiques of every new curve were sure to be plentiful. Ava didn't want to look like she gained weight. So far she had two strikes. A third, and she'd be out. Out of going to her parents' house.

She could opt to stay home, but hadn't seen her parents or her brother and his wife in weeks. And if she continued to be too antisocial, her inquisitive mother would come at her with a list of questions.

Lately, all she wanted to do was lie in bed or on her sofa and eat, drink, and try to be merry. Going to work because she had to and church, every once in a while, because she needed to was the extent of her travels. And then of course, there were the frequent drive-through visits.

Ava desired to call Rene, but the past week every time she dialed her number she received the same response: four rings and then voicemail. Rene probably looked to see who it was and chose not to answer. So since her best friend, who was the sister she never had, wasn't speaking to her, and with good reason, Ava finished getting dressed and left her apartment to spend time with her biological family.

The door opened as she approached the front steps. Her father grinned and said, "Hey, baby girl. Glad you made it. Come give your old man a hug."

Her father's inviting embrace was the only thing she truly looked forward to. However, she didn't need to stay there too long for fear he might sense something was wrong. He was special that way and so was their connection. "Hey, Daddy. Missed you guys." *Well, missed you.*

"We missed you too. Go on inside. Your brother and Elaine are in the kitchen witcha momma."

Ava pulled the top of her pants across her stomach, fixing her shirt to lie smoothly over her jeans. Well, somewhat smoothly. Running her fingers through her hair, she eased into the kitchen. She wouldn't give her mother anything to pick on her about if she could help it.

"Ava's here." Her mother smiled, put the knife down she used to cut the potatoes, and bustled around the island to give Ava a hug. "You're looking healthy."

Gah dawg! I ain't been here two minutes. "Thank you, Momma. Good to see you too."

Before the moment became too awkward, her brother, Alex, chimed in. "Hey, sis. It's really great to see you. Where you been hidin'?"

"Nowhere. Just doing my same thing, work, church, and home. What up with you, bro?" She hit him in the arm then hugged him. Turning to Elaine, she said, "How are you, sister-in-law?"

"I'm good. Busy, but good." Elaine gave Ava a hug.

Ava smiled and bounced her head. "Yeah, I bet y'all are busy. Momma told me you two were trying to get pregnant."

"Momma, dang!" Alex frowned. "You just had to say something."

Popping an olive in to her mouth, Ava asked, "What? Your own sister can't know?"

"It's not that." He put his arm around Elaine.

Elaine shook her head. "It's okay, she didn't know."

"I didn't know what?"

Rubbing Alex's shoulder, Elaine took a deep breath. "We've been trying for a while now and not sure it's going to happen. I've been to the fertility doctor and everything."

"Oh, it will happen." Ava needed it to happen. Her mother might get off of her case once she held her first grandchild in her arms. "God gives you the desires of your heart, right?" *I need to remember that for myself.*

"Thank you, Ava." Elaine flashed a smile. "I'll hold on to that."

Giggling, Ava went on. "And you know I just can't wait to spoil my niece or nephew and send the little sweetie back home."

Alex set a stack of plates on the table. "Are you going to be that type of auntie? Spoil the baby and then when he or she gets to crying and pooping, you ready to send them back our way."

Ava's mother slapped Alex's shoulder. "Don't talk about bowel movements in the kitchen." She picked up a casserole dish from the counter and walked it over to the kitchen table. "Ava, you better do right by your brother because if and when you ever have any of your own, Alex will do the same thing to you."

"Now see, Momma. Why you gotta say it like that?" Ava placed her hand on her hip.

"Like what?" Her mother scrunched her face.

"If and when. I plan to have kids. Just when the time and the man are right."

"Amen, sis. No need to rush thangs." Her brother extended his hand in the air and high-fived Ava.

Her mother moved to the stove to stir a pot that was boiling over. "You know what I mean. Don't be so sensitive."

Ava's father put his arm around her. "Lydia, leave our little girl alone. You always say she don't come over here enough. She's here now, so let's enjoy it."

"I am enjoying it. I'm just saying." Her mother grinned.

Glad her father shut her mother up, Ava helped her brother set the table. Alex set the plates at each place setting, while Ava filled the glasses with ice and Elaine put out silverware. After everything was completed, they sat down as a family to eat. When Ava's father completed his prayer over the food, Ava noticed her brother rubbing Elaine's hand. He then handed her the potatoes and kissed her on the cheek.

Ava wanted that intimacy. Was it too much to ask? A man like her father or brother? In her family there were not one, but two Christian men with a sense of humor and ambition, who valued women and treated them with respect. Even though the good man count was down in the world, knowing her family produced high-quality marriage material gave Ava hope, but admittedly her hope was dwindling.

Her mother took a bite of her Caesar salad. "So, Alex, what's going on with you?"

"Same ol' same ol', Momma. Work's good. Home's great." He kissed Elaine's hand.

"That's wonderful. You've always made me so proud." Cutting her meat, prim and proper with her bony fingers, she looked at Ava. "And how's everything with you? Last time we talked you had broken things off with Xavier."

Here we go. Ava put her glass down. "We're still not together, Momma, so leave it alone."

"Yeah, Momma. If Ava is through with him, let it go." Alex winked at Ava.

"I just want her to be as happy as you and Elaine are. Is that such a bad thing?"

Who said Ava wasn't happy? Well, she wasn't but her mother didn't know that. "If you think I was happy with Xavier, you're going to love this."

"What, Ava?" Her mother set her utensils down and stared at her with her frown lines front and center.

Ava paused. *Why am I opening up this can of worms?* Sadly, adding disappointment to her mother's day became a pastime for Ava. If her mother was going to continue to highlight her flaws, Ava would hold the neon marker. "Well, you're going to find out anyway." She shrugged her shoulders. "Rene and I haven't spoken in over a month. I slept with Ishmael."

Her father spit out his water. "You what?"

"It was just one of those things that happened. A big, bad mistake. And now she's called off the wedding and not talking to me anymore." There. It would be in bad taste to take a picture of her mother's face, but that didn't mean Ava didn't want to do it.

Her mother hung her head. "See, that's why you need a man of your own."

Ava rolled her eyes. "You know, Momma, your comments don't help me at all."

"Yeah, Lydia. Leave the girl alone." Her father put his head down, seemingly like he didn't want to make eye contact after hearing the words "I slept with" come out of his daughter's mouth.

"You're going to blame me now?"

"I'm not blaming you, Momma." She waved her finger back and forth, while her neck swayed. "I'm just letting you know I could do without your little comments." Ava's chair legs split. Crashing crackle sounds shuddered as she hit the floor.

"Oh, Lord!" Her father jumped out his seat. "Are you okay, baby girl?"

Alex hopped out of his seat and sprinted around the table. Lifting her up, he asked, "You all right, sis?"

Just what she needed. "Yeah, I'm fine. My tailbone and pride are damaged a bit, but I'm okay."

Her mother shook her head. "I've tried to tell you, you need to lose weight. You broke the patio chair last summer and now this one."

"Dat gum it, Lydia. The girl just fell. Can't you cut her some slack? Anyway, you know we've had these chairs since the beginning of time. Jesus sat in 'em chairs." Ava, Alex, and Elaine laughed while her father sat down in his seat. "Don't worry about it, Ava. We was goin' to get some new chairs anyhow."

"Thank you, Daddy. It was great to see you all, but I believe me and my embarrassment are going to go on home." Ava kissed her father on the forehead, hugged her brother and sister-in-law, and patted her mother on the shoulder. "Y'all take care and I'll talk to you soon."

"Oh, Ava, don't leave." Her mother reached for her hand.

Jerking her hand back and picking up speed in her footsteps, Ava fled through the kitchen. By the time she sat down in her car, tears streamed down her face.

Chapter 15

Toni and Eric sat on the patio of an Italian bistro in downtown Houston awaiting the arrival of Rene with Eric's court papers. When things got out of hand at Ava's apartment, Toni and Rene were not able to exchange paperwork and information concerning his charges and Roderick's attempted rape.

Toni drummed her finger on the table, looking at Eric. "Talk about Ava? Don't talk about?"

He shrugged his shoulders. "I don't know. See how the conversation flows, I guess."

Toni spotted Rene's car. She watched Rene park in the open parking space in front of the patio, wondering if she and Eric sat there looking like a couple, and if Rene would say anything about them resembling a couple again.

Rene exited the car with her briefcase in hand, and closed the car door. Opening the gate that separated the bistro from the sidewalk, she made her way toward Toni and Eric's table. "Good to see the two of you." Rene turned to Eric. "Glad you could make it. Wasn't sure you'd be here."

"Yeah, I was supposed to show a million dollar home today, but I pushed it back an hour." He smiled. "I felt this was more important."

"I thought it was too." Toni tapped her fingers on his hand, then moved her eyes to Rene. "Good to see you, girl. Can't wait to hear this good news you have for me."

"Well, most of it is good news." Rene placed her briefcase on the table. "Like I told Toni, the charges were dropped against you, Eric; but, Toni, you will have to face Roderick in court."

"No problem. I can handle that. Eric said he'd be there with me as a witness and a support system." Toni pointed at Eric's chest. "He'll be the one we need to watch." She wasn't sure what Eric would do when he laid eyes on Roderick. His protective demeanor was flattering, but she didn't want to see him in handcuffs. Again.

He sipped his tea, then said, "I'll be cool as long as the court handles it like they should."

The waitress interrupted their conversation to take their orders. Toni and Eric asked for a refill of iced tea and Rene ordered a glass of water. The ladies chose grill chicken salads, while Eric ordered nothing.

Rene removed her shades, unhooked the latch on her briefcase, and gathered a small stack of papers. "Okay. Here are the documents you need to look over, Eric. Basically, it says you are aware of the charges and that they've been dropped. Sign the last page and have it notarized. Then all you have to do is drop them off at the police station to be filed, and your part is done."

Eric took hold of the papers. "Thank you, Rene. Sounds easy enough."

"You're welcome. The sooner you take care of it, the better." Rene turned her attention to Toni. "And as for you, Toni, your court date has been set for July twenty-second."

Toni frowned. "Why so far away? What's the hold up?"

"Girl, that's good. The courts are so backed up, you usually have to wait a lot longer. But I have a friend in the records office who moved your case up as high to the top of the pile as he could."

"Well, be sure to thank him for me." Toni needed this debacle to be over. Roderick, a fake and a phony, had wasted enough of her time with his lies and violent ways. Not only was he not a production assistant at a TV station, he didn't own the Range Rover he drove that night either. Turned out he was a small-time drug dealer and a frequent visitor of the county jail.

Rene dug into his background while working the case, and found all sorts of holes in his story. Something told Toni to cancel on him that night. She wished she would've listened to her inner voice.

"There's not much to your case. We'll need to meet a time or two before to go over questions the defense may ask you. Just be honest and it'll go smoothly. And with you, Eric, giving your testimony of what you heard and rolled up on, it should be a piece of cake."

"Ooh, cake." Toni's eyes lit up. "That sounds good. Since I've been off work, my sweet tooth has gone wild. I may have to do some of that cardio you were telling me about."

Rene smiled and leaned in to examine Toni. "Your face looks a lot better. Will you be able to go back to work soon?"

"Hope so. I went in a week ago after I could hide the bruise with make-up, but wasn't sure I was ready emotionally."

"I can understand that."

Toni cleared her throat. "I feel like posing for pictures gets guys like Roderick thinking they can attack me just because I flaunt my body in front of a camera. Well, that's how I felt the first time I went to see my agent. But it's all I know how to do."

"Girl, you can't let that fool put a negative spin on your dream job. He's crazy and guys who think like that are crazy. You have the right to model and no idiot can take that from you. And you are not flaunting, offering free advertising, or anything else. That's why he's going to jail for what he's done." Rene placed her hand on Toni's leg. "You've done nothing wrong."

"Well, thank you for that. After I leave here, I'm headed to my modeling agency to meet with my agent. He wants to see the physical damage and if it's healed completely. *And* if I'm completely healed as well. Hopefully, I can start going out on jobs next week." Toni couldn't wait to get in front of the camera again. Posing for pictures was all she'd ever known. And with that not an option for the past month or so, boredom ruled her daily life.

"I received a copy of the pictures of your injuries taken the night the attempted rape happened, and with you having to take off work because of your bruises, Roderick doesn't stand a chance."

After Eric thanked Rene again and excused himself to get to his real estate meeting, the waitress returned with the ladies' grilled chicken salads. As they ate, they discussed the happenings in their families. Toni missed Ava's presence. She wanted to throw Ava's name in at several pauses in the conversation, but couldn't find the right words to ease into their chat. Or she could've just been scared to utter the three little letters that would probably send Rene to her unhappy place. Either way, Toni's curiosity was heightened.

After her last bite, Toni couldn't take it anymore. "So, you still giving Ava the silent treatment?"

Rene scowled, looking at her like she was crazy. "You know I'm not talking to her."

"I was just hoping you had a recent change of heart."

"Not a chance."

"I know she misses you." Toni sipped her tea.

"She should have thought about that before she slept with Ishmael."

"I know, Rene." She shook her head. "Ava is real sorry and ashamed about what she did. She feels terrible for hurting you like that."

"I really don't care how she feels." Rene placed her shades back on her face. "And if you're going to start talking about Ava, we can end this conversation right now."

Taking a deep breath, Toni put her hands up as if to surrender. "Okay, my bad. I thought you might want to know how your girl was doing. I mean she seems depressed and barely leaves the house."

"She brought it on herself. Now let's change the subject."

"No problem." Toni tried her hand at mediation. But maybe it was too soon. "Have you been to church lately?"

"I went a couple of weeks ago, but I didn't want to have to answer questions about why my engagement ring wasn't on my finger. I'll go when I'm ready."

"Yeah, I understand. Well, I went yesterday and Pastor Monroe was on it. As always. His message was extremely timely. It was about putting action behind your faith from the Book of James, I think. Faith without works is dead."

Rene sheepishly laughed. "Yep, could've used that."

"Also, he touched on relationships and having faith in God and what He can do to heal your marriage. He spoke specifically to those who are considering divorce. You know he jacked me up on that one." Toni promised herself at that very moment to read over her notes from the sermon later. Perhaps the words would sink in better.

Eyebrows raised, Rene asked, "Are you having second thoughts?"

"Sort of. I want to believe Eric's changed, but I'm not interested in getting hurt again if he hasn't. He did ask me if we could go to church together some time, and if I would go to couples counseling with Pastor and his wife, Sandra."

"Do you want to go?"

"I'm thinking about it." Toni shrugged her shoulders.

"Let me know how it goes." Rene took her wallet out of her purse. "Well, girlfriend, I gotta run." She laid a ten dollar bill on the table.

Toni snatched it up and handed the bill back to her. "I got it. It's the least I can do. I truly appreciate you taking this on, Rene. I know you're a busy lady."

"Thank you for the lunch and you're welcome. And it's not a problem, really. The busier I am these days, the better. Like I said, piece of cake."

"I think I'll order that piece of cake now." Toni smirked. "It goes great with salad."

"Enjoy, and hope all goes well at the agency."

Rene walked through the gate and got into her car. Leaving the eatery, she dug her cell phone out of her purse when she was out of Toni's sight. Rene scrolled through her contacts to Ava's number, imagining Ava sitting at home alone. Part of her was disheartened for her friend and even missed Ava's companionship. But then she envisioned Ava and Ishmael in bed together. Rene smacked her lips and tossed the phone back into her purse.

Chapter 16

Toni called Ava as soon as Rene pulled out of the parking lot and headed down the street. She prepared her words to leave a voicemail since there was no answer. Just as she went into her message, Ava's picture appeared on her screen and she answered the call. "Hello."

"Sorry, I didn't pick up in time."

"Are you asleep?" It was the middle of the day and her friend's groggy voice made Toni check her gold wristwatch.

"Yeah." Ava cleared her throat. "I came home early from work. Had a headache."

"Oh, well, you can call me back later when you get up."

"No, it's okay. What's going on?"

"I'm about to head to the modeling agency to see if I'm cleared to start going out on shoots again." *Please, Lord, let it be a yes.*

"I know you're ready to get back working. Has your face completely healed?"

"I think it has, but Eddie, my agent, will have the final say-so." Toni was prepared to offer him a bribe to even give her the smallest of jobs. Makeup could do the trick of covering remnants of any injury.

"Good luck and I'll be praying for you, girl."

"Also, I just had lunch with Rene."

"You did?"

Toni couldn't tell if the surprise in Ava's voice was a positive or negative response. "We met to discuss Eric's charges and the court date for my case."

"Everything all right?"

"Better than that. Rene said with the evidence against Roderick, the case will be as easy as giving candy to a baby."

Ava giggled. "Glad to hear that. So how was Rene?"

There. The door was open for Toni to go to work as the mediator. "She seemed okay. I think she misses you as much as you miss her, but wouldn't admit it for the world."

"I do miss her. I still can't believe I committed the very sin I was trying most to avoid. And against one of my best friends. How do you explain that?"

As much as Toni had discussed the situation in her head with a judgmental slant, none of what would come out of her mouth would be uplifting. Could the Lord intervene for her? Toni remained in thought for a second. "What's that scripture about the things I want to do, I don't do, and the things I don't want to do, I do?"

"I believe that's somewhere in Romans. I'll have to look it up. But I don't feel like doing much of anything these days. Including reading my Bible."

"Ava, you need to get up and do something. At least get out of the house. Take a walk. Anything."

"Mmh. I will."

Toni pictured Ava rolling her eyes at her suggestion. But she could only do so much to help her friend through this tough time in her life. Ava would eventually have to snap out of the funk.

After hanging up with Ava, Toni got into her ride and turned the radio up. Jamming to the upbeat music, she looked forward to what she hoped would be good news from her agent. At a red light, she brought the rearview mirror down, checking her face. Confidence set in as she carried on en route to the agency.

Pulling into the parking lot, a fellow model waved as she drove by. Toni, a few minutes early for her meeting, parked and then turned the radio off. "Lord, your will be done in this situation. I believe I am ready to work again, so I hope Eddie sees it that way." She smiled. "And Lord, your will be done with Eric and me, too, please. I love him. Very much. And I know you know that, but I do not want to be hurt again. Please help me to guard my heart and move at a slow pace. Amen."

She bounced through the front door of the Midtown Modeling Agency. Greetings and smiles were passed around as she made her way to Eddie's office. Nothing had changed. She felt as though the place was still a whirlwind of average-looking people catering to the needs of the stunningly gorgeous. She stopped in her tracks to view the whole scene.

Was Toni's nose that high in the air when the assistants served her beverages? Did she say please and thank you? The surroundings may have been the same, but Toni saw herself and her counterparts in a different light. The past couple of weeks had done a number on her humility and she welcomed the change.

Before she could knock on the open door, Eddie looked up. "Toni." He lifted up out of his chair and offered her a hug. "How are you, girl?"

She received him with open arms. "Great. I feel like it's been longer than three weeks."

"Yes, me too." He pointed to the large sofa by the window. "Come on, sit down. Let's catch up."

They sat facing each other and talked over the major parts of the case with Roderick. Then they focused on her health and what her first job back might be. After they finished the conversation of particulars, Eddie walked over to his desk to search for an itinerary of possible shoots Toni was requested for.

His secretary brought them each a bottle of water. "Toni, you have a delivery at the front. Would you like me to bring it in?"

Toni's forehead wrinkled. "Um, yes. Thank you."

The secretary said, "Don't worry, you'll like this. I'll be right back."

She returned moments later with a bright bouquet of yellow roses. Puzzled with anticipation, Toni reached for the flowers. "Ooh, these are beautiful. I wonder who they're from."

"There's a card, but I didn't want to pry."

Toni accepted the bouquet. Smelling the bunch, she set them next to her on the sofa. Even though the thought crossed her mind that Roderick may try something like a remorseful gesture to get her to drop the charges, the only person who knew her whereabouts was Eric. However, he had never been the flower kind of guy.

Eddie jerked his neck toward her. "Well, aren't you going to read the card?"

"It can wait." If the lovely floral goodness was from Eric, she wanted to read the note in private where her emotions could run free.

"No, it can't." He chuckled. "I'm nosy and I want to know now."

Picking up the flowers, she removed the card from the plastic holder. She slid the card out of the mini envelope and read it aloud through a grin. "Just wanted to brighten your day. Thinking of you, Eric." Her grin turned into a full-fledged cheese from ear to ear.

Eddie drifted around his desk and reclaimed his seat by her on the couch. "That's sweet. But I thought you and Eric were separated."

"We are, but with all that has happened, we've been talking. Moving slow, but moving."

"Okay. Well, he gets points for this, right?"

"Of course." He was making big strides forward to regain his place in her life. She could stand to give him a few extra points.

"Good. Hope it all works out."

"Thank you, Eddie. So, that's it? I'm cleared to work, right?"

He put his hand on hers. "As long as you are ready, I say yes. Everything's good on the physical side of things. But only you can make the decision if you're ready."

"I am. I've been so bored these past few weeks. Eric has helped a great deal with the emotional part of the attempted rape. And all this free time has given me a lot of time to talk to God and work through some things." She never thought she'd be one of those folks who waited until tragedy struck to open their Bible and have a little talk with Jesus. Why couldn't she have done that beforehand? From now on, she'd make prayer and studying God's Word a priority.

"All righty then. Let me get your go-see sheet, and I'll e-mail you the details for the next photo shoot this Friday. We'll get some new shots to vamp up your portfolio."

"I appreciate everything you've done." She stood. "All the rescheduling that was needed and just being here for me."

"No problem. That's my job. And since I actually enjoy it, I feel like it's my calling. You take care and I'll see you in a few days."

She took the sheet out of his hand and gave him a hug. "See you in a few."

When she left his office and walked past his secretary, she giggled like a schoolgirl and smiled all the way to the parking lot. Eric knew she'd be there, but she never expected the beautiful-scented surprise accompanied by the heartfelt note. She couldn't wait to get in her car, locate her cell phone, and call him.

"What's up, Toni? I was hoping you'd call."

"I was hoping you'd answer. Some sweet person sent me flowers here at the agency, and I was wondering if you happen to know anything about that?"

"Maybe."

"Well, I just wanted that person to know how thankful I was. Could you pass the message along for me?"

He chuckled. "Why of course."

"That was very thoughtful. And you have such great timing."

"I wanted you to know I was thinking about you and hoped all went well in your meeting with Eddie."

"It did and I'm back working again." She brushed her hand over the flowers.

"That calls for a celebration. How 'bout we meet for an early dinner?"

Toni repressed her eagerness to see him again and threw in a hint of a nonchalant attitude. "I'm not that hungry. But we can meet for coffee."

"Sounds good to me. Our old place?"

"That'll work."

He cleared his throat. "Shoot, if I would have known all I had to do was whoop somebody to get you to talk to me, I would've done that a long time ago. Just found anybody in the street and start kickin' they butt."

Toni laughed. "Eric, you are stupid, boy. But yes, I appreciate you literally fighting for me. Also, I see a change in you, so whatever you've been doing, keep doing it."

"Not much to it. Just enjoying a real relationship with our Lord. He's opened my eyes to a lot of things. So I truly hope you'll agree to go to counseling with me. Maybe we can talk about that some more over coffee."

She stared out of the driver's side window. Everything Eric said sounded good, but she didn't want it to be too good to be true. Toni decided she would let the Lord handle the situation from there on out. Prayer and seeking His guidance would become her new daily activities. Ever since Eric sought comfort outside of their marriage, she put her faith aside and fell out of fellowship with the Father. She reduced herself to only praying over a meal, and turning to alcohol and a gripe session with friends for comfort. And Eric was further gone than she was. Toni wasn't sure what he did spiritually or in any other area as many nights as he spent away from their home.

She loved Eric with every part of her being, but knew one of her many mistakes in their marriage was putting him before God. As they started over, she'd be sure to keep the Lord first. Peace lived inside of her as she took small steps forward to restore her relationship with her husband. She was hopeful for what might happen in the months ahead. Her faith this time, though, would not be in Eric, but in God.

Chapter 17

Ava planned the perfect menu for a pastors' luncheon, and after three weeks, the event was finally here. As she prepared the meal in the kitchen of the Lanson Hotel, she missed her best friend. Wishing Rene was there to talk to, Ava finished the second round of appetizers and wrapped up the main course when nausea hit

One of her assistant chefs walked over to her. "Are you okay? You don't look so good."

She put her hand on her midsection. "Why don't you take over for a minute? I'll be right back."

Pushing past two servers, she covered her mouth and zigzagged through the back hallway to the restroom. The smell of roast beef and potato hash aggravated her stomach. The noises coming out of her stall would've alarmed an ER doctor.

The woman next to her asked, "Ma'am, are you all right?"

"Yes, I'll be fine." *I think.*

"Okay. Just wanted to check."

Ava held on to what was coming next until the lady washed her hands and left the restroom. After a few more belches, she got up from her bent-knee position and sat on top of the toilet. What did she have to eat that day? She bit her lip. Was her monthly visitor, as her mother called it, on its way? She frowned. *When was my last period?*

"Couldn't be."

"Couldn't be what?" a voice from two stalls over asked.

"Sorry, ma'am. Thinking out loud." So much had gone on the last few weeks, Ava couldn't remember when she last traveled down the aisle in the grocery store most men try to avoid. Now she'd need to visit the aisle for a different reason.

Once Ava completed the dessert course and paid the crew she'd hired for the day, she bustled out of the hotel. She was almost home when she zoomed into the parking lot of a local drug store. Strolling down the female needs aisle, Ava peeked over her shoulder periodically to make sure no one she knew was in the store.

She grabbed three pregnancy tests and stuffed them under her arm. Ava snatched a bottle of water and threw it on the checkout counter as well. She needed to be sure she'd be able to complete the tests.

When she arrived at her apartment after purchasing the tests, she dropped her keys on the bar and bolted straight to the bathroom. She followed the printed directions step by step on the rapid results pregnancy test. After one minute had passed, she read the plus sign. Something had to be wrong with the test. It was only 99 percent accurate. Sure that she was the one percent, Ava quickly opened the second box and repeated the procedure. Same results. She planned to take the third test, but couldn't relieve herself anymore. *I should've drunk more water on the way home.*

After cleaning everything up, she called Toni and told her to drop everything she was doing and come over as soon as possible. By the time Toni blew in the front door, Ava was on the couch in tears, holding the two positive tests.

"Ava, what's the matter?" Toni sat on the coffee table in front of her friend.

Ava could barely lift her head. "Everything."

Toni reached for the indicators. "What's in your hands?"

Ava yanked them back before Toni could palm them. "You don't want to put your hands on those. I just used both of these pregnancy tests."

"You did what?"

"You heard me right. I ran out of liquid or I would've taken a third test." The third one probably would've read the same scary positive results. She dropped them on the floor, and cupped her hands over her face. "This can't be happening."

Toni picked up the tests with her index finger and thumb on both hands, walked into the kitchen, and threw them away. She washed her hands and then sat next to Ava. "So are you thinking you're pregnant by Ishmael?"

"I'm not thinking, I know." Her situation just kept getting worse and worse. She felt God was punishing her for her terrible choices in life.

"How can you be sure? Could it be X's?" Toni handed Ava a tissue.

"It's not. The last couple of months of our bootleg relationship, I chose to withhold sex from him. I was trying to do the right thing. So I'd have to be like nine months pregnant by now, about to give birth." She wiped her tears. If only she could go back to that night of sulking and sipping wine and take a nap instead.

"I see."

"It's Ishmael's. I cannot have the child of my best friend's ex-fiancé. That sounds like a bad soap opera. I can't go out like this."

"Hold on now, Ava." Toni put her hands over Ava's. "I don't like you talking like this. It's not the end of the world. We'll figure things out together."

Ava pushed Toni's hands off of hers. "No. I'm serious. How can I show my face anywhere, pregnant with Ishmael's kid? I can't go to church. Or work. How embarrassing. And I can hear my mother going off in her colorful way. I can't handle it anymore. I should just dive into hell right now."

"Ava, stop it. You are really scaring me. Now look, I don't want to hear you say another word like that. In fact, where's your laptop?"

"My what? What do you need with my computer?"

Toni rose up and looked around the room. "Because, I'm going to search Christian counselors in the area. I think you need to talk to somebody more qualified than me."

Ava leaned back on the couch while Toni continued rummaging in the apartment until she found the computer. She placed it on the coffee table, lifted the screen, and turned the power on. Toni searched the Web as Ava stared at the ceiling and wept.

Her life was over. What kind of friend treated a close friend like she treated Rene? Ava understood God was a forgiving God, but how could even He forgive this act? And the poor innocent child that would be born into a world of mess. Its father, a no-good fool, and its mother, a backstabbing, promiscuous floozy. The child didn't stand a fighting chance.

After a few minutes, Toni said, "Ah ha! Here's a place close by. It's called the Christian Counseling Center, or CCC. It says here, they help people who need grief counseling, have drug dependency, and suffer from depression. Their slogan reads, 'Changing lives, one at a time, with the Word of God.'"

"Well, I'm not grieving, addicted to drugs, or depressed. So what I'ma go for?"

"Are you kidding me? I'm taking over now. You just do as I say." Toni clicked on a few links. "Here we go. Look, Ava."

"I don't want to."

Toni pulled Ava's head around by her chin. "I said look." She turned the laptop toward Ava, but Ava looked away. "This is Dr. Glory Moses. That's a unique name. She's been at the CCC since it opened almost ten years ago and deals mainly with patients experiencing depression. She looks nice enough and she's a Christian. You need to give her a call. Do you hear me?"

"I hear you. But she's not going to be able to fix the fact that I'm pregnant by Ishmael. I've got to be the dumbest broad on the planet." No one could repair her muddled mess. What did Toni know? Nope, what Ava needed to do was move across the country, maybe even overseas, change her name, and start a new life elsewhere. No Dr. Glory Moses was going to help her out of this chaos.

"Ava, you're not dumb. And you're not the first woman to make a mistake. You want what we all want. Someone to show us some attention and love us. Granted, it was with Ishmael, but we'll chalk that up to bad judgment mixed with good wine."

"Whatever." Ava grabbed her fleece blanket, and put her feet up, kicking Toni in the process. She had heard enough. Toni could leave now. Toni was trying to help, but she was trying to help someone who didn't want or need it. Ava just needed to be left alone. She could think more clearly after a nap.

"Oh, let me get out of your way." Toni scooted over.

"Sorry, girl. I'm tired though. I'm going to lie down for a bit."

"Well, I'm going to write Dr. Moses' number down and put it on the fridge. First chance you get, you call her. Do you hear me? I'm going to check and make sure you did. And if you don't, I'm going to call her for you. Got it?"

Ava sighed. "Got it."

Toni stood and fumbled through her purse until she found a pen and a piece of paper. She copied the number down for Dr. Moses at the CCC. She marched into the kitchen and affixed the piece of paper under a magnet on the fridge. She walked over to Ava and kissed her forehead. "I'm here for you, girl. No matter what. Call me if you need me."

"Will do."

"It will get better, Ava. I promise." Toni patted her on the shoulder. "Love you."

"Love you too." Ava lifted her head. "And, Toni?"

"Yes?"

"Thank you." She was grateful for Toni caring so much, but right then, tiredness overruled everything else.

"You're very welcome."

Ava pushed out a half smile and pulled the blanket up, covering her head. Too bad she couldn't just as easily cover her sins.

Chapter 18

Rene sat in front of her computer, scrolling through her Facebook page. After removing Ava as a friend, she then switched to her profile pictures. Any sight of Ava and the delete button was pressed. She resisted the need to leave a message on her wall about what friendship was and wasn't, betrayal, and how you could lose trust in others. All of the above resided in her heart, but she didn't want to put her business in the street like that. Especially on Facebook. Then everyone would have something to say, and somehow it would get back to Ava. Who knew what would be said about her ex-friend? And she didn't want to hurt her. Necessarily.

When Toni's photo appeared on the screen of her phone, Rene hesitated. If Toni was calling about Ava, she didn't want to hear it. Against her better judgment, she answered the phone.

"Wanted to thank you again for taking care of Eric's issues along with mine."

"No problem." So far, so good.

"Are you busy?"

"Just getting home." Rene slid out of her heels. "About to make me something to eat, and then chillax."

"Well, you wanna meet for dinner? We can hang out and catch up."

"Yeah, we can." Rene's less-than-enthusiastic tone didn't sound like her heart was in the meeting, but being social would be nice. What were Toni's motives behind the offer? They had never been out to dinner, just the two of them, to "hang out." Nor did they have anything to catch up on that required a conversation longer than two minutes.

"There's something I need to discuss with you, so we might as well do it over a meal."

"What is it?"

"It has something to do with Ava."

She knew it. "There's no need to meet to talk about Ava. I told you I'm not interested."

"Rene, you need to listen. I know you're upset and I understand, but you will want to know this."

Breathing deep, Rene rolled her eyes. Why did she answer the phone? "Listening."

Toni sucked her teeth. "First off, Ava has been real depressed lately. This whole situation is wearing her down."

"And she brought it on herself." Rene wasn't going to let Ava slide on this repulsive incident one bit.

"Just listen."

"Okay, dang." Rene could appreciate what Toni was trying to do, be the liaison between her and Ava, but Rene wasn't ready for a mediation and didn't want to be forced into one.

"I'm not just talking about feeling sad or down about something, but saying comments like she can't go on and stuff like that." Toni paused. "Are you sitting down?"

Rene remained silent, propping herself up on a barstool. "I am now."

"Ava's pregnant. And says it's Ishmael's."

Dropping the phone on the floor, Rene's expletives echoed throughout the house. "Ahhh! You've got to be kidding me!" She needed to wait for her initial reaction to play out before she picked up the phone again. Toni would have to wait. This information was something Rene needed to know, but truly didn't care to. Now there'd be a child walking around in the world looking like Ava and Ishmael. Her best friend and the man she loved. A forever reminder of the horrid betrayal. That could be the kid's name. Horrid Betrayal Alexander.

Rene's spirit fell as she realized she was putting her friend's sins on an innocent child. She digressed, yet her temples pulsated and she clutched her cell so hard, her tensed knuckles made it difficult to hold on to the phone. "Well, this just keeps getting better and better. I can hardly wait to see what happens next."

"I know this is hurtful, but I'm worried about Ava. She feels likes she's alone, and you and God are so upset with her that she has no business on this earth."

Keeping her sobs as silent as she could, Rene spoke through sniffles. "I know she's hurt, but this is the bed she made and now she needs to lie in it. I hope nothing bad happens to her, but you just dropped a brick in my lap and you want me to be automatically be okay with it." *Ain't happening.* "I need time to process all of this."

"Okay, I just thought you should know."

"The best I can do right now is pray for her. And I need to pray for myself as well. I'll talk to you later."

Rene sat frozen on her sofa. It was going to take all of God's power to keep her behind in that seat. Driving to Ava's apartment and finishing the butt whooping she started the last time they saw each other sounded like the greatest plan. But she couldn't hit a pregnant woman. Even if Ava was wronger than wrong. Rene wasn't made of stone. Part of her wanted to be there for her estranged friend and walk with her through this nightmare, but her pride and anger wouldn't let the rest of her emotions have any room in her mind. Or heart.

And violence directed toward Ava wouldn't be the best solution anyway. Rene could, however, take it out on the male responsible. She sent Ishmael a text: Meet me at your mom's house. NOW!

Rene then changed into fighting clothes and tennis shoes. Snatching her keys off the table, she stormed out of the house.

Chapter 19

Ava looked at the TV with a glaze over her eyes. The noises and sounds from whatever show was on ran together, confused in her head. She picked up the remote, turned the television off, and sat still in the dark. She deserved to be alone. Not only did she let the celibacy promise slide, she engaged in sex with her best friend's man. *If I could just lose weight, I could get my own man. I'd be the prize on his arm instead of him the prize on mine.*

"God, please fix this. I hate feeling like this. I'm a terrible friend, and deserve whatever I get, but I pray Rene can move on and be happy. Wherever she is, please let her know I love her and miss her. I need you, Lord. I can't go on living like this. I'm embarrassed, ashamed, and a hot, pitiful mess. Something's gotta give." Ava never figured herself to be the suicidal type, but understood why people felt the way they did. Things would be easier if she stopped breathing all together.

She slumped off the sofa, feeling as gloomy as the April showers outside of her window. A glass of wine would make her feel better. Or at least support her deep sleeping habit she'd picked up the past couple of weeks. Walking over to the fridge even seemed like a daunting task. Ava couldn't shake her funk.

She frowned as she removed the bottle from the fridge. Not sure if pregnant women were allowed to drink wine, she opened the cork and breathed in a nice whiff of sweet red grapes. She remembered her prescription pain pills from her tooth extraction in her medicine cabinet. *If I take only a couple pills and drink the entire bottle of wine, my death could look like an accident. Rene would be sorry for giving me the silent treatment and my mother would realize how hurtful her comments truly were.*

"Lord, what's wrong with me? I need your help." Shedding a few tears, she placed the bottle back in the refrigerator and closed the door. Her colorful magnet that read GOD IS IN CONTROL seemed to be magnified. The piece of paper the magnet held in place was in Toni's handwriting:

Dr. Glory Moses (832) 555-4545
God is our refuge and strength, a very present help in trouble. Psalm 46:1

Ava recalled Toni saying she'd put the number on the fridge, but was equally grateful for the scripture. She hadn't paid much attention to it the past couple of days. Could this be the answer she was looking for? Could God have already known on this day she would really see the note, and the scripture would be exactly what she needed? Taking the written counsel as a sign, she called Dr. Moses' office and made an appointment. That was all she could do for now. She crawled into bed for a nap.

The next day at work, Ava stayed in her office, only coming out to use the restroom and warm up her lunch in the microwave. When she got back from the office lunch area, she saw she'd missed a call. On her voicemail, the automated attendant for Dr. Moses' office called to confirm her afternoon appointment.

She was glad Dr. Moses was able to see her so soon, but a little nervous about what emotional junk would be uprooted. By the workday's end, all sort of scenarios back-flipped in her mind. Would she be labeled depressed and put on medication? Be asked to come back? Or asked not to come back? She trotted to the restroom to wash her face. Ava breathed in deeply, found her keys, and left her office.

As she entered the CCC, she looked around to see who saw her go in the building. A handful of people huddled over to the side of the walkway, talking and smoking cigarettes. She smiled, but quickened her steps to avoid inhaling the smoke or it creeping into her hair.

"Hello, ma'am." The animated receptionist at the counter beamed. "Welcome to the Christian Counseling Center, aka the CCC. Where God meets you right where you are."

What was she so dang happy about? Ava threw up a hand.

"Do you have an appointment?"

"Yes. With Dr. Glory Moses at four-thirty. My name is Ava Alexander."

The receptionist found her name on the appointment registry. "Ah, yes, Dr. Moses' office and waiting room are just down that hall to the right. I could show you if you like."

"No, I think I can manage."

"Have a great rest of the day."

"You too." Whatever the receptionist was on, Ava wanted some.

Strolling toward Dr. Moses' office, she spoke to the people who spoke to her. Two people stood by the coffee pot in the main lobby, seeming to be in a deep conversation. Another group of folks were in a circle holding hands and praying for the person standing in the middle. She didn't want to seem nosy, but listened in on the powerful prayer belted out by the solidly built brother who laid hands on the individual crying in the center of the circle.

With every step Ava took in the direction of Dr. Moses' office, peace came over her being. She needed to be there and was thankful God brought her out of her solitary hole, and into the CCC. When she reached the private waiting room, she grabbed a magazine from the table and got as comfortable as she could in the firm microfiber chair.

A tall, thin black woman with warm eyes soon opened the door and walked out. "Hello, you must be Ava."

Ava stood. "Yes, I am."

"I'm Dr. Moses. How are you today?"

"Okay. I'm here, so that's progress." She forced a smile.

"Progress from what?"

"Staying in the house and sulking."

Dr. Moses nodded. "That is progress. Let's see if we can't talk through some things today." She motioned for Ava to walk into her office.

Ava plodded through the door and plopped down on the neutral-colored couch. A heavy sigh escaped her lips. Dr. Moses closed the door and sat in the armchair across from Ava. She then picked up a legal pad from the coffee table, flipping a couple pages over.

Leaning back in her seat, she crossed her legs. "So, Ava, would you like to tell me what's going on in your life? Where do you think the source of your depression originated?"

Ava chuckled. "I don't think. I know."

"Well, tell me about it."

"The past few weeks have been an emotional roller-coaster. I've made some terrible choices. I made the bed, and lay in it. With my best friend's fiancé. Well, ex-best friend and her ex-fiancé."

"Mmh."

"I know I struggle with insecurity in a lot of things, but my weight and self-image are the worst. I recently broke off a mentally abusive relationship. Then after vowing to be celibate all it took was a few glasses of wine and a few compliments from the guy, and I gave up my promise real quick. And not only have I hurt my best friend by sleeping with her fiancé, I went to the doctor and found out I'm almost twelve weeks pregnant. So more hurt is headed her way."

"I see." Dr. Moses scribbled on her pad for a minute.

"Yeah. I know it sounds like an episode of *Jerry Springer.*"

"Oh, don't mind me. I take notes to better understand the situation."

Ava switched from one hip to the other. She had plenty for Doc to take notes on. "I can't stand myself and what I've become. I want to make everything right with Rene, but she's not talking to me right now. I'm at a loss for what to do." Not wanting to come off as a crazy, weak woman, Ava hesitated sharing the whole story, but something in her urged her to spill the beans. Or pills in her case. "And last night, I seriously contemplated suicide by way of prescription drugs and wine. Having thoughts like that scared me."

Dr. Moses looked up from her writing. "Have you paused in all of this to pray?"

"Yes. Well, I prayed for Rene and for God to help me with my insecurities."

"Have you asked the Lord for forgiveness for what you've done?"

"Not really." Ava folded her arms. She couldn't remember if she had or not. Besides her tears and loneliness, everything else had pretty much been a blur.

Dr. Moses put down her pad and pen and extended out her hands toward Ava. "Let's pray together."

Ava held Dr. Moses' hands.

"Lord, we come to you in prayer right now thanking you for this life you've given us. We know we don't always make the right decisions or choices, but you love us anyway. We thank you for your unconditional love and guidance." Dr. Moses squeezed Ava's hands. "Father, I ask right now that you would meet Ava at the point of her need. You know her heart, Lord. You know what she's feeling. Nix the plans of the enemy. He likes to fog our minds with doubt, fear, and shame, so that we cannot see or hear from you clearly."

Dr. Moses' words were perfect. Ava wanted to pull out her phone and record every word for later.

"You have made us in your image, Lord. Please help Ava to see that she is fearfully and wonderfully made like it says in your Word. Please forgive her, Lord, for the choices she made and the consequences that are now set before her. Guide her every step of the way. Help her to forgive herself and give Rene time to heal and come to a place of peace. And if they are to restore their relationship, let it be your hand that turns Rene's heart. In Jesus' name we pray in faith, believing, and trusting in your goodness. Amen."

Yep, she'd need to hear that again. Ava reached for a tissue from the box on the coffee table and wiped her tears. "Thank you, Doctor. I needed that."

"You're very welcome. The Bible says in Matthew 18:20, 'Where two or more are gathered in my name, I am there in the midst of them.' So He has heard your concerns and our prayers, and He'll meet you right where you are. But you must believe He will deliver you out of your circumstance the best way possible. Seek a relationship with Him. Seek His heart and not His hand. You have some homework before we meet again."

Ava frowned like a teenager in class. "Homework?"

Dr. Moses laughed. "It's nothing too hard. I want you to study the following scriptures. Here, write them down." She handed Ava a legal pad and pen. "And from now on, bring a journal or spiral notebook, so you can write down thoughts or scriptures we talk about."

"Okay." Ava removed the pen cap and sat at attention.

"When I was praying, I said that you are fearfully and wonderfully made. That comes from Psalm 139:14, but you can read and study verses thirteen through sixteen as well. Also, look up Ephesians 2:1–7. Highlight especially verse five, which says, 'Even when we were dead in our sins, God made us alive together with Christ because of His grace that saved us.'"

Ava copied down the scriptures, feeling lighter in her spirit.

"If you take anything from this first meeting, and I hope you do come back, I want you to understand you don't have to feel condemned in your situation. Everything around you may be messed up, but God can turn things around in an instant. He cares about everything you care about and will lead you to the other side of your miracle, if you follow Him."

Nodding, Ava placed the top back on the pen.

"Oh, one more scripture." Dr. Moses sat up in her chair. "I'm sure you've heard that there is no condemnation for those who are in Christ Jesus. That's Romans 8:1. Meditate on those words and see what God does."

"So next Tuesday same time?" Ava tore the sheet from the legal pad.

"Yes. Your insurance will cover twelve sessions with me once a week. Also, I'd like to recommend you come to our group session on Thursdays. That'll give you two sessions a week. A greater chance for success." Dr. Moses grinned. "The group session is a small meeting of believers who share and pray for one another. And someone is usually going through or has been through what you are going through and can tell you what worked for them."

"I appreciate you inviting me. I'll plan on being here." Ava smiled. "Lord willing."

"Great, I'll look for you. Also, don't eat dinner because we come about six and it's kind of a potluck thing. Then the meeting starts promptly at seven o'clock. You can share, not share. That's up to you, but I think it'll be beneficial for you."

"Thank you for everything."

"You're welcome. Be blessed and see you Thursday."

God had snapped His fingers while Ava was in Dr. Moses' office. Her gloomy situation looked better already.

Chapter 20

Toni sat silent in Pastor Monroe's office at the House of the Lord church.

"I know I messed up." Eric's eyes focused on the patched floor rug under the coffee table. "I want Toni to know I'm aware I hurt her, and if I could go back and do things differently, I would. I'm asking for a chance."

Pastor Sandra, Pastor Monroe's wife, turned toward Toni. "What do you think about that?"

Toni tapped her fingers on the bright-colored throw pillow that kept their legs from touching. She agreed to come to a counseling session, but wasn't sure why. Opening up wounds wasn't anywhere near the top of her list of fun things to do. "I'm not sure what to think. I want to believe that's true, but when he chose to step outside of our marriage, our home, our life together, I was devastated. What's to say that a few years from now—shoot, a few months from now—it won't happen again?"

Clearing his throat, Pastor Monroe scooted to the edge of his seat. "Nothing in life is certain but God. Eric and I have been meeting for some time now, and I believe for certain God has changed his heart. Now, I can only speak from my perspective. Eric will have to earn your trust back."

Eric placed his hand over Toni's fingers and she stopped tapping. "And, Toni, I'm ready to do that."

"That's a good starting block. Take things slow and move forward only if you both are at peace. Also, pray separately and together. My wife and I wrote a couples prayer, and in it we talk about God's grace. So, Toni, I urge you to exercise the same grace toward Eric that God has shown you." Pastor Monroe picked up his Bible from the table. "According to God's Word, divorce is not in His plan. I encourage you to give the Lord a chance and see if He can restore this relationship."

Toni didn't want to make any promises she couldn't keep. "I can pray about it. In fact, I'd like to hear more about the couples prayer."

Pastor Sandra walked over to the silver, thick-edged frame hanging on the wall. She unhooked the frame and handed it to Toni. "Here it is. We usually wait until our last counseling session for our couples who are in premarital counseling. But you can look over it and anytime you guys are ready, you two can recite the prayer together."

Eric leaned over Toni's shoulder. They both read the prayer together. Certain words seemed to leap off the page: love, respect, forgiveness, purpose, and grace. God could do all things. So if it was His plan to heal their marriage, they would be open at least to the possibility.

Toni and Eric cruised out the church doors that morning wearing smiles. Had this been a few months ago, Toni wouldn't have been able to even imagine them walking anywhere together. Some hurtful and helpful issues were discussed in their counseling session, yet when she left, hope crept into her heart—hope of what could be, and could be healed in their relationship.

Eric's desire to go to the pastor's office showed he was trying. Before issues had turned too rocky in their relationship, Toni suggested couples therapy, but he repeatedly blew her off or ignored her request all together. What a change of events. He asked about counseling, then shared with her what God's Word said about divorce. And now, this step forward was a step toward reconciliation.

Eric put his arm around Toni's shoulder. "You want to grab a bite to eat?"

"I'm up for that." Why not spend a little more time with him? It could be like a small celebration for their new direction. "Where do you want to go?"

"Doesn't matter to me." He rubbed his stomach. "I'm just hungrier than a mug."

"How 'bout that new place off of 610? The Chicken Shack."

He chuckled. "Now that's a ghetto fabulous name if I ever heard one."

"You know it's the hole in the wall places that have the best food."

"True that. I'll follow you." He hustled to his car.

Toni, ecstatic on the inside, didn't want to show her hand just yet. She coolly veered to her car. She got in, buckled her seat belt, and waited for him to pull behind her.

As she entertained herself with the good memories she and Eric made in the past for a few miles down the road, thoughts of Ava interrupted her journey down memory lane. She dug her cell phone out of her purse and dialed her friend's number.

"Hey, Ava. How you feeling?" she inquired after Ava picked up the phone.

"Much better these days. What are you up to?"

"Just left my first counseling session with Eric and the pastors."

"Ahh, you said 'first.' So there's going to be a second?"

"For now there is. I want to remain hopeful, but not be stupid." She glanced in her rearview mirror at Eric following behind her. "Enough about me. How are you and the baby doing?"

"We're good. The week didn't start off too hot, but I did call that Dr. Moses whose name and number you left on my fridge. And thanks for the scripture. I seriously needed it."

"That was a God thing, girl. I felt led to do it, so I did it."

"Well, my session with Dr. Moses was a God thing too. I met with her on Tuesday and then went to the group session on Thursday."

Toni bounced her head to an imaginary beat. "Yeah! That's wonderful, Ava. I'm glad you made the call."

"I'm actually glad too. I met some good people with struggles of their own. Helps me to remember I'm not alone."

"Great. But you will never be alone, girlfriend. I will bug the bejesus out of you before you think you're alone." Toni meant it, too. She could easily move in with Ava until she came out of her mood if she needed too. Glad the situation didn't come to that though, because now she and Eric may need some privacy every now and then.

"You know what I mean. But there were a few folks with a lot more skeletons in their closet than I had. Not proud of what I did, but I know I can recover after talking with them."

"Awesome. So what's next?"

"I don't know. Just take one day at a time, I guess."

"That's what they say works best. That's what I plan to do with Eric."

"So there is a plan?"

"There is. I'm going to throw mine out of the window and give God's plan a try." *Lord, I sure hope You know what You're doing.*

"Sounds promising. I'll do the same."

Toni pulled into The Chicken Shack. "Well, Eric and I are getting a bite to eat and we're here, so I'll give you a call a little later."

"Okay, that'll work."

"And Ava." Toni turned off the car. "I'm really glad you're doing better. You had me worried for a minute, but I knew you'd eventually come around. Now if we can just get you and Rene to make up, that'd complete the task at hand."

"Yeah, well, one miracle at a time please. And like Rene said, I won't hold my breath. I'll continue to work on myself and take care of this baby, and we'll see what happens. But if you talk to her, please let her know I miss her."

Grabbing the strap of her purse, Toni hopped out the car. Eric's handsome swagger was headed her way. There were so many tangibles about him she loved, but one that could never be mistaken or misplaced was the way he carried himself. His clean-cut persona, tailored suits, and confident steps drew her in. In more ways than one.

Toni always believed he could be a model as well. A dream of hers was for them to one day do a shoot together. Even if the pictures were for their eyes only. They were a beautiful couple on the outside, no doubt. What she was concerned about was their inner man and woman. Mainly his. Their relationship was in God's hands now though. And Toni wouldn't move until He said move. And not a step sooner.

Chapter 21

Rene paced in front of Ishmael's mom's house. As she hit the twenty-minute mark waiting for him to arrive, anger grew and surged through every part of her body. Focused on Ava giving birth to Ishmael's child, she wasn't sure what she might do when she saw his face. She feared one of her many emotions might take over and she'd heave an object through the window, but she didn't want to end up on the five o'clock news. Her cell phone read a quarter to four. That'd be just enough time for the local station to get a camera out to Ishmael's mother's house and film the breaking news.

Loud music caught her attention. She looked up to see Ishmael's car bumping down the street. He turned into the driveway at a snail's pace. Rene's hands shook. What did the word "now" mean to him?

When he stepped out his beat-up car door, she darted at him and swung at his face. "Ava is pregnant! And you're the father." Just saying those words fueled the anger that already resided in her. It was like Rene hovered over the scene, watching herself. Holding anything back was not an option. She wanted to watch herself knock him out.

"What?" He put up his hands to block her right hook.

She nicked his head, knocking off his baseball cap. "You heard me, you son of a— "

"Rene!" Ishmael's mother yelled out of her window as she pulled behind his car in the driveway. She exited her vehicle and hustled to the scene.

Exploding into tears, Rene pushed his broad chest. "I can't believe this is happening. What is wrong with you? Shoot, what is wrong with me?"

Ms. Carter inserted herself between Rene's and Ishmael's stern stances.

Ishmael held his mother by the arm. "Momma, I got it. Go on in the house."

"I'm not going anywhere, son." She removed his hand. "Rene has every right to be upset, but I'm staying to make sure she doesn't do anything she'll regret later."

Rene laughed in relief. "Ms. Carter, sorry to say, but your son's not even worth it. I'm glad I found out before I walked down the aisle."

"I know I'm wrong, but please don't make any hasty decisions. Everything's just messed up right now." He stepped closer. "Rene, I love you and still want to marry you."

Was he serious? Maybe his past chicks took him back after infidelity, but this chick wasn't having it. "Don't do me any favors. Not only are you a dog, but you will now have two baby mommas you'll be dealing with. I can't stand to see you or Ava's face."

Ishmael conjured up some tears. "Rene, please. I'm sorry. That was a moment of weakness that will never happen again. I need you in my life. I'll fix this."

Rene stepped back. What was he smoking? "Fix this? You can't do nothing to fix this."

Ms. Carter pushed her son back from Rene. "Baby, just leave her be. I don't know why you feel you gotta lay down with everythang that looks good to you."

"Not now, Momma." Ishmael put his hand up as a sign to silence his mother.

"Well, Ishmael, you're going to have to live with the consequences of your actions."

"Listen to your momma and leave me alone. I'm done. Forever!" She marched to her car. Ishmael sniffled. "Rene, you'll see. I'll take care of it. We'll be back together. You watch."

Could he hear what he sounded like? A stalker in denial. She was finished with his mischievous ways and all the pain he'd caused her heart.

As she opened her car door, he yelled, "I'm here when you're ready to patch things up."

Rene paused and shot him a glance that could've sent the fibers of his shirt into a blaze. Going back and getting in one more lick would somewhat satisfy her rage, but she was ready to get out of there. She planned to never have to lay eyes on his face again. And if he continued to pursue her, the lawyer in her had no problem getting a restraining order.

Why had she always been attracted to bad boys? The relationship always ended poorly. Rene was the walking definition of insanity. Going after the same type of man, yet expecting different results. Hopefully, this would be the last time she got taught this lesson.

Ava studied the scriptures Dr. Moses had given her in their session. As she read, she prayed for understanding and the ability to live out the scriptures daily. *I am fearfully and wonderfully made.* That verse didn't match up with what she thought of herself. At least she could admit it, and work toward thinking that way about herself. She could fake it until she made it.

Two knocks on her front door interrupted her quiet time. She walked over to the door and looked through the peephole. "Who is it?"

"It's Ishmael. I need to talk to you."

What in the heck was he doing at her door? The only person she hated more than herself was Ishmael. "What do you want?"

"I just want to talk. Can you please open the door?"

He wouldn't get back in her apartment easy like the last time. She hooked the chain onto the latch and opened the door enough to show her face. "We have nothing to talk about. You should leave."

He flicked the chain. "Really, Ava. Is this necessary?"

"Yes, it is. I don't want you thinking you are welcome in my apartment for any reason. Now, if you have something to say, say it."

Ishmael folded his arms. "Rene told me you're pregnant and you think it's mine."

Think. She rolled her neck. "It is yours."

"And you plan on having it?"

"Of course. I haven't decided if I want to give the baby up for adoption, but I am going to have it. It's not the child's fault we couldn't control ourselves." Adoption did sound like the best option. The poor child would have a better chance of making it in the world the farther he or she got away from Ava and Ishmael.

"Do you really think that's a good idea? I mean you're supposed to be Rene's best friend."

"And you were supposed to be her fiancé." Ava could admit her responsibility in the fiasco, but Ishmael acted as if she performed the act alone. He assumed no blame and no concern for anybody but himself. She figured what his solution was, but wanted to see if he'd come out and say it. "What do you suggest I do?"

"You need to get rid of it."

Ava scrunched her face. "Get rid of it?"

"You heard me. You don't need this baby any more than I do. When Rene and I get back together that kid will be a constant reminder of us sleeping together."

Ava chuckled. Ishmael was as delusional as he was coldhearted. "You and Rene getting back together? Sorry to bust your bubble, but the Rene I know is done with the both of us. So you can hang that up now."

He scratched the back of his head. "Listen. I don't care what you think. I know she loves me and will eventually forgive me. And I don't need you and this kid standing in the way of that. I can get you the money for the abortion if that's what you're worried about." Yep, she knew it. Calling him coldhearted had been an understatement.

She placed her hand on her hip. "Get me the money? You couldn't even put gas in Rene's car when you had it. And what I'm worried about is not ending the life of an innocent child." Ava pushed the door to close it.

Ishmael stiffened his hand against the door to stop it from closing. "Ava, you're not ending anything. It's not even born yet."

"I feel this baby growing inside of me." A flutter tugged at her soul.

"Look, I'm giving you a chance to do the right thing. Next time I come back, I won't be so nice."

"There isn't going to be a next time. And I am doing the right thing. It's about time I start doing the right thing. Now, leave me alone or I'll call the cops." She slammed the door and bolted the locks. Who did he think he was?

"Either get rid of it Ava, or I will," he yelled through the door.

Ava heard his footsteps thunder down the steps. She leaned against the wall and slid down to take a seat on the floor. Tears uncontrollably ran down her face. Who could she talk to? Rene wasn't talking to her. Toni and Ava's brother would overreact. And the embarrassment of walking into the police station to file a report of his threat would be too much.

A voice inside her spoke aloud. *I am fearfully and wonderfully made.* "Yeah, right."

She wallowed on the floor a few minutes more, and then waddled to her bedroom. The best thing to do would be to go to her group therapy session. Confiding in her newfound friends would hope to prove easy. Instead of receiving judgment, she could receive prayer. Maybe someone would have an answer for how to handle Ishmael's threats.

When she arrived at the CCC, folks cleared out from the five-thirty session while others for the seven o'clock meeting time strolled into the building. She headed for the beverage station and poured herself a cup of coffee.

A well-built man brushed against her arm. "Excuse me, ma'am."

"It's all right, but I'm not a ma'am." She looked into her cup and stirred her coffee.

He grinned. "It's a respect thing, not an age thing."

"Oh, well, thank you."

"You're welcome." He stuck out his hand. "I'm Kevin."

"I'm Ava."

She smiled, then turned to walk to her meeting room and remembered seeing that same man pray a powerful prayer over someone during her first visit to Dr. Moses. Was he single? Married? Ava couldn't get a good look at his ring finger. *Lord, help me to stay focused.*

During the group meeting, a handful of people shared their stories and how they affected their lives the past week. Ava went to speak up a couple of times, but couldn't quite put the right words together. And whether it was the embarrassment of her situation or the fear of Ishmael that resided in her, she chose to keep quiet.

By eight-thirty the meeting came to a close. Dr. Moses asked if anyone wanted prayer. Ava's heart beat fast against her chest. She was sure everyone in the room heard it.

"I'd like prayer, please." She took a deep breath, not sure if she wanted to divulge all the details of her personal life. "My current situation has taken an ugly turn and I ask that you pray for wisdom and protection for me."

Dr. Moses led the group's prayer, highlighting all the requests and thanking the Lord for handling them in His own way. A few yeses and amens were added by members of the group. As she prayed, one lady spoke in tongues during the entire prayer and this seemed to put Ava at ease. Only God knew what the woman said, but the scene caused Ava's eyes to swell with tears.

When Dr. Moses finished speaking, everyone hugged and said their good-byes. Ava threw her paper cup in the trash and spun around to find Dr. Moses standing behind her with a big Kool-Aid smile.

"Glad you came."

"Me too. I didn't feel like coming either, but I felt I needed to be here."

"Well, happy you did." Dr. Moses grabbed Ava's hand. "When you don't feel like it, that's when you need to be here the most. Things not going so well?"

Ava looked down at her shoes and rubbed her midsection. "No, not really. The father of this baby is pressuring me to have an abortion."

Dr. Moses took Ava by the arm and pulled her over to a more private corner of the room. "And you told him where he could go with that, right?" She smiled. "In a godly manner, of course."

"Yes, I did. It's just I was hoping to never see him again and wasn't prepared when he popped up at my house talking that mess."

"Remember Who you serve, and remember the fact that you don't have to listen to any of his garbage. Stay prayed up. And if you need to, get a restraining order. Be encouraged. God is with you."

"Thank you, Doc."

"You're welcome and we're here if you need us."

Ava dug her keys out of her jeans pocket, while Dr. Moses sashayed over to a man who stood waiting to talk

to her. She waved at a couple of people on the way out
then settled into her Chevy Cavalier.

On the drive home, Ava switched back and forth between the R & B station and the Christian station. She
wasn't interested in hearing any commercials. As she
passed McDonald's, the thought of a juicy cheeseburger
ran across mind and taste buds, but she decided to pass.
She had a good-sized portion of her chicken and veggie
casserole in the fridge. *One small change at a time.*

When she turned down the winding road that led to
her apartment complex, a car zoomed up behind her
and flashed its headlights. Someone must've been in a
hurry. She slowed down and moved over to let the car
pass, but the vehicle was glued to her tail. Ava pushed the
electronic button to roll her window down and motioned
for the driver to go around her.

The automobile revved up and bumped her car. A few
choice words escaped her mouth as nervousness flared in
her body. *Lord, forgive me.* What was going on? She sped
down the dark street. Ava just needed to get to the gate.
People were always standing out in the parking lot of the
apartment complex. *Just get to the gate.*

One more turn to make, then she'd be at the front of
the apartments. She reached for her phone, but it slipped
down in between the seats. As she hurriedly approached
the turn, the car behind her revved up louder than before
and blasted her car across the other lane. Losing control
of the wheel, her car bounced up off the curb. Her vehicle
headed straight for a massive oak tree. Ava's body tensed
up as she braced herself for the impact.

Everything went black.

Not sure how much time passed, she made out a voice
coming out of her rearview mirror speaker. "Hello, this is
your OnStar operator. What is your emergency?"

Ava moaned.

"Hello. Ma'am? Sir? Are you okay?"

It felt like somebody must've smacked the front of Ava's head with a hammer as she grabbed her head and replied, "I . . . I don't know."

Chapter 22

Ava's eyes opened enough for a slit of light to come through. The sandpaper that replaced her esophagus gave her a constant desire to cough. Her right arm and forehead were competing for the award for most painful part of her body. She recognized faces and heard mumbling, but couldn't form any words of her own.

The smell of sterilized metal and mopped floors bothered her nose. Plain white sheets, walls, and window blinds tipped her off that she was in a hospital bed. She recalled someone hitting her from behind and losing control of her car, but not a thing after that.

What happened between that moment and now? What was the extent of her injuries? Who was going to pay for the hospital bills she was sure to stack up? Sure, she had insurance, but nowadays the 20 percent co-pays were through the roof, and all of her extra money was tied up in her catering business.

When she uttered a weak moan, the mumbling around her ceased and she heard a familiar voice. "Alex, get the doctor. Your sister's awake."

Somebody's hand slipped into hers. "Ava, baby. It's Daddy. We're all here."

"Ava? It's your momma." She caressed her daughter's cheek.

Ava lifted her head. Hearing familiar voices soothed some of her worry, but she'd rather be at her house in her own bed.

Her brother entered the room. "Hey, sis. We're glad you made it out all right. The front of your car was toe up from the flo' up." He pointed to the ceiling. "God is good."

"All the time." Elaine patted Ava's leg.

Ava's father kissed her forehead. "You can't be scaring us like that, baby girl."

The doctor entered the room, clipboard in hand. "Hello, everybody. I'm Dr. Griffin." He ambled to the side of the bed. "Ah, Ava, you're awake."

"Doctor, she hasn't said anything since she woke up." Her mother's worry lines were front and center.

"Don't be alarmed. That's normal. Her mind is still wrapping itself around the accident and she's in pain. I gave her something for that so she should be a little more comfortable. And when she does speak, she may not remember many details of the accident so we'll need to be patient. She has a minor concussion." He turned to Ava. "And, Ava, I believe your right wrist is broken. Looks like you tried to brace yourself with your hand against the dashboard as the air bag popped out."

Ava nodded as a tear fell down the side of her face and into her matted black hair.

The doctor silently read from his clipboard. "I'm not certain where the break is because we haven't done an X-ray yet. We put a brace on it for now and that should keep everything in place. There are some complications with the pregnancy. We're going to keep you here and monitor the baby until I feel it's safe for you to go home."

"Baby?" Her mother walked over to the doctor and looked over his shoulder. "She never said anything about being pregnant. Are you sure you have the right paperwork, Doc?"

Shoot. If only Ava had been awake when she arrived at the hospital, she could have told the doctor to act as if he were playing a baby shower game, and couldn't say the words "pregnant" or "baby" in front of her family. She'd wanted to tell them in her own time.

"Yep. It says Ava Alexander right here at the top. We did an ultrasound and she looks to be right at about twelve weeks." He looked at Ava with raised eyebrows.

Her mother stepped away. "Twelve weeks?"

"Well, I'll let you all get back to spending time with her. A nurse will come in few minutes to take her for X-rays of her wrist now that she's awake. Also, I told the detectives on your case to come back tomorrow. It's important to keep your blood pressure down." Turning to her mother, Dr. Griffin said, "Please be sure to keep her calm."

Ava's mother waited for the doctor to leave the room. "Ava, you're pregnant?"

Lowering her eyes, Ava turned her head to face the wall.

"Shake your head, nod. Something." Her mother couldn't contain her anger. "What is everybody at church going to think? That I raised some floozy?"

"Now, Lydia, what did the doctor say about keeping her calm?" Her father grabbed her mother by the arm. "Come on. Let's go down to the coffee shop and sit awhile."

As her father escorted her mother out of the room, Alex slid a chair next to the bed, his wife standing right behind him. "Ava, please tell me it's not Ishmael's baby."

The warm sting of guilt rushed to Ava's face. There was no need to start lying to her brother now. He could read the difference between the truth and a lie in her face anyway.

"Ah, sis. What are you doing?"

"I don't know, Alex. I truly don't know."

His eyes lit up. "You're talking?"

"I could talk before. I just didn't want to say anything." She needed to save fielding questions from her mother for another time. Ava pointed to the paper cup on the table next to her bed. "Can you hand me the water?"

He lifted the cup to her mouth and assisted her in taking a sip. "Well, we were going to wait 'til all of this kind of settled to share our good news, but I guess now is as good a time as any."

Ava lifted her head. "Yes, please. I could use some good news."

Alex looked back at his wife. Elaine stepped forward and put her hand on Alex's shoulder. "I'm six weeks pregnant!"

"That's awesome. I told you, girl." At least someone had great news to bring to the family. Ava was elated for them and also knew her mother would now be preoccupied, so this news worked out for everyone involved.

"Looks like our kids will be born within months of each other." Alex tapped Ava's hand. "They'll be close in age and get to grow up together."

"I'm happy for you guys. I know you've been trying quite a while. And them growing up together sounds great, but I don't know. I can't keep Ishmael's child." Ava hung her head. "I'm thinking giving it up for adoption would be the best thing to do."

"That would work too." Ava's brother shook his head. "Now, look, Ava. I know Mom and Dad may be unhappy about you being pregnant, but I know they'd want to know you're able to talk."

"I know. I needed a minute first. I didn't want you guys to find out like this. Can you give Toni a call for me?"

"Already did. She's on her way." He kissed her hand. "I'm going to get Mom and Dad. I can't sit here and let them think you can't speak. Come on, baby." He grabbed Elaine's hand. "We'll be right back, Ava."

She knew Alex would be able to vent his real thoughts to his wife on the way down to the coffee shop. Ava understood he didn't want her feeling any worse than she already did, nor did he want to say what he truly felt in front of his mother. Ever since Ava and Alex were little, he had been her protector. Their mother found fault with almost everything Ava did. Or didn't do. So the brother and sister team consistently displayed a united front.

Ava lifted both hands to pray, but her right forearm screamed at her to keep it still. She closed her eyes. "God, please heal me and the baby. I don't understand all this, but I know I don't have to. All I have to do is draw close to you and you can handle everything. Please help my family deal with the news of the pregnancy the best they can. And, Lord, guide me through all of this mess. Thank you for all that you do. In Jesus' name."

Praying to God was the only thing and the best action she could do from that hospital bed. She'd need to go to the Lord a lot the next couple of days. Her head settled into her pillow as she closed her eyes. Maybe if and when her parents came back, they'd think she was asleep and leave.

Only a few moments of alone time were granted. Toni knocked and opened the door at the same time. "Ava?"

"I'm in here."

"Oh, Ava." Toni covered her mouth, scampering over to Ava's bedside and gently hugging her friend.

"It's all right, Toni. I'm going to be okay." She pushed out a smile.

"Okay? Ava, you are in the hospital. What happened?" Toni wiped the tears from her eyes.

"I don't know. I remember a car following close behind me. It hit me and I woke up in here."

"And your family? Where is everybody?"

"They went down to the coffee shop. Finding out from the doctor I'm pregnant didn't sit too well with my mother."

Toni's eyebrows rose as she took a seat. "Oh."

"Well, at least it's out now. There are no secrets."

"Yep, no secrets." Toni struggled to get comfortable in her seat. "Speaking of secrets, I couldn't let you sit in here and not tell Rene. I called her on my way over here."

"You didn't have to do that. I'm sure she doesn't care." Sadness controlled Ava's eyes. Rene coming to visit her would be nice, but she suspected Rene wanted to stay as far away from Ava as possible, injury or no injury.

Toni scooted closer. "I don't care what's going on between you and Rene. She has the right to know. Plus, I know she cares about you, Ava. She sounded worried."

Ava scoffed. "Mmh."

"I'm serious. I wouldn't be surprised if she showed up here to visit first thing in the morning."

Ava lightly shook her head. "Rene is not coming here to see me."

"You don't know that." Toni leaned on the bed.

A knock at the door interrupted their conversation.

Toni yelled, "Come in."

The door slowly swung open. Rene stood there in tears.

Chapter 23

The lump in Ava's throat increased her need for more water while her heart danced the hokey pokey in her chest. Ava couldn't believe Rene stood in the doorway of her hospital room. For all three ladies, words were scarce, but tears were plentiful.

Toni bounced up out of her seat and gave Rene a hug. "Hey, Rene." She looked back at her other friend. "See, I told you, Ava. Nothing can separate you two."

Rene strolled over to Ava's bedside and sat down.

"Thank you for coming." Ava wiped tears with her healthy hand.

"I had to." Rene interlocked her fingers on the bed and stared down at them. "I know we haven't been speaking, but I'd never wish any harm on you. I was so scared when Toni told me what happened. I'm upset with you, Ava. But I still love you."

Watching from a corner of the room, Toni said, "You know, I'm going to head on out. I'll check on your parents. Visiting hours are almost up. We can all just come back in the morning."

"You don't have to go, Toni." Rene tossed her hair out of her face.

"No, it's quite all right. You and Ava need to catch up." Toni placed her hand on Ava's leg. "Do you want me to bring you something from your apartment?"

"No, I don't need anything." Ava smiled. All she needed was in the room.

"Okay, girl. You hang in there and I'll see you in the morning."

Rene, keeping her eyes on Ava, put her hands in her lap. "So what exactly happened?"

"Details are still foggy, but someone chased me down the street. I was almost home. They hit me from behind. I lost control of the wheel and that's all I can remember. The doctor said details may be foggy for a while."

"Did you see anything?"

"Nope. I couldn't tell what kind of car it was."

"Mm. A hit and run." Rene's attorney's mind was in full effect. "Are there any witnesses?"

"Not sure. I just woke up a little bit ago. The doctor instructed the detectives to come back in the morning to get my statement. He said I needed my rest."

"Oh, well I can go."

Ava cleared her throat. "I wish you would stay."

The two sat in silence. When the nurse entered, Rene moved out of her way and watched as she checked Ava's blood pressure and heart rate. Soon a second nurse came in the room and together they wheeled Ava to the X-ray room. Hopefully, Rene didn't leave before she got back. She may've just come to see that Ava was okay, and decide to leave after she found that out.

Ava went through the process of taking pictures of her wrist from all sides, complete with the lead shield apron over her belly to protect the baby. By the time Ava returned to her room, Rene was busy spreading out a blanket on the boxy recliner chair.

"I told the nurse I was your sister and wanted to stay the night."

Hearing this decision of Rene's to stay the night made a warm feeling travel through Ava's body. God really did answer prayers. And fast, too. "I'm glad you decided to stay. We can catch up."

"That'll be nice." Rene smiled. "Looks like the verdict is out on your wrist. They put a cast on it, huh?"

"Yep. The doctor says it's fractured in two places."

"Well, Toni and I can help you for the next couple of weeks."

Ava grinned. "I'd like that." Soon, the dose of pain medicine kicked in and she was out like a base runner at home plate.

When morning rolled around, Ava heard Rene rustling around in the bathroom. Ava adjusted herself in the sheets.

Rene turned off the water in the sink and walked out the restroom. "Good morning, Ava. How are you feeling?"

"I'm better. I think. My side doesn't feel too great."

"You want me to get the nurse?"

"No, I'm sure it's nothing." Ava pushed herself up. "Wait." She placed her hand on her side. Something didn't feel right. "Maybe you should get the nurse."

Rene dashed out of the room.

Ava's right side of her stomach felt like someone was drilling a hole in it. She nervously reached for her cup of water and knocked it over on the ground. The aggravating pain came in shots. "Ahh." If this was what it felt like to have a baby, Ava wanted no part of it.

Rene scurried back into the room a few seconds later with the doctor on her heels.

Dr. Griffin eyed Ava's heart rate from the monitor that was hooked up to her index finger. "What is the problem, Ava?"

"My side hurts and I think I just urinated on myself."

Dr. Griffin lifted the bed covers. Blood covered the sheets under where Ava lay. Rene stood back in the corner of the room wide-eyed. Once Ava saw the blood-drenched sheets, panic set in. What was happening? She took back what she said about wanting no part of giving birth.

"Ava, it's going to be all right. It's an effect from the trauma of the accident. We'll get you into an operating room and do another ultrasound to assess any damage."

"It will be okay, Ava. I'm here with you." Rene moved over and held Ava's hand as the nurses wheeled her out of the room.

Chapter 24

The colorful, vibrant flowers Toni held in a glass vase immediately lifted Ava's spirit when she returned to her room.

"Thank you, Toni. They're beautiful."

"You're very welcome. Everything okay? When I came in you were gone. Rene filled me in on what happened."

Ava pushed herself up into the pillows. "Just a scare. The doctor says some bleeding is normal, but with the accident they'll have to watch me closely."

Toni placed the vase on the windowsill. "Well, I called your parents and they're on their way."

Ava jeered. She wished Toni hadn't done that. Sitting with Rene and Toni alone would prove to be the best medicine. "Mmh. Thanks."

Rene slid the drapes back. "We need some light in here. It's too dreary. The sun and flowers will brighten up the room."

"That is better." Ava reached out for Toni to help her sit up all the way.

After this maneuver, the trio caught up on each other's happenings at the job, in their families, and what was the new gossip at church. Everything seemed like old times. Ava relished the conversation. If you had asked her a week ago if this would ever happen again, her answer would have been a no to the tenth power. But here all three ladies sat in the room sharing pleasantries. Ava didn't care how it came to be that Rene was talking to her again. She only knew that she would do her best to make things right and stay that way.

Dr. Griffin opened the door. "Hello, ladies."

Ava grinned. "Hey, Doctor."

"You have some visitors, Miss Alexander. But only if you're up for it. The detectives handling your case are in the waiting room."

"I'm okay. I'm ready to get this part over with." Ava grabbed Rene's hand. She valued her being there. Rene would never know how much. "Can my girls stay with me?"

"That's up to the detectives. I'll let them know they can come on in." Dr. Griffin looked over the blood pressure monitor. "If you start getting worked up, they'll need to leave."

"Yes, Doctor."

Ava, not sure what the detectives would ask that she would know the answer to, rubbed her forehead. However, the support of both her friends in this confusing and difficult time was appreciated.

A woman with a stocky build and a tall gentleman with chiseled facial features entered the room.

"Hello, Ava." The woman nodded. "I'm Officer Roberts and this is Detective Jones. We want to ask you some questions. Dr. Griffin told us your memory is a little cloudy. Just do the best that you can. No pressure, okay?"

"Okay." Ava ran her fingers across the cast on her arm.

Detective Jones opened his notepad. "First off, do you know of anyone who'd want to bring harm to you?"

"No, not like this." Ava glanced at Rene. Glad she was there, but telling of Ishmael's visit to her apartment earlier that day made Ava uneasy. She wasn't sure if Rene would be repulsed and hurt even more than she already was, or take up for him. "I don't think."

"Okay, tell me what you remember."

"Well, I was almost home. A car came up behind me and rode my bumper close. I slowed down to let them pass, but the driver stayed on my behind." She took a sip from her paper cup. "I sped up and went on. Then a few seconds later, they hit me and my car jerked forward. I remember trying to find my phone. After that, I was hit again from behind and lost control of the wheel. The last thing I remember, a huge tree was in my direct path." Ava paused. "Sorry, that's all I can recall."

Detective Jones wrote notes at Ava's every word. Officer Roberts moved closer to Ava's bedside. "No, you are doing fine. Now, Detective Jones has details he'd like to share with you."

The detective looked up from his pad. "Yes, I have some information from the scene I'm hoping you can help us with." He opened a manila folder and pulled out some papers.

"I'll try." Ava locked her eyes on Rene.

"Let's see. There was one witness coming out of your apartment complex and he told the police he saw a dark-colored car leaving the scene. And your vehicle was marked with navy paint on the bumper." Detective Jones thumbed through the paperwork. "Also, the two sets of tire marks found at the scene were very distinct. One set, of course, were the tires from your Chevy Cavalier, and the other type of marks found were P235 black-wall tires, which are usually found on GM cars, and specifically Buicks. Do you know anyone who owns a Buick?"

"All cars basically look the same to me. I couldn't be sure." She wasn't much help.

Hopefully, they could solve the case without her testimony. Uncertain, foggy, and cloudy were just a few words to describe the details in her head.

He closed the pad. "The witness says he thinks it was a Buick Regal."

***

Rene's body heat rose. She rubbed her chin and stood, throwing her purse over her shoulder. "I need to go see about something."

Ava's worried expression saddened Rene's heart. "Are you sure, Rene? You can stay. I enjoy having the extra support."

"I'll be back before you know it." Rene rustled in her purse and found her keys. Ishmael's mom's car was a Buick, but Rene wasn't sure what model. *Could Ishmael have gone that far?* A sick feeling in her stomach guided her out of the hospital, to her car, and all the way to Ms. Carter's house.

Chapter 25

Rene parked her car in front of Ms. Carter's house. There was no vehicle in the driveway, but she needed to make sure no one was home. She wasn't sure what she would do if Ishmael answered the door, but at this point, she didn't care. She wanted the truth.

Ms. Carter opened the door before Rene could get to the threshold. "Hello, Rene. This is a nice surprise."

"Ms. Carter, I'm not here for a social visit."

"What's the matter?" Ms. Carter pushed the screen door and invited her inside.

"A lot." Rene stepped in, arms folded. "Where's Ishmael?"

"He's out with somebody. Mike, I think."

"Is he in your car?"

"No, my car is at the repair shop. What's this about, Rene?" Concern read in Ms. Carter's eyes.

"My friend, Ava, the one Ishmael got pregnant, has been in an accident. She's in the hospital. Last night, she was run off the road and hit a tree." Rene squeezed the side of her neck. "A witness told police it was a dark blue car. The driver fled the scene."

"Oh no. I'm sorry to hear that." Ms. Carter covered her mouth.

"There are more details about the car. Isn't your car a Buick?"

"Yes, why?"

"What model?" Rene's lips tightened.

"Well, it's . . . it's a Regal." Ms. Carter stepped back. "But you think my Ishmael did this?"

"Did he have your car last night?"

"Yes. He was with friends at some club. He said someone hit him in the parking lot. And he'd take care of the damage. He took my car in just this morning."

"Mmh." Rene shook her head. Ishmael lied to everybody. That was probably the only way he was like God. He was no respecter of persons.

"I know he was upset and wanted to make things right between you two, but Rene, you can't believe he would do such a thing."

"I not only believe it, but I plan to tell the police what I know."

"Rene, you can't believe he did this. You just can't. Ishmael wouldn't do that to me. Or to Ava. I know my son." Ms. Carter opened the front door. "You can leave now."

"Gladly. You may be in denial but I'm not. He did this and you know it. You need to get him some professional help." Rene trudged through the doorway then turned her head back around to Ms. Carter. "And a lawyer."

She stomped to her car in front of the house as Ishmael pulled into the driveway.

He jumped out the car and hustled in her direction. "Rene, I can't believe you came to see me. I've missed you so much." He reached out to her.

Rene slapped his hand. *He must be crazy.* "Don't touch me. I know exactly what've you done."

"What are you talking about?" His brow wrinkled.

"Nice try. But you can save the act for the judge. I will urge Ava to press charges and represent her as well. You will get everything coming to you. I can promise you that."

On her drive back to the hospital, she phoned the police station and asked Detective Jones to meet her there. Ishmael had transformed into a monster before her eyes. This was what she was rushing down the aisle to marry? A man who could bring harm to another human being without even a thought about the consequences, physically or spiritually?

She sent up a prayer of healing for Ava and the baby she carried. Then Rene expressed her gratitude to God for keeping her from making such a colossal mistake. Being joined in holy matrimony with an individual who harbored such demons as Ishmael would have proved to be a detrimental move on her part. A decision she would have surely regretted.

Rene, determined to seek justice, would flag Ava's case as her top priority. And she'd do everything in her power to put Ishmael behind bars.

Ava listened while Rene filled Detective Jones in on everything she knew about the awful accident that put her in a hospital bed. She couldn't believe Ishmael would actually go that far. What did he think was going to happen? He'd remove Ava and the child inside of her and Rene would automatically run into his arms?

As Rene and the detective put all the evidence together of times, damaged vehicles, motive, and Ishmael's threats, Ava feared what he might do next. She kept quiet while the conversation came to a close with the exchanging of contact information.

Rene closed the door behind Detective Jones and turned to Ava. "Why didn't you say anything to the detective the first time about Ishmael threatening you?"

"I don't know." Ava knew. She knew she didn't want to speculate without knowing exactly how Rene felt about the situation.

"Well, of course, I'll represent you. I'll lobby for your case at the state prosecutor's office. Someone owes me a favor." Rene sat down next to the bed. "I'll go down to the station tomorrow and get copies of the case files and formally press charges against Ishmael on your behalf since you're in the hospital. He will get everything he deserves."

Ava yanked the sheet over her midsection. "Do you think that's a good idea?"

"What do you mean?"

"I don't want to make matters worse." Ava had done enough the past few months. "I'm concerned with the health of the baby and restoring our friendship."

"Ava, we cannot let Ishmael get away with this. People can't go around handling situations however they see fit. Why do you think I became a lawyer?"

"I know. But I don't want to shed any more light on what I did to you." Sadly enough, her sins were smack dab in the middle of the situation. Whatever God wrote down in His book on this one, Ava didn't want to highlight His words any longer. "I want it to go away as quickly as possible."

"Do you think Ishmael will go away? Look at what he's done already. He has no regard for you or that baby." Rene's fingers combed through her hair and settled her curls behind her ears. "What's done is done. Things between you and me may never be how they were, but I can forgive you and try to forget. But justice must be served. Not to mention we'll have a daily reminder when the baby gets here. We'll have to work through this somehow."

Ava took a deep breath, tapping her fingers on the bed. "I plan to give the baby up for adoption."

"You do?"

"I think that's best. There are plenty of good families who will love on this baby and take care of him or her better than I ever could. Plus, like you said the baby will be a daily reminder of how wrong I did my best friend."

"Just because you give the child away doesn't mean the situation goes away." Rene cupped her hands over the sides of her face.

"Well, I have a great deal to think about." Ava shrugged her shoulders. "Let me think and pray about it. We can pick up this conversation tomorrow."

"What conversation?" Ava's mother entered the room right in stride.

"Nothing, Momma." *Shoot.*

"Oh, hi, Rene." Ava's mother welcomed Rene into an embrace. "Looks like you two are talking again. That's wonderful."

"Hello, Momma Alexander."

"What conversation? I hope it's about what you plan to do to clean up this mess you've made."

Rene stood and picked up her purse from the chair next to her. "I'm going to let you two talk."

Ava sat up. "Rene, please don't go."

"I'll come back in the morning and we'll get a fresh start on everything." She smiled. "Take care of yourself."

"I will. Thanks for being here." Ava waved.

Ava's mother stared at her. Ava didn't feel like discussing any details of anything. The case, the baby, or her thoughts about giving the baby up for adoption. She closed her eyes and wished the doctor would miraculously give her *I Dream of Jeannie* powers to blink herself out of the room. Or at least come in with the hospital release papers at that very moment. If Ava had been healthy enough, she'd have hopped out of the bed, rolled out with Rene, and left her mother sitting in the room alone with her judgmental comments that were sure to come.

Chapter 26

The smoldering July heat didn't bother Toni and Eric as they seemed to skip out of the court hearing that handed Roderick jail time, community service, and embarrassment among his peers. Toni owned a sense of pride. She'd done her part to keep a rapist off the streets. At least for the four years before he got a chance for parole. And when he became a free man, hopefully his appetite for attacking women would be curbed.

Eric, handsome as ever in his navy suit and picture-perfect tie, attached himself to Toni's side when he picked her up that morning, and hadn't moved since.

"Thank you, Eric." Toni turned her head and flung her hair back behind her shoulder. "I appreciate you being there for me and giving your testimony."

"Where else would I be?" He grabbed her hand.

Her initial reaction was to shake her hand loose, but this used to be one of her favorite displays of his affection. The warmth of his hand, familiar and comfortable, meant a lot more to her these days. Eric was in full courting mode while Toni prayed her way through the decision to start seeing him again. She and God discussed her rollercoaster thoughts. If she felt at peace after all the court happenings, she'd reciprocate his attempts to win her back.

"So, what are your plans for the rest of the day?" Eric squeezed Toni's hand and added a smile dripping with charm.

"I'm going to visit Ava before visiting hours are over, but that's about it." She wouldn't mind hanging out with him a little longer. But not too long. The more time she spent with him, the better chance of her guard coming down prematurely.

"How about we do a little celebrating?" Eric's expression resembled a young child asking for a second cookie.

Toni put her hand on his broad shoulder. "I'm down with that."

When they arrived at Eric's cherry red Jaguar, he led her to the passenger seat, opened the door, and helped her into the seat. The two of them played eyeball tag on the ride to downtown Houston as they reminisced on the good times. Toni giggled like a schoolgirl. They were the young kids again who fell for each other back in high school. Minus the red and white cheerleading and quarterback uniforms.

She wanted to erase the previous six months of infidelity from her memory. Eric morphed back to who he was before the problems arose in their marriage. If the Lord could help Toni forgive him and move past the trust issues, their relationship, or whatever it was for the moment, might have a chance.

The Houston Pavilions swarmed with people in each corner of every restaurant. Eric pulled in front of Guadalajara's Fine Mexican Grill and valet parked his ride. They walked into the restaurant, Eric's hand on her back.

After they were seated and the waitress took their orders, Eric took hold of Toni's hand. "Can I be real with you?"

"Of course. You always have been." She grinned, but hoped he wasn't too real with her. Especially about what happened in their past. Trying to throw that whole scene out of her mind of him with another woman was hard enough. She didn't need to be reminded of any details.

"I want to sincerely apologize for all the pain I caused you. You didn't deserve any of that. I was a selfish idiot. I hate myself for being so nonchalant about the vows we took on our wedding day." He wiped the corners of his mouth. "I have never stopped loving you and never will. You are all I want and need in this world, Toni. I want to ask you to really consider giving me another chance. I'll do whatever I can to make it up to you."

Toni breathed deeply. Did she really want to travel down that bumpy road again? Had he truly changed? "Not sure what to say. I . . . I . . ."

"Take your time." He caressed her hand. "I don't need an answer right now. Believe me. I ain't going anywhere until you tell me to."

"Well, Eric. It's just . . ." She bit her bottom lip, wanting to choose her words carefully. For once. "I want to believe you mean what you say. But it was extremely difficult to get through the whole ordeal. And I am just starting to move past it. My hesitation lies in being able to trust you again. I do not want to dive back into this and end up with the word 'fool' stamped on my forehead." She had been there and done that many times over.

"Toni, I understand and will give you all the time you need to see the change in me. At the head of my life is God. Hitting bottom made me look up and I have strengthened my relationship with the Lord. He not only opened my eyes to what I've done." Eric placed his hand over his heart. "But He has opened my eyes and heart to all I could be in Him. And all I could be to you."

Tears formed in Toni's eyes, but she held them captive in her sockets. He didn't need to know he could still stir up emotion in her just yet. "I'm actually speechless. That's never happened before."

They laughed as she gripped his hand a bit tighter.

Toni's cell phone buzzed in her purse. "Bad timing, I know. But it may be Ava. I told her to call me if she needed me to bring her anything. Mind if I take it?"

He waved his hand like an usher offering a row of seats in church. "No please, go ahead."

She looked at the screen. "Oh, it's Rene."

"Toni!" Rene sounded distressed.

"Yes?"

"You need to get to the hospital as soon as you can."

"What's wrong?" Toni's body tensed, bracing herself for whatever came next.

"Ava has gone into surgery." Rene sniffled as she talked through tears. "She was complaining of cramping and started bleeding heavily."

"Oh, my goodness." Toni, frazzled, stood and grabbed her purse.

Eric walked over to her side of the table.

"Are her parents there?"

Rene cleared her throat. "Yeah, they're here. Her brother too."

"Okay. I'm on my way." Toni hit the end button on her cell phone and looked into Eric's eyes.

He removed his wallet from his inside coat pocket and dropped forty bucks on the table. "Let's go."

Glad that Eric was with her and doing the driving, Toni called on God to heal Ava right where she lay. She also sent up a prayer that Ava's dad had some packaging tape with him. He'd need to place it over Ava's mother's mouth. Her mother stressed Ava out more than anything else in the world. And she didn't need any added stress in the condition she was in now.

Toni would've gladly told her mother off herself, but she was brought up to respect her elders. And Ava seemed to handle the comments pretty well on her own.

However, if Ava's mother did add to the stress of the current situation, Toni would personally escort her out of the hospital room herself.

Chapter 27

"Momma Alexander, Ava is a grown woman!"

Ava heard Toni's raised voice as she approached her hospital room. The nurse wheeled her into the room and all conversations ceased. Her family and friends filled the small quarters. Her parents, brother, Rene, Toni, and Eric all wore soothing smiles welcoming her into the room. After looking in everyone's eyes, Ava hung her head. The nurse helped her out of the wheelchair, slowly and carefully, and into bed.

Her lower half was in pain, but her heart suffered more. "I lost the baby."

"Oh, Ava, I'm sorry." Toni covered her mouth.

Sad expressions rested on everyone's face, but nothing was said. Ava knew it was a hard situation to comfort her in, since she didn't want the baby in the first place. What had her life become? It seemed like shame on top of shame. First, having slept with Ishamel. Then ending up pregnant by him. And now, she couldn't even carry the baby to term.

"Ava?" Her mother walked over to her bedside.

"Yes, Momma?"

"How you feelin'?" She pushed Ava's hair out of her face.

Not sure what to say, or if she even wanted to say anything, Ava shrugged her shoulders. If another word came out of her mouth, tears would follow and flow like a running faucet.

Toni moved in closer. "Are you in any pain?"

"A little." Faucet on. Ava's cry was shrill and disheart-ening. Her father grabbed the box of tissues and handed her a few.

Her brother maneuvered his way through those around the bed and leaned over to give her a hug. "Ava, it's okay. Everybody in this room loves you and we are here for you no matter what."

His words were true and meant to be comforting, but she wanted to be alone. How could she relay that message without hurting their feelings? Rene sat in a chair by the window, seeming to be deep in thought. Ava wanted to ask Rene how she felt about her losing the baby, but couldn't ask her with everyone in the room.

Yes, Ishmael was responsible for causing the accident that led to her miscarriage. But if she could've stopped herself in that moment of weakness they shared together, none of the other tragic events to follow would've even happened. Was God punishing her for the choices she'd made?

Dr. Griffin stepped into the room. "Hi, everybody. I've come to explain exactly what happened."

"Yes, Doctor?" Ava's father held her hand, wearing an intense expression.

Rene looked up from her train of thought.

"You may want a little more privacy, Ava." Dr. Griffin looked around the room and then at his clipboard.

Eric and her brother turned and left the room.

The doctor moved closer to Ava. "Shall I go on?"

"Yes, Doctor. My parents aren't going anywhere and my girls are the sisters I never had. You can say whatever you need to say." The worst was out now. She breathed a breath of preparation.

"Well, we knew you had issues with bleeding and cramping." He rubbed the side of his five o'clock shadow.

"But at some point between your last ultrasound and before your emergency surgery, your membranes ruptured. You passed blood clots and tissue."

Her mother's face dropped, while her father's eyes read deep concern.

"Is there anything I could've done to avoid that happening?"

"No. The impact from the car accident affected the cervix. We couldn't be sure how and when your body would react, that's why we kept you here for observation. You passed most everything, but just to be sure, we performed a D and C."

Ava glared. "D and C?"

"That stands for dilation and curettage. I like to call it dusting and cleaning. Basically, it's an emptying of the uterus. You may have some cramping and bleeding for the next couple of days, but other than that you are okay." He cleared his throat. "Physically anyway. Having a miscarriage can be an emotional thing. I suggest you talk to someone you trust, a counselor or pastor."

Someone knocked on the door, slowly pushing it open. "Did I hear someone say counselor?" Dr. Moses carried a huge bouquet of flowers and balloons that read GET WELL SOON.

Ava smiled for the first time that day. She missed Dr. Moses and all of her wisdom and encouragement. They hadn't had a chance to really talk since the night of the accident. She had called Ava after Toni called her to let her know why Ava wouldn't be attending her counseling sessions for a while. Dr. Moses prayed a quick prayer of healing, but they only spoke a few minutes.

Ava had so much to hit her with that Dr. Moses' head would twirl around several times. The doctors exchanged pleasantries and then everyone said their good-byes, so Ava and Dr. Moses could talk. She should've shown up sooner if she had the ability to clear the room like that.

Dr. Moses placed the flowers and balloons on the table near the window. "The card is signed from all the folks at group. They're thinking about you and praying for you."

"Please tell everyone I said thank you, and I'll be back as soon as I can."

"So how have you been?"

"Not so good. I just came out of surgery." Ava's eyes focused on her twiddling thumbs. "I lost the baby."

She touched Ava's arm. "I'm so sorry."

Ava was sorry too. And she didn't know where to start. Dr. Moses would counteract everything she said with an encouraging word or a scripture. She wasn't sure she wanted to hear it right then. Feeling sorry for herself sounded better than continuing to put a spotlight on all the wrong she'd done.

"Also, we found out it was Ishmael who caused the accident. I guess it was his way of getting me to have the abortion I told him I wouldn't have."

Dr. Moses looked confused. "How'd they find out it was him?"

"Rene figured it out. He used his mother's car. Rene's been great. We're not only talking again, but she's going to be my lawyer in my case against him." Ava halfway smiled. "It's funny how things turn out."

"Yep, I believe there's a plan in everything. Even our mistakes."

"Can I ask you something?"

"Of course, that's what I'm here for."

Ava stared into Dr. Moses' eyes. "Do you think the miscarriage is God's punishment for what I've done to Rene?"

"Absolutely not, Ava. Don't you even tell yourself that. God doesn't punish us when we sin. He allows things to happen as a result of the choices we make, but it's not like He's out to get you. He loves you more than you could ever think or imagine." She reached in her purse and took out her Bible, complete with a hot pink cover that brightened up the room.

Relaxing her shoulders, Ava waited patiently.

"There's a scripture that comes to mind." Dr. Moses thumbed through the pages of her Bible. "Here it is in Romans. It's Romans 5:20: 'Moreover, the law entered that the offense might abound, but where sin abounded, grace abounded much more.' Do you see that, Ava?"

"What scripture was that again?"

"I'll write it down for you." She dove back into her purse and retrieved a pen and a small notepad. "What I want you to understand is God prepares for our mess-ups. He knows what's going to happen even before the idea ever pops into our head. His plan is grace. And His grace is sufficient."

Ava reached out for the paper.

"In fact, Second Corinthians 12:9 says, 'My grace is sufficient for you, for My strength is made perfect in weakness.'" Dr. Moses gently snatched the paper back and scribbled the second scripture. "Let me write that one down for you too."

"Thank you so much, Doctor. I needed to hear that." Ava wiped a tear from her face. "Will you pray for me?"

"You don't even have to ask." She grasped Ava's hands in hers. "Lord, we want to thank you for who you are in our lives and for all that you've done. We come to you right now asking for your healing power over Ava. Healing for her body. Her mind. Her spirit. And help her find peace throughout this situation. We know that you are in control of everything and can change this around with a wave of your hand. Please give her wisdom in what to do next and understanding where confusion lies."

Ava let the waterworks flow. The words Dr. Moses spoke were the words that rested in Ava's heart. She felt a cleansing of sorts move throughout her soul.

Dr. Moses went on. "Also, Lord, please give her an understanding of how much you love her and about the grace you have covering our lives and choices. As she moves forward, be with her every step of the way. In Jesus' Mighty Name, we pray. Amen."

"Amen." Ava opened her eyes to see Dr. Moses in tears as well.

"The Lord just showed me that everything will work out for your good. That's Roman 8:28. You must believe that and walk in it. Do not be afraid going forward. Rest in His power."

"I think I can do that."

"You can, Ava. You are stronger than you give yourself credit for. You are God's daughter. Walk in that too." Dr. Moses smiled and gathered her things. "I'm sorry to cut out on you, but I have to get home and get dinner started. My husband's coming in from working out of town and he texted me all of his favorites. Seems he missed my cooking."

"That's sweet." Ava looked forward to the day her husband would come home with the same request. "I appreciate you coming to visit me. And for the scriptures and prayer. You are really good at what you do, Dr. Glory Moses. I feel blessed to have walked into your office that day."

"God planned that, too." She winked and then exited the room.

Ava felt ten pounds lighter. God had outdone Himself on Dr. Moses' words alone. She knew He had to be in the room, surrounding her with love. He did care about what happened to her and He was making Himself more real to her every moment. And He sent Dr. Moses there at the perfect time. *God's got me.*

A knock on the door interrupted Ava's thoughts. "Come in."

Rene slipped in with two bags of McDonald's. "I was hoping you'd be alone when I returned. I'd feel guilty if I didn't have anything for Doctor Moses."

"I didn't realize you were coming back." Ava was all teeth.

"Well, we didn't get to talk earlier." Rene emptied the bags, placing her salad in front of herself and a chicken sandwich and fries in front of Ava. "I wanted to know if you were okay."

"I'm better than when you left. Dr. Moses worked her spiritual flow over me." Ava tossed a fry in her mouth. "Are you okay?"

Squeezing her dressing over the salad, Rene answered. "God knows I wasn't prepared for any of this to happen. I mean the last few months have been extremely hard. I was supposed to get married next month. But I'd be willing to bet our marriage wouldn't have lasted a year. Ishmael's true colors would've come out sooner or later."

Ava thought how Ishmael had shown an entire rainbow several times before, but Rene turned her head to his colorful schemes. However, she wasn't about to muddle this revelation of Rene's as their friendship took another step forward. And seeing as Ava owned one of the paint brushes, it was better not to say anything on any front.

"I hate this is the way you found out about him. I can't say I'm sorry enough."

Rene swallowed her bite of salad. "Well, I don't want to dwell on the past. I want to move forward."

"Sounds good to me."

"Have you given any more thought about pressing charges?"

"Yes, I have." She gulped down a drink of sweet tea. Ava would let faith lead her instead of fear. "I want to proceed with the charges. I can't let him get away with this."

"So true. He will go down for attempted vehicular manslaughter."

Ava scrunched her face. "Attempted? He's the reason I lost the baby. He killed an innocent child."

Rene shook her head. "Not in the state of Texas. It's sad, but if the baby isn't born yet, the best we can do is press charges against him for what he did to you."

"Well, he'll get his one way or the other. I'm sure of it. He'll answer to the courts first and then God will deal with him later."

"That's the attitude to have." Rene shared a smile. "I'll call the detectives on my way home."

"Thank you so much, Rene. I appreciate you taking the case. I know it must be difficult to be in this position." An awkward road lay ahead, but Ava believed in God. And God could do anything. Even bring the sinners and the sin together face to face with the one offended by the sin in the middle of it all. The Lord not only worked in mysterious ways, He worked in mysteriously, crafty ways.

Rene sternly peered into Ava's eyes. "What would be difficult about this whole situation is if you got the wrong lawyer, and Ishmael walked. I couldn't live with myself." She reached for Ava's hand. "Together, we'll bury that fool under the jail. Where he belongs. I promise you that."

Chapter 28

The following day, Ava was discharged to go home. Dr. Griffin assured her that outside of some cramping she should feel fine. Glad to be leaving, Ava packed her belongings and took down the flowers and balloons from the windowsill. The card from her group therapy friends sat on the table, unopened. She picked it up and read all the messages written on the inside.

A smile resided on her face as she silently read each heartfelt message and prayer. There were words of encouragement and prayers for healing and protection. Thankful for the love shown her way, she placed the card back in its envelope and tucked it in her suitcase.

People were actually thinking about her and wishing her well. It had been a long time since she felt special. Wanting to hold on to that feeling a little longer, Ava fished the card back out, sat down on the bed, and read through each message again.

After getting through half of the messages, Toni busted in the door. "Ava, you ready, girl?"

Rene came in behind her. "Yep, we're breaking you out of this place."

"Thank you, Lord. I miss my own bed." Ava could've chosen a different piece of furniture to vocalize her missing the apartment, seeing how the bed was the scene of the crime. She'd need to be more careful in her choice of words from now on. Especially when Rene was around.

Toni cut her eyes at Ava, seeming to feel Ava's thoughts. "Well, if you're packed and ready to go, let's be out."

"Do you want a wheelchair?" Rene picked up one of the bags.

Ava grabbed the balloons. "No, I'm okay."

"Well, let's ride." Toni picked up the suitcase and opened the door.

Waving good-bye to the nurses on the way out, Ava wore a solid smile. On the way down to the car, Rene communicated to Ava how through God's grace she'd made it out of the dangerous accident alive, as well as managed to catch the culprit. Ava concurred, and although she didn't understand why the miscarriage happened, she walked out of the hospital with more peace than she rolled in with.

Dr. Moses' visit and prayer had helped her to open her eyes and see the situation differently. The word that was imprinted on her mind was grace. When she returned home, digging deeper into her Bible and the scriptures concerning grace would be at the top of her list.

"You want to stop and get some real food on the way home?" Toni grinned.

"No, I just want to get home. We can order pizza or something." She lifted her arm with the cast on it. "I need to figure what I'm going to do about this event that's coming up in a few weeks. It's sort of a welcoming in the fall sort of celebration and is a good piece of change, but I don't know if I can fix all the meals they ordered, even with extra staff."

Rene bent forward toward the front seat. "You have a catering gig? I didn't know that. I'll be able to include that in our case against Ishmael. We need to write down all the things you can't do that you normally would be able to, and what is hindered as a direct result of the accident. Emotionally, physically, your safety. Whatever you can think of."

Out of all the phrases Rene put together, one word stood out to Ava: our. They were taking Ishmael to court together. God sure could turn circumstances around. And heal relationships in the process.

Ava turned to Rene. "We can do that today, if you feel up to it."

"No problem."

"Pizza and preparation for the case it is." Ava placed her good hand over her stomach. The pregnancy had come and gone so fast, which saddened her heart. She would do her part to put the murderer behind bars.

Ava couldn't comprehend how Ishmael could be so cold. Or, how Rene couldn't see that side of him before. *I guess people show what they want to show when they want to show it.* He couldn't have thought that causing Ava to lose the baby would win Rene back. He was definitely crazier than she thought. Ava was just happy Rene saw that horrific side of who he was before the marriage license displayed their signatures at the bottom.

Toni pulled into Ava's apartment complex. "Well, I can make sure I'm free whenever the event is. I can help you with the catering, Ava. You'll have to tell me what to do. You know I don't cook. But I'm pretty good at following directions."

"That'd be great. Then I'll just have to get some extra staff to bring out the food."

"I can ask some of my model friends." Toni smiled. "At least you know they won't be sneaking food off the trays."

They laughed, and then Ava took out her cell phone and ordered dinner for the ladies.

Heading up the stairs, Ava sent up prayers of thanks. She was at home by way of her closest friends in the world. Toni was going to be there for Ava with her struggling catering business, while Rene, who she had caused a great deal of pain, represented her without hesitation as her determined lawyer.

She was thankful to have such amazing friends. Skinny and beautiful, yes. But there was character behind that beauty. And that was the most attractive part of all. The Lord had taken care of all of Ava's issues despite her poor decision-making skills. Maybe that was the grace Dr. Moses was talking about.

Ava delighted in all of the blessings God placed in her life. And she couldn't wait to see what else He had in store.

Chapter 29

Ava's catered event went off without a hitch. Toni and her friends proved to be exactly what she needed. They not only acted as waitresses, but turned out to be pretty good banquet decorators as well. Ava's client purchased all of the fall décor and the ladies worked together to make the guests feel like they were sitting in an autumn painting. Tired and ready for a nap, Ava did just the opposite and put her tennis shoes on. She wasn't sure where her energy came from, but she enjoyed it just the same.

After ten minutes of walking down the block, her feet, sore and aching, didn't offer much support to her stiff back. But her will to start feeling better about herself was much stronger. She meditated on Philippians 4:13 as she strutted to the end of the street. When she turned around to walk back to her apartment complex, the tree she had ruined with the front end of her car stared back at her.

Seeing this tree brought up an awkward feeling. Tragic as it was, the scattered dent of bark in God's creation also represented a turning point in her and Rene's relationship. And brought back to memory the conversation that led to Dr. Moses' prayer, which, Ava believed, sparked the fire she needed to get moving in the right direction. Everything was far from perfect, but as she walked toward God, hope lived inside of her now.

After returning from her walk, as she opened the door to her apartment, her phone's ringtone played the upbeat song that matched her new attitude.

"Hey, Ava, just calling to let you know the police picked up Ishmael today." Rene seemed pleased.

"Well, that was fast." Ava took a bottle of water out of the fridge.

"They had all the evidence they needed. I don't know if he'll make bail. His momma will probably end up paying it, but we should go to trial soon. My friend in the office will move your case to the top like he did Toni's."

"This friend of yours seems to hook you up a lot. You sure he just wants to be your friend?"

Rene giggled. "He asked me out once or twice, but I told him I wasn't ready. He said when I was he'd be happy to show me a night on the town."

"Sounds promising."

"First things first. I need to get Ishmael out of my system before I dive into anything else. Even if it's just a date or two."

"I hear you. As always, I appreciate all you are doing for me." Ava gulped her water.

"Justice is justice. And of course, I love you, Ava."

"Love you too, girl. See you at church on Sunday?"

"I'll be there."

Closing her cell phone, Ava said a little prayer for Rene's peace of mind and strength to move on. And that their friendship would continue to flourish.

The next few days included ignoring the humiliating comments the young inmates made toward her as she visited the county jail, and walking twenty minutes a day despite the pain, and sticking scriptures all over her apartment. The more she read and thought about the scriptures, the bigger the invisible earplugs became at work, and the easier her walks were on her limbs.

On her bathroom mirror, she taped a sticky note that read:

Psalm 139:14 I am fearfully and wonderfully made.

By her bed, on the nightstand, the paper read:

Proverbs 18:22 The man that finds a wife, finds a good thing.

Hanging on the fridge, her pink stationary note had scribbled on it:

2 Corinthians 12:9 My grace is sufficient for you.

And finally, by the front door where she hung her keys, she wrote:

Romans 8:28 All things work together for good for those who believe.

Every word in each scripture was inscribed on her heart. She spoke these words into her spirit and truly believed each one of them.

Thursday evening came before she knew it. After her daily walk, she showered and got dressed. Group therapy started in an hour and a half. She noticed her jeans fit a little better and it wasn't an uphill battle to put them on. Putting on makeup crossed her mind, but she didn't want to go too far. One step at a time. Some lip gloss would be enough for now.

Her mother wanted her to put on the whole face: foundation, powder, eyeliner, mascara, eye shadow, and blush. Ava figured she could work up to that, or only do it on special occasions. Like her wedding. Yeah, the full-face war paint could make a debut on her wedding day. For now, simplicity was best.

Before she left her apartment, she smiled into the mirror over her bar and was surprisingly satisfied with what she saw in her reflection. Maybe she'd do the lip gloss thing.

When she arrived at the counseling center, she scoped out the coffee, knowing she'd need the caffeine to stay awake. Two Sweet'N Lows and three creams. She created hot chocolate actually, but it tasted good.

She turned around and stepped toward her meeting room. Right behind her, a white shirt covering a firm chest bumped her hand. All the coffee turned the shirt to a caramel color.

"Ahh!"

"Oh, I'm so sorry." Ava snatched napkins off the table. "Here you go."

"It'll be okay. I've had worse pain before. Ava, right?" The classically handsome gentleman smiled.

"Yes, how'd you know?"

"We've met at this spot before. I'm Kevin."

A lot had happened since then, but Ava didn't want to offend him. Even though she didn't remember him, she played it off. "Oh, yeah. I remember you."

"No, you don't." He laughed. "Just lying. And in the Christian Counseling Center, too."

She hung her head and chuckled. "You got me." *I must've been going through quite a bit to forget your handsome face.*

He tossed the soaked napkins in the trash. "This should help you remember. You got on me for calling you ma'am."

Smiling, she pointed her finger at him. "I do remember you." She really did this time. "But you explained yourself. A respect thing. I got it. I've seen you pray over people out here in the lobby."

"That would be me."

"Do you attend one of the counseling sessions?" She wrapped a napkin around her coffee cup, analyzing every line in his face. Ava guessed he was in his late twenties or early thirties.

"Yes. Actually, I'm the leader of the drug recovery group down the hall."

"Oh, okay. Sorry about your shirt. Hate you have to lead the group with a big coffee stain on the front of it. I didn't see you."

"Man, I gotta step up my game. You don't see me. You don't remember me. What's a man to do?"

She recalled him all right. Just figured he was one of many who didn't pay her no mind, so she carried on about her business. "What made you remember me?"

"Well, along with that pretty smile, you have a sweet spirit about you. A little feisty I bet, but sweet all the same."

No, he didn't. "Thank you."

"You're welcome. We should hang out sometime after group. What do you think about that?"

"Depends on what you mean by 'hang out.'" She'd "hung out" plenty before which usually led to hanging in. Between the sheets.

"What does hang out mean to you?"

She smiled. "How about you tell me what it means to you?"

He shrugged his shoulders. "Have lunch, dinner, or maybe go get a cup of coffee. Something like that. But I'd be sure to wear a dark-colored shirt though if we got coffee."

Ava laughed. "I like your definition. Sure, we can hang out some time."

"How about tonight?"

Her heart vaulted into her throat. "I guess that'd be all right."

"If you'd rather wait, that's fine. I don't want to rush you. Just interested in getting to know more about you."

That's a first. "No, you just caught me off-guard is all."

"If asking you out for a cup of coffee caught you off-guard, get ready for a fun ride."

Ava wasn't sure if she was ready, but she didn't care. She'd just be sure to wear her seat belt.

Chapter 30

All week, Ava counted down the days until group counseling Thursday. Going to group meant she'd get the chance to converse with Kevin. Last week after their meetings were over, she told him they could postpone hanging out until the next time they met up at the center. Not wanting to seem too eager, her need for male companionship would have to wait another seven days.

Dr. Moses said she was progressing right along in overcoming her insecurities and self-pity. Her main issues remained the sensitivity it took to restore her relationship with Rene, and the ongoing problems that stemmed from her involvement with Ishmael.

Ava hadn't been in any pain since she'd left the hospital, but emotionally, it was like riding the Titan at Six Flags. A part of her wanted to have the baby, so she'd have someone to love and someone to love her back. But maybe her losing the baby happened for a reason. The child would be dropped into a world of chaos. Who knew what would've become of him or her?

So other than trying to figure out the "Ishmael baby accident court case" situation, she had a positive outlook on life. In fact, between studying God's Word and her walks where she could meditate on His Word, she felt and looked better than she had in years.

On her way out the door, Toni called. "Headed to your counseling session?"

And to Kevin. Ava chose to keep quiet about him. She didn't want to put the cart before the horse by spreading any news about her new friend. Especially, if their talks turned out to be no news at all. "Yes, I am. Looking forward to it."

"That's good to hear. You seem to be feeling better these days."

Ava smiled. "God is good."

"All the time."

"And all the time . . ."

"God is good." Toni laughed.

When Ava and her girlfriends used their "God is good" catch phrase, it meant all was good in their lives. Ava wanted to utilize that phrase much more in the days ahead. "So how are things with you and Eric?"

"Well, that's part of the reason I called you. Wanted you to know he and I are starting our relationship up again. I'm liking what I see in him, so I'm diving in. Needed to ask you a favor?"

"Anything."

Toni took a deep breath. "Could you please keep us in prayer? This is charted territory, but uncharted feelings. It's weird. I love him, but in a different way. It's a new him. Dating him again is almost like I'm cheating on the old him with the new him."

"Yep, you're right. That does sound weird. But just enjoy it, girl. I'd love to see you two mend and finish skipping down that path you started together way back when." Toni and Eric were meant to be together. They completed one another, and when he stepped out of their relationship shock was the biggest emotion Ava walked around with. And ever since, Toni felt incomplete. Moving toward reconciliation excited Ava as much as it did Toni. Well, maybe half as much. Toni loved her some Eric.

"I would too. But don't want to get my hopes up too high." She paused. "The higher they are, the further they have to fall."

"Just move slowly. And before any moves forward, make sure you have peace."

"Will do."

Ava couldn't be happier for the reuniting couple. It was obvious love still resided between them. She just hoped Toni would never have to go through what she went through that sparked talk of a divorce. So as promised, she began to pray for Toni and Eric.

Lord, your will be done. Protect Toni's mind and heart, and only have her move forward with your peace. Keep Eric on the straight and narrow, and if they are to return to each other, then cover their relationship with the blood of Jesus. Only you know the plan laid out for them. I ask you to have them follow it to a tee, so they can be blessed as individuals and as a couple. In Jesus' name.

Now almost to the CCC, she threw up a quick prayer for herself. "Father, I pray your will be done in my life as well. I trust you with my future. Please continue to restore my health, physically, mentally, and emotionally, as well as restore my relationships. And if Kevin is to be a friend of mine and maybe more, help me to let him lead. Remind me that I can be nobody but who you've created me to be. I am fearfully and wonderfully made. Thank you, Lord. Amen."

Later during group, Ava barely heard two words anyone said in the group session. Her eyes travelled back and forth between whoever was speaking at the time and the thin, vertical rectangular window in the door. Catching a glimpse of Kevin was at the front of her mind. She hadn't seen him in the lobby before the meeting started.

Was he avoiding her? He must've had second thoughts about going out for coffee afterward. Maybe he didn't want to be seen in public with her. Xavier avoided being in public with her by pulling from any one of his lists of excuses. Too tired, no money, or not feeling well. Surely, the Lord wouldn't dangle Kevin in her face only to have him be a replica of Xavier.

She should've just gone out with him last week before he had a chance to dwell on what he had done by asking her out.

Dr. Moses broke into Ava's train of thought. "Well, that's it, everybody. Thanks to all who shared tonight. Let's have a closing prayer." She bowed her head. "Lord, thank you for changing us from the inside out. Please let everyone have a safe trip home and keep us in your care until we meet again."

Ava waved to Dr. Moses on her way to the door. "See you next Tuesday."

Upon entering the lobby, she looked straight over to the coffee pot to see if Kevin was in what had become their meeting spot. When she didn't see him there, Ava walked toward the hall where the recovery group met. No one in sight. He probably bolted out of there, so he wouldn't have to make up an excuse about not being able to go.

She pushed open the exit door and headed to her car.

"Ava?"

Turning around, she saw Kevin's baby-faced smile and inviting, dark eyes. He held his hands up in the air. "Are you trying to skip out on me?"

"I thought the same thing about you. Thought you might have forgotten our plans."

"Nope, just in the restroom. We got out a little early." He reached in his pocket and took out his keys. "If you're ready, why don't you follow me down the street to the Coffee House."

Oh, I'm ready. "Okay, sounds good." *Calm down, girl. He's just a man.*

It was almost nine o'clock. The Coffee House was fairly full for a Thursday night. On the patio, there was a little band playing tunes. Inside, college students with mounds of books studied in groups with coffee in one hand and notes in the other. The scene was public, yet peaceful. The perfect spot to get to know Kevin better.

After they received their orders, he led Ava to a small table in the corner. He pulled out a chair for her. "So, Ava, are you from Houston?"

She placed her coffee on the table and sat. "I was born in Dallas. Lived there until junior high school. But then my dad got transferred to Houston and I've been here ever since. What about you?"

"I'm from here. And never wanted to leave. My whole family's here," he replied, now situated in his chair.

"Do you have a big family?" As she heard herself ask that question, she didn't want it to lead him to asking about her family. She'd only be able to talk highly of her father and brother.

"Pretty much. I have two sisters and two brothers. We're all close." He removed the top from his coffee cup. "So how'd you end up at the CCC? If you don't mind sharing."

Ava's lips tensed up. "Well . . . that's probably a story for another time." She was not prepared to reveal all her dirty laundry yet. Maybe after a few more coffee dates.

"Don't worry about it." He smiled. "I can tell you how I ended up there."

"Okay."

"I used to be a heavy cocaine addict. God delivered me." Ava read confidence in his laid-back demeanor. "He completely changed me."

So he had some laundry that could stand to be thrown into the washer too. Ava could work with that. Meant he wasn't without flaws. And God was using those flaws to help others. "Amen."

"My family was there for me, but I couldn't kick the habit. Even with their tough love. Finally, I became sick of myself and called on the Lord. He answered me almost immediately."

"That's an awesome testimony."

"Thank you. I've been clean for ten years and serving as a counselor at the CCC for the last six and some change. I'm also a sponsor, and have about five people I sponsor right now." He rubbed the palm of his hand over his bronze bald head. "Well, four and a half."

"A half?"

"Yeah, my newest former addict hasn't decided if he really wants to get clean. And that's something I can't do for him. So he struggles, but knows I'll be here when he's ready."

"That's nice of you." He seemed good on all fronts. Hopefully, he wasn't too good to be true.

"Someone did it for me. I'm just doing what was done for me."

Ava relished how easily the conversation moved along. She enjoyed listening to him speak. His deep baritone voice soothed her nerves. He smiled as he talked, which seemed to act as a calming agent as well. They swapped info about their jobs, friends, and families. The chat continued smoothly with bouts of laughter mixed in. Before they knew it, ten-thirty had rolled around.

Kevin looked at his watch. "I hate to cut us off, but I have to get up at five in the a.m."

She shook her head and picked up her cup. *I hate to cut it off my dern self.* "Don't worry about it. I need to get up early too. I enjoyed talking with you."

"Hopefully, we can hang out again some time." He raised his bushy eyebrows. "Next week after group?"

"Sounds like a plan." Ava was all in to hang out again.

They strolled to her car. After she disarmed the alarm, Kevin reached and opened her door for her. "You have a good night, Ava."

"You too."

Ava couldn't remember the last time she had a great cup of coffee and a great conversation with a man. And the added bonus was there were plans to do it a second time. The whole drive home Ava's smile grew larger along with her inner hope in this new relationship.

Chapter 31

Toni waited for Eric to pick her up so they could ride as a couple to their weekly small group Bible Study. They had attended it together for almost a month now. Each week, she grew accustomed to seeing a new surprise in his character. If he was faking this newfound zeal of living for Christ, he was playing a mighty good part.

As she peeked out the window, a stimulating sensation filled her body. The butterflies fluttered around again. She'd missed that feeling. He pulled up in front of her house. Toni grabbed her Bible, picked up her purse from the table, and walked out the door.

"Toni, what are you doing?" Eric walked up to her.

"What do you mean?"

"You're supposed to wait for me to come and get you." He welcomed her into his arms.

She leaped into his embrace and his enticing scent. *I could stay here forever.* "I'm not worried about those formalities. I was excited to see you, so I came on out."

He showed all thirty-two teeth. "I love that answer. I'm excited to see you too. Been thinking about you all day."

The house where Bible Study was usually located was only about fifteen minutes away, so when ten minutes passed of them driving around and Toni saw nothing familiar to her, she needed to know where he was headed. "Did they move the group tonight to someone else's house?"

"Nope."

"Would you care to elaborate?"

"Nope." Eric grinned.

The corners of Toni's mouth turned down. "Are you sure about that?"

"Yep." His thin eyebrows vibrated over his eyes like a party clown.

Toni didn't want to jump to conclusions, but nerves set in as they drove into a nice neighborhood, yet unfamiliar. He couldn't be taking her to his parents' house. It was too soon. Toni hadn't seen his mom and dad in over six months. And the last time wasn't pretty. When his mother asked Toni to overlook his cheating ways because no one in her family had ever gotten a divorce, Toni let a few choice words escape her lips. She didn't want to disrespect her elder, but in that moment being respectful wasn't on the top of her list.

Surely, Eric knew her better than to just surprise her with an unannounced trip to their house. She'd want to have time to get her mind right before seeing his parents again. Here she was feeling on top of the world, and he was about to mess it up.

Eric pulled into the driveway of a large, pewter house with a trimmed yard. Someone with class had to be the owner.

"Who lives here?"

"No one right now." He opened his door and stepped out, carrying his Bible, and then drifted over to Toni's side.

She stepped out. "Then why are we here?"

"You'll see."

I'll see. Did he forget how quickly her attitude could change? "Eric, I don't want to just be dropping by some-body's house I don't know."

"I told you no one lives here."

"Then what are we doing here?" Aggravation swished around in her belly.

He slipped his hand into hers. "Come here on the porch with me."

She obliged. She wondered what was he up to and why he was so hush-hush about it. Was he trying to spice up the regular routine of Bible Study? They could've easily gone to a coffee shop, a park, the church. Toni was there now, so she decided to just go with it.

Eric flipped through the pages of his Bible. "In Romans 4:17 it says, 'As it is written, I have made you a father of many nations, in the presence of Him who he believed— God, who gives life to the dead and calls those things which do not exist as though they did.'"

Toni, not sure what to say, remained silent.

"That's what I'm doing, Toni. I'm calling things that don't exist as though they do." He closed the Good Book. "My love for you has never changed. I know I had my idiot months, but I am back now. Stronger than ever. In God's strength. I am the man you've always wanted and deserved."

Still not able to form any words, she listened.

"I'm starting with this house. I put a bid on it this morning. My family-to-be will live here and we'll make memories together." He pulled out a small, velvet box from his pants pocket and knelt on the ground.

Toni swallowed hard. Was she ready for this? "Eric, what are you doing?"

He opened the tiny box to reveal a lustrous rock sitting on top of a smooth silver wedding band. "Antoinette Yvonne James, I love you more than I ever have. And that's difficult to do. You are the only woman for me and I want to spend the rest of our lives making memories, babies, and being all God has called us to be. Together."

"Oh, Eric." Tears dashed down her cheeks. Could this proposal really be happening?

"What do you say? Remarry me? We can renew our vows and light a new match to our old flame."

Toni internally asked God for peace. He gave it to her. She smiled and kissed Eric's soft lips with passion and excitement. "Yes . . . yes . . . yes!"

He jumped to his feet and picked her up off the ground, twirling her like a merry-go-round. Eric was the man she loved and craved since they were teenagers. God did His part in changing him and returning his heart to hers. She had no problem reaping the benefits.

She'd never actually filed for the divorce. The paperwork lay on her desk at home. Whether she knew in her heart she really didn't want to get divorced, or if it was God's plan all along to keep them together, that didn't matter. The first thing she would do when she returned home would be rip the divorce papers in half, and throw them away.

Chapter 32

The hot summer sun beatdown on Ava's face as she headed into the CCC for her last one-on-one session with Dr. Moses. Ava rode into the office on top of a cloud. She couldn't believe she'd been seeing Dr. Moses for almost three months now. Between her Tuesday one-on-ones, and her Thursday group sessions, she felt like a different woman. God was doing His thing inside her and she hoped others could see the change on the outside. She could feel the difference already with only a fifteen-pound weight loss. Her back wasn't hurting as she walked, which fueled her to want to do more.

Upon entering the waiting room, she noticed a young couple sitting with their daughter. The girl looked to be about six or seven years old. Ava didn't know Dr. Moses held family counseling sessions. She may have to take her up on that once God gave her a family. There was no shame in receiving help.

Ava signed in at the window and paid her co-pay.

"Mommy, how is she going to fit through that door?"

There was no way Ava could've acted like she didn't hear the little one's comment. Here she was a dress size smaller, feeling better inside and out, and someone just had to try and stomp on her mood.

"Shh. That's rude."

Ava turned around. "It's okay." *They need to whip her butt.*

The red-faced father sheepishly said, "Sorry, ma'am. She didn't mean it maliciously."

Sitting down across from them, Ava assured him. "Really, it's okay. Kids say whatever's on their mind."

Proud of herself for how she handled the situation, Ava recalled a time when she would've told the mother, father, and their daughter off without hesitation. She was growing. And no matter the comment or who said it, she was valued by God. Seeing herself as the Lord saw her was clearer to her now. Her value was wrapped up in the person she was and how she treated others and lived her life. Not in what someone else thought.

Dr. Moses was all smiles when Ava walked through the door. "I can't believe this is our last one-on-one."

"Me either. I'm kind of sad." Ava poked out her bottom lip. Dr. Moses had done so much for her already that a part of her would miss their talks. Unloading her emotions and situations in that hour proved to be extremely beneficial. She felt lighter in more ways than one. "I'm glad I've come a long way and don't feel depressed anymore, but I'll miss you."

"You can come by anytime and visit." She hugged her. "Plus, Thursday group sessions are open meetings, so come as needed."

Ava, thankful and content, took a seat on the couch.

"So what's new?" Dr. Moses sat down next to her.

"I've been walking a mile a day and plan to kick it up to two miles soon. My catering business is doing well. I'm a little bit closer than I was a year ago to being able to do my catering full time. And I have some good spiritual news." Ava's dream was still alive. "I'm signing up next Sunday for baptism class."

"Awesome. When you do it, let me know and I'll come if I can." She squinted her eyes. "You've never been baptized? I thought every black kid in America's been baptized even if they didn't know what they were doing."

Ava laughed. "That's just it. I was dipped in the water as a child at my grandmother's church, but didn't fully understand why."

"Well, awesome, Ava. I'm glad for you and all that God is doing in your life."

"Speaking of which, Rene and I are becoming close again; almost like old times. The Lord works in mysterious ways. I still can't believe she's prosecuting her ex-fiancé on my behalf—the woman who split them up." God was all in her situation. That was the only explanation that made sense.

"Don't forget Ishmael had his part in that breakup too. So it's not all on you. And I'm not a prophet or anything, but the way he was going, I don't think they would've walked down the aisle."

"To tell you the truth, I didn't either. I believe she dodged a bullet not marrying him. I just hate I was the one who shot the gun."

Dr. Moses chuckled. "Remember, you are forgiven. Move on in peace and understanding of her feelings. But move on. You can't dwell in the guilt. God has forgiven you, and you need to forgive yourself. "

Ava was prepared to move on. She'd love it if everything returned to normal. Things between her and Rene might never be normal, but she'd like to get as close to normal as possible. Forgiving, however, was a whole other issue. She'd do her best. "I can work on that."

"In regard to your forgiveness, have you forgiven your ex, Xavier?"

Ava put a hand up. "I'm working on that, too."

"Well, Ava, please understand that forgiveness is for you, not for him. He's gone on about his business."

"I'll pray on that."

"That's a start." Dr. Moses leaned forward. "Now, with the court case coming up, are you ready to face Ishmael and Rene in the same room?"

"All I can do is let God handle it. Spending the past few months with you, I've realized I need to thank God not only for what He has done in my life, but for who He is. And He's my protector. My guide." Ava wrote a reminder in her notepad. "I know He will go before me and make every crooked place straight again. I wholeheartedly put my trust in Him."

"You have definitely made a one-eighty."

"Thank you. I'm trusting Him for everything. Something in me wants to step out and take the leadership class at church, so I can become a prayer partner." A tingle went through her body. "Prayer has been my lifeline and I want to help others experience that."

"Great, Ava."

"Also, I'm trusting God for friendships with the opposite sex."

Dr. Moses tilted her head. "Oh, is there someone in the picture?"

"Actually, you know him. Kevin, the counselor over the drug recovery group."

Dr. Moses smiled. "Yes, I do know him. He's a great man of God. You have my approval."

They shared a laugh. If Doc okayed him, he must be all right.

"He's been here since this building's been open. In fact, he came on board almost seven years ago to the date."

"Good to know."

"Our anniversary's coming up soon. January second to be exact." Dr. Moses touched Ava's knee. "You should be the caterer for our party. We have a celebration every year to thank God for all He's done. We used to meet in someone's house, then rented a building for a while, and then got a place of our own seven years ago. The Lord continues to grow us and allow us to point hurting people in His direction."

"That's great. I'd love to cater for you guys. Just let me know what you want on the menu." Ava was elated to share her culinary skills in celebration for the CCC and the people who had been blessed by its services over the years. She knew counselors, patients and their families, and other special guests would all taste her food.

But one person stuck out in her mind. Kevin. If the saying "the way to a man's heart is through his stomach" was true, then for the anniversary party, Ava was about to cook the meal of her life.

Chapter 33

After anxiously waiting for months to be able to stick it to Ishmael, the date was finally here. Ava found herself sitting opposite Ishmael in a dreary courtroom, Rene posted up between them. The scene couldn't be any more uncomfortable. Ishmael's not guilty plea seemed to anger Rene in more ways than one. She'd asked Ava to meet her outside the courtroom an hour before the proceedings started to go over the questions for the one hundredth time.

The fall weather cooled off the outside, but inside that courtroom Ava recognized a fire in Rene's eyes that seemed to send the thermostat soaring. That flame showed up in cases she was extremely passionate about. Her passion for this case was off the charts.

Toni walked in with Ava's father ten minutes before the case was to begin, both exhibiting concerned expressions. Her father made a beeline for her and welcomed her into a firm embrace. He seemed as if he didn't want to let go.

"Where's Momma?"

He bowed his head. "She said she'd rather not be a part of this."

Ava shrugged her shoulders. Her mother's decision to stay away from the case was probably a smart one for all parties involved. Knowing her mother would put her two cents in every chance she got, Ava wasn't sure she'd be able to handle it in an honor-your-mother fashion. Ava would need stitches for all the biting of her tongue she would do.

"But she sends you her love and is praying that all works out." Her father's face looked like he was adding a positive note to what her mother said. Ava loved him for many things and especially for that. No matter what she and her mother did, her father always did his best to keep the peace.

As the judge—a short, pale-faced woman with a confident presence about her—walked into the room, everyone stood.

The bailiff stepped forward, towering over her. "All rise. The honorable Judge Powers residing."

Everything suddenly became more real. Opening arguments were made with Rene highlighting all the evidence against Ishmael: the holes in his alibi, his mother's car paint on Ava's vehicle, and his threats toward her about having an abortion. How did her life get to this? People say everything happens for a reason, but the reasoning in this was so farfetched Ava couldn't grasp it. Learning from her mistakes was the only takeaway she could come up with at that time.

Rene first called Neil Gallagher, the man she had as the only eyewitness. He'd pulled out of the apartments as Ishmael sped off.

After he was sworn in, Rene moved with slow steps and purpose. "What can you tell us about the night in question?"

"When I pulled out of my apartment complex, I saw a dark-colored car, like a black or navy, back up and speed off," the witness stated.

"You told police you believe it was a Buick?"

"Yes, ma'am." He shook his head. "My daddy used to own a Regal when I was younger. I practiced with his car to get my license." Neil paused to look at the judge. "Only in parking lots of course."

Judge Powers, smiling, nodded.

Looking over her notes, Rene asked, "Is there anything else you can remember about that night?"

"Um. Not really." He wiped his hand over his mouth. "Well, I'm not totally sure, but when the driver saw I was coming over to help, they backed up and burned rubber away from the scene. Like they did it on purpose, and wasn't concerned if the person in the other car was all right."

"Objection." Ishmael's lawyer, in an expensive suit, stood. "Your Honor, Mr. Gallagher is speculating."

"Mr. Redmon, your client is pleading not guilty, correct?"

"Yes, Your Honor."

"Then the witness is only telling what he feels the perpetrator did. If your client is innocent, then the speculation toward him won't hold up." Judge Powers grinned.

Rene said, "I have no more questions for this witness. Thank you."

When the defense had his turn with Mr. Gallagher, he danced around the ifs and the whens. The jury didn't look enthusiastic about any of what Ishmael's lawyer had to say.

"Counselor, please call your next witness."

"Yes, ma'am." She picked up a handwritten note. "Your Honor, and people of the jury, the defendant's mother did not want to be summoned as a witness against her son, and so my client and I accepted a handwritten note that has been notarized. I'd like to approach the bench."

Ishmael's lawyer stared at him as if to ask, "What the heck?" Ishmael shrugged in his seat and looked downward. His mother was nowhere to be found in the courtroom. The embarrassment over her son was enough to keep her home.

Ava realized that both she and Ishmael had one thing in common. Well, two. They hurt the person they loved while disgracing their mothers to the extent that they didn't want to be seen in court. Ava did not appreciate being lumped in with Ishmael in any kind of way. She would have to do better and improve her decision-making skills. Running things by the Lord first was her best bet.

After the judge read the note silently, she handed the piece of paper back to Rene. "I will allow it."

Rene turned to the jury. "To whom it may concern. I love my son. And many will call me a terrible mother for what I am putting in this letter. But I cannot rest knowing I could've helped someone when I know something isn't right. The day that Ava Alexander was struck by a car, Rene had broken things off with Ishmael and he told me he would do anything to get her back. He borrowed my car and returned the next morning with the front end gravely damaged. I didn't know what to think except for what he told me about it getting hit in the parking lot of a club."

Pausing to seemingly allow the jury to absorb that piece of evidence, Rene took a deep breath and then continued. "I can't believe that he would do such a thing, but I cannot be sure. This breakup has hit him hard, and I've never seen him in this type of pain before. I love him and will be there for him either way, but want justice to be served so that any wrongs done can be righted. Sincerely, Mavis Carter. Mother of the defendant."

Had the case already been won with the issuance of this note? Rene's face looked like it had. "Members of the jury." She sauntered over to the jury box and then motioned toward Ishmael. "I just want you to ask yourself this question. If the defendant's own mother is unsure of his innocence, what does that tell you?"

Ava smiled on the inside. Rene was good, and Ava was blessed to have her as her attorney. She had so much to pay her friend back for, she'd deplete her emotional bank account before she turned thirty.

It was now Ava's turn to take the stand. She shuffled to the front of the courtroom, and sat at attention as she was sworn in. Placing her hand on the Bible served two purposes. Sure, only the truth would flow from her lips, but the Good Book also reminded her of Who she served and how far He had brought her along. And one thing she knew beyond the shadow of a doubt, was that He wasn't about to leave her now when she needed Him the most.

Rene's questions were a carbon copy of the many practices she and Ava had prior to the trial. The faces of the jurors soothed Ava's soul. Even though there were only four women in the jury box, each expression seemed to exude sympathy.

Ishmael's attorney stood and fastened the buttons on his suit jacket. He looked downward, shuffling papers, as if to take his time. Clearing his throat, he moved toward Ava. "Miss Alexander, I just have a few simple questions for you."

Ava braced herself for the worst. Rene assured her that words like "simple" would not be anywhere near the defense's cross-examination.

Defense Attorney Redmon leaned an elbow on the edge of the witness stand. "Ava, could you tell the jurors why you think my client could've committed this terrible crime?"

Glancing at Rene, she said, "Well, Ishmael and I made an enormous mistake by sleeping together. It was a terrible thing to do to my best friend. She didn't deserve that." Ava looked down at her hands. "I soon learned I was pregnant. When he heard I was pregnant with his child, he came by that day of the accident to try to talk me into having an abortion. He didn't like my answer and told me he would be back."

"So, let me get this straight. You slept with your best friend's significant other, and then planned to have a baby by him. Is that correct?"

"That's not all there is to the story."

"But we're just interested in facts today, Miss Alexander. So do I have the facts straight?" He turned and walked over to the jury.

"Yes." *Here we go.* All of her dirty laundry was about to be strung out on the line.

"Good. Now you say he didn't like your answer, but there is someone else in your life who didn't like your answer either."

Nervous tension shot through Ava's body. What was he going to bring up now?

He flipped over his legal pad. "Isn't true that one Xavier Thompson, your ex-boyfriend, was not happy with you as well? You broke your relationship off with him around the time of the accident. Is that correct?"

"Yes."

"So you sleep with men, use them, and then do away with them when they've served your purpose."

A curse word was on the tip of her tongue, but the thought of being held in contempt and carted off to the jailhouse calmed her need to add an outburst. But it didn't stop her face from burning, or the cracking of her knuckles. When she remembered what Rene told her about not letting the jury see her upset or frazzled at the defense's line of questioning, she ceased the cracking and placed her interlocked fingers on her lap. "If that's how you want to spin it."

"Thank you, Ms. Alexander." He paused, seemingly pleased with himself. "There is one other thing I need you to make clear for the jurors and myself today."

Ava nodded. *He'd better watch himself.* Courtroom or no courtroom, God was the ultimate judge, and if Ishmael's lawyer continued to skip over Ishmael's part in all of this, making her look like the criminal, Mr. Redmon would have heaven to pay.

Picking up a photograph, he slithered over to Ava and put the picture in front of her face. "Is this a picture of your car?"

"Yes, it is."

"Well, the detectives found navy paint on your vehicle, which you say came from Ishmael's mother's car, am I right?"

"Ishmael's mother said it too." Ava chuckled. She was glad to be able to throw something back in about the incriminating letter.

"Please answer the question." His brows crinkling down over his eyes let Ava know she hit a nerve.

"Yes, the detective found navy paint on my car."

Rubbing his chin, he asked, "So do you believe my client's mother's car is the only navy car in this area?"

Ava's neck rolled. What kind of question was that? "What do you mean?"

"Well, I'm just saying, you visited the mall that week, work, and I'm sure a lot of other places. Restaurants, et cetera. Couldn't another driver at any number of those places have swiped your car at one point or another?"

"At the exact place where my car was hit?" She was no detective, but he did his best to make her look like an idiot. Reading the jurors' expressions and a smile on one of the men's faces made an uneasy feeling ooze into her pores. Would Ishmael go free because of the crafty viciousness of his lawyer?

Ava soon was able to take her seat next to Rene, who assured Ava everything would turn out okay. Rene's words consoled her until Ishmael took the stand. Butterflies did a number on her stomach. It was too late to pray for a recess. Ava had to suck it up and hope for the best.

Ishmael avoided making eye contact with Rene, who seemed to be on a mission. She drilled him about his visit to Ava's apartment earlier that day and his strong push for her to have an abortion. Rene then shone a light on his weak alibi and his mother's note. All evidence pointed to guilty. But people could never know how jury members would process the information, construe the facts, or what questions they would have. And juries did do crazy things sometimes.

The tainted closing arguments of the defense included suggestions of Ava's careless promiscuity, the lame argument of several cars all over the Houston area being dark blue, and that Ava was only envious of what Ishmael and his fiancée shared. Rene's name was left out of the statement. Ava guessed it highlighted the fact that same Rene was the one prosecuting him.

Rene's closing arguments brought to the forefront Ava's traumatic experience in the hospital and ultimately losing the baby, which would have emotional effects for the rest of her life. Following that unfortunate issue, her friend called attention to Ava having to take a week off work, and the catering offers she had to turn down. The whole fiasco, from which Ishmael tried to remove his responsibility, had turned Ava's life upside down and sideways.

But the most crucial part of the argument was Rene's powerful words. "Being that I was thrown into this nightmare, at first I was resentful and hurt. I am still hurt and saddened that my relationship with my best friend will never be the same. However, I love her and can forgive her." She put her hand on Ava's shoulder and smiled.

Ava grasped her hand with a tear in her eye. *Glory to God.*

Rene cruised over to the jury box. "But more importantly, this case is not about what Ava and Ishmael did, but about how he reacted to the result of what they did, the poor choices he made trying to fix things, and the effects his actions will have on everyone involved. Emotionally, mentally, and physically. People can't go through this world thinking they can fix things their way. Even Ishmael's mother said it in her own words. Justice needs to be served." She looked to the jury box. "Members of the jury, the power is in your hands."

Water filled Ava's eyes. God had a hand in everything and she knew He would not let them down. Ava, sure the Lord would deliver, prayed without ceasing. Her heart was filled with gratefulness toward her Father and her lawyer. Her support system was strong and her faith was even stronger.

An hour and a half went by as the jury deliberated. Ava, Rene, and Toni ate lunch in the courthouse cafeteria, mulling over every word said during the trial. Rene's cell buzzed and she read it aloud. "The jury's in."

Sweat formed on Ava's hands as they trekked back to the courtroom. No sound or movement was made. When the twelve jurors crept in, most of them with their head down, a sick feeling developed. Why didn't they want to look her in the eye? Hopefully, it was because they didn't want to reveal the good news with a smile and not the fact that they were sorry for how things turned out.

Ava sat, back straight and fully enveloped in the proceedings, hoping for the best.

"Members of the jury, have you reached a verdict?" Judge Powers tossed her hair out of her face as the bailiff stepped forward to hand her the verdict.

The lead juror stood. "Yes, we have, Your Honor."

With her heart throbbing in her chest, Ava listened with purpose. Her life and relationship with Rene might never be the same, but certain troubles would subside with Ishmael behind bars. She breathed a deep sigh.

"To the honorable Judge Powers and those in attendance: we find Ishmael Kane Carter guilty of attempted vehicular manslaughter."

Cheers rang all over the room. The butterflies in Ava's stomach flew free. Toni and Ava's father jumped to their feet, clapping.

Judge Powers pounded the gavel firmly until everyone quieted down. "I take outcomes like this very serious. The actions of one individual against another. People taking matters into their own hands." She peered down through her glasses. "Crimes against women are on the rise and I want to do my part to see that the offenders are brought to justice."

Rene sat forward like a rabbit with a dangling carrot in front of her.

"In the case of Alexander versus Carter, the defendant, Ishmael Carter, found guilty of attempted vehicular manslaughter, is hereby sentenced to ten years in prison, serving seven before he is eligible for parole." The judge tapped the gavel again and said, "Court is adjourned."

Ava and Rene stood and hugged. The tight embrace was reassuring on so many levels. As the arresting officers took Ishmael away in handcuffs, he yelled words of apology to Rene that she seemed to tune out. Ava's friend had come to do a job and she did it. Well. Justice prevailed, and now putting the case and Ishmael behind them could give them the push forward they needed in their lives.

The ladies chose a fine-dining restaurant to celebrate the case against Ishmael going in their favor. Ava was relieved the trial was over.

Toni held the wine list in her hand. "You ladies really want to party and pop a bottle of champagne?"

Ava shook her head. "No, thank you. I'm slowing down on the alcoholic beverages. I haven't had a drink since . . ." She looked at Rene.

"It's okay." Rene waved her hand in Ava's direction. "If we're going to be friends again, then we need to move on."

Hearing the same words Dr. Moses had spoken, Ava felt it was confirmation from her Father on high. She would do just that. Move on. So much had changed between her and Rene, but much had also stayed the same. Rene had always been a forgiving person. She believed in forgiving people as God forgave her. Ava needed to accept that part about her and move past the guilt once and for all, and be sure to never put herself in that position again.

"Speaking of moving on." Toni's bright smile and radiant eyes spoke volumes. "I have some good news. Well, not about moving on, but moving in another direction."

"Don't tell me you're moving." Ava had just gotten one friend back. She didn't want to lose another.

Toni giggled. "No, I'm not moving. At least not from Houston. I *am* moving fifteen minutes down the road to a new home with my husband."

Both confusion and excitement were all over Ava's and Rene's body language and facial expressions. Ava's grin was hard to hide. "What?"

"That's right." Toni pulled the engagement ring out of a small pocket in her purse. "Eric asked me to remarry him. Renew our vows."

They all looked back and forth at each other and then screamed. "Ahh!"

"Oh, my goodness. I knew it." Ava feigned dabbing invisible tears. "I'm so happy for you, Toni."

"Thank you. I am too. I wasn't sure this would happen, but God is good!"

Ava chimed in. "All the time. And all the time . . ."

"God is good." Toni completed the phrase.

Sitting back in her chair, Ava asked. "But tell me this, Ms. Toni."

"Yes?"

"Why are you just now telling me? Thought I was your best friend."

"Well, Ava. You two were busy with the case and all. And I needed some time for his proposal to sink in. He re-proposed in the most romantic way, too." Toni batted her eyelids. "He asked me in front of the house he purchased and read a scripture first about calling things that are not as though they are. I was floored."

"OMG! That's awesome." Ava relished the fact that things were starting to look up for all of them. God was showing up and showing out.

"Yep, I went home that evening, tore up the divorce papers, and threw them away." She bent her chin. "I do have one request though. Would you two mind helping me plan the ceremony? I'd like to have it on Valentine's Day. So that gives you about five months to create magic."

"Of course. You know I gotcha on the food. You just pick out a dress. And Rene and I can hook up the decorations and get a DJ."

Rene said nothing, seeming to be deep in thought.

"I can understand, Rene, if you don't want to." Toni raised her eyebrows.

"Please, I'm not letting Ishmael steal one more thing from me. This day is going to be about you and Eric. And I'm happy for you both."

"Amen." Ava smiled, lifting her hands. "Looks like we're planning a vow renewal ceremony!"

Chapter 34

Sunday after church, Ava and Rene got together to start putting some ideas together for Toni's vow renewal ceremony. With February only a few months away, that time seemed liked the perfect day for the "renuptials" to take place. It was the day of love, but there was also some time for Toni to make sure going a second round with Eric was something she really wanted and could do.

The bride-to-be-again assured Ava this time around would be for good and she wanted it to be more special than the first. Toni's specific requests included a Friday evening start time, held in a church, and a huge reception in the banquet hall of the church afterward. She gave Ava free rein to handle the rest of the particulars. Of course, Pastor Monroe would lead the service and she wanted her and Eric to recite the couples prayer they read in a counseling session.

As Ava prepared Sunday dinner, Rene wrote down their ideas. They hung out just like old times. She cherished every moment spent with Rene. And although it may never be exactly the same between her and her friend, they were close again and Ava was grateful.

Juggling plates of Rene's favorites over to the table, Ava looked like a skilled waitress in a diner.

"Here, let me help you with something." Rene jumped up, grabbed a dish, and set it on the table. "Hey, guess what I got in the mail the other day?"

"What?" Rene's question made Ava a little nervous. She wasn't sure why.

"A letter from Ishmael's mother."

"Really?" Ava, intrigued, scooped out modest-sized portions on their plates. "What did the letter say?"

"Basically, she apologized for spoiling him and raising him thinking he deserved whatever he wanted. She said I was the best thing that ever happened to him and she had looked forward to not only calling me her daughter-in-law, but me being her daughter. "

"Ahh." Ava smiled, but felt responsible for causing that split, too. *You were half the problem. Now move on.*

Rene filled glasses with ice and poured sweet tea in both of them. "Yeah, she ended the letter with how she wished things had turned out different, but she definitely understood my decision to call off the wedding. Her PS told me to tell you sorry for what Ishmael did to you with the accident and all. The letter was very sweet and brought tears to my eyes."

"Well, that was a nice way for her to reach out." Ava reflected on her own relationship with her biological mother. They hadn't spoken since the day she was discharged from the hospital. Their relationship worked better that way. She kept up with her mother and vice versa through her father. Ava was a daddy's girl, which worked out perfect since she couldn't stand her mother sometimes with her stinging tongue.

Ava and Rene devoured the Italian feast. The aroma of the fresh baked Italian bread and hearty tomato sauce made Ava want to stuff her belly, but she aimed to do better where her eating was concerned. She ate until she was full and satisfied, or all her walking would have been for nothing.

Reaching for more salad, Rene asked, "So how is everything with your counseling going?"

"Actually, my one-on-ones with Dr. Moses are done. I still have my group meetings on Thursdays and that has been an eye-opening experience. You find out you're not the only one going through difficult situations, even though it feels that way." Ava hoped that Rene wouldn't bring up the fact that Ava brought most of her difficult situation on herself. "It's been a big help."

"Good. I'm glad for you. And I can tell God is changing you. I'm happy to have my best friend back." Rene leaned over to hug her.

"I'm happy to be back. I love you, Rene."

"You know I love you too, girl."

Ava couldn't believe how God had turned her life around in just a few short months. He reached down and pulled Ava out of the pit of depression, healed her from the injuries stemming from the car accident, sent her to a doctor who not only understood her, but fed her with scriptures that lifted her up and helped her to grow spiritually, and now, He restored her relationship with Rene. He was beyond amazing.

"Also, I've been able to make new friends at group." Ava sipped her sweet tea, knowing her googly eyes would tip Rene off to know exactly what she was talking about.

"Oh, yeah? Tell me all about him." She smirked.

"I haven't said anything because I didn't what to get too excited and it turned out to be nothing." Ava wanted it to be something, but planned to keep herself in check. "His name is Kevin."

"That's a strong name. Good sign. Good sign."

Laughing, they continued to pick at the bread.

"I actually met him in the lobby. He's the counselor over the drug recovery group and has been clean for ten years. Which he gives God full credit for."

"Awesome. That's a big plus that he has a relationship with the Lord."

"Yep, so far, so good. We've only hung out a handful of times, around the coffee pot at the CCC, and a few dates for even better coffee after group sessions on Thursdays. He's very respectful and we are becoming friends." Ava wouldn't have minded moving a bit faster, but whatever God wanted to do in that relationship, she was down for. He knew better than she did. "He hasn't asked for my number yet, but I'm hoping he will soon."

"Well, cool. I'll include you and him in my prayers tonight."

"So, what's up with you and that friend of yours who's always so eager to put your cases on top of the stack for you?"

"Girl, I'm not ready for him. He seems nice and like a good guy, but I need to get Ishmael all the way out of my system."

"I hear ya." Ava needed to get Ishmael out of her system as well. He was on the list with Xavier and her mother of people to forgive. Right then, she was zero for three. However, she was hopeful her emotions regarding each of them would come to a settlement and be able to forgive them for her own sake and wellbeing.

Rene grinned. "It's good to know I still got game, but right now I'm taking myself on a timeout."

Ava probably could've called timeout for herself too, but it had been so long, or maybe never, since she had a man of decency and integrity interested in her. So if she needed to forgo her timeouts and even skip half time to move forward with Kevin, she had no problem with that at all.

Chapter 35

Ava prepared all the food and beverages for the CCC's tenth anniversary. Filled with gently used decorations from someone's New Year's Eve party, the lobby was packed with folks from one wall to the other.

Ava kept watch on the hors d'oeuvres and her famous orange sherbet punch, making sure the partygoers didn't run out of either. But occasionally, her wandering eye for Kevin's likeness stayed occupied. Toni and Rene were in attendance, which made Ava nervous for the moment when it came time to introduce him. Did she introduce him as a friend? An acquaintance? Someone she's seeing? She prayed the right words would come whenever she did get the chance to have her friends meet Kevin.

"Ava, everything tastes so good." Dr. Moses talked through stuffing her mouth with cornbread balls. "What'd you put in this, girl?"

"A little of this. A little of that." Ava smiled. "Can't tell my secrets."

"I understand. How about we have you cater every year? This is the best food we've ever had at one of these functions."

"Thank you, Dr. Moses. I'll put you on my calendar from here on out." Ava's catering ventures were finally starting to pick up. Maybe with the great reviews from all the different people at the anniversary party, the word would spread like a good rumor.

She strategically placed flyers and business cards throughout the dishes set up on the buffet-style tables. Ava viewed having to market herself as a colossal, terrifying adventure, but she'd have to overcome her fear if her business was going to grow. She had overcome so much the past nine months and with God's help she could jump that hurdle, too.

"You don't have to call me Dr. Moses anymore. It's like you've graduated. Just call me Glory."

"Okay, Glory. How's everything going with you?"

She waved her head side to side. "Could be better."

"Oh, care to share? I could switch roles with you. Lord knows I've dumped all my issues in your lap." Ava smiled, yet hoped she hadn't offended her, and what it might be that she was going through.

"I appreciate that. I could use a listening ear every once in a while myself." Dr. Glory looked down into her drink. "My husband is out of town. Again. He's been looking for work since he got laid off a couple months ago. He can't seem to find anything in town, so he's been traveling to Dallas or Austin every other week. But I'm not so sure I'm ready or willing to move."

Ava realized at that moment everyone had troubles. No matter how put together people may seem on the outside, behind closed doors and on the inside of their flawless body, they could be in torment. Look at Toni and all she had gone through the past year. And she was a model. Problems weren't just reserved for the average-looking person.

"I'll be sure to put you and him on my prayer list tonight. And if I hear anything job wise, I'll let you know."

"We'll work it out some way. I know God is faithful."

"Yes, He is." Sensing the air diminishing from Dr. Glory's mood, Ava offered a distraction. "Would you like to try any of my bacon-wrapped shrimp? I stuff them with a special cream cheese mixture."

Glory was sold. She disappeared into the crowd surrounding the smorgasbord of goodies. The punch bowl looked a little skimpy, so Ava retrieved the Sprite, fresh pineapple slices, and sherbet from the kitchen and commenced creating her concoction.

Kevin interacted with others across the room. He seemed to be working his way over to where Ava was posted up by the kitchen. People stopped him to make small talk. She anticipated his arrival, as she checked her teeth in her makeup compact for any particles.

A few days ago, Ava decided to spruce herself up a step at a time. She added a smoothing powder and peach lip gloss to her simple makeup strides forward. And she found the mirror in the compact to be doubly helpful in avoiding a potentially embarrassing incident. Her teeth were free of broccoli and chicken. Ava quickly stuck the compact back in her bag and continued attending to the tables' needs.

She didn't want to focus on any negative aspects of the night, but couldn't help wonder if Kevin would even pay attention to her with Toni and Rene in the same room. He was different. *Right?*

Toni and Rene wandered up, speaking to guests on the way over.

"Need any more help with anything?" Toni threw the empty bottle of soda pop in the nearest trash bin.

"I believe everything is done." Ava stirred the punch, grateful for her friends. "You guys want some punch?"

Rene scooped up a cup. "Sure."

Pouring the punch with the silver ladle, Ava's midsection did somersaults. "I have someone I want you two to meet and he's coming this way."

Kevin worked his way around those stacking their plates with Ava's specialties. His deep, boyish dimples appeared, bringing Kool-Aid smiles to all of the ladies' faces.

A finger stuck out from his massive hand. "This must be Toni, the model. And this must be Rene, the lawyer."

Toni shook her head. "Yes, you got that right. And you are?"

"Kevin. Kevin Adams." His muscular build was the star of his rugged good looks. "Nice to meet you ladies. I was looking forward to it."

Here we go. Again. Why did Ava invite her girlfriends?

"It's nice to meet you as well." Rene extended her hand with a friendly smirk.

He hugged Ava sideways. "Yes, I wanted to meet the women who are special in Ava's life. She's a special lady, and I've enjoyed getting to know her. So naturally, I want to meet the people important to her."

Ava beamed. "Well, thank you, Kevin. I've enjoyed getting to know you too." She watched with excitement as his dark brown eyes glowed while he shared his testimony to Rene and Toni of how God had moved in his life and he ended up at the CCC.

A heavyset woman dressed in a skirt suit walked up to him and whispered in his ear. Kevin nodded, and then the woman shuffled off and stepped onto the stage. Rene and Toni glanced at Ava.

Kevin drank the last of his punch, tossed the cup in the trash, and then turned to Ava and her friends. "Excuse me, ladies. I need to grab the mic and get to work. I'll just be a minute."

Ava, relieved the mystery woman didn't seem like a threat to her courtship with Kevin, smiled at Rene and Toni, who also looked more at ease.

Kevin sprang up on stage as the woman handed him the microphone. Tapping the microphone, he cleared his throat. "Um, excuse me; can I have your attention?"

He needed to repeat himself a couple times before all was quiet. Dr. Moses drifted to the platform with a few other people who looked to be important in some way or another to the CCC's cause.

"Mr. Brooks, could you join us on stage, please?" Kevin used his hand to usher him to the stage.

A tall, lanky white man scampered up. Those assembled in the lobby clapped their hands.

The mystery woman handed Kevin a small plaque. "First, giving honor to God, the Big Boss Man who sits on high and loves on us unconditionally, we thank Him for all He has done for the Christian Counseling Center, aka the CCC. And we'd like to honor the CCC's founder and pastor, our boss man, Mr. Harold C. Brooks."

He handed Mr. Brooks the plaque. Proud to be associated with the man who was making the introductions, Ava gazed toward the stage, imagining what life might be like if she were connected to him permanently. *Slow down, chick.* She giggled internally at herself and how quickly her emotions could get carried away.

"Mr. Brooks, we just want to thank you for all you do for the people here: staff, counselors, and patients of the CCC. We love and honor you. And want you to know we are truly blessed because your vision has become a reality. God bless you."

Kevin leaned into Mr. Brooks for a manly one-arm hug as he handed him the microphone. Ava didn't hear a word Mr. Brooks said. She was caught up in how Kevin carried himself as he stepped back from the front of the stage and intently listened to the man giving the speech.

Finding herself imagining a little bit too much, she ducked into to the restroom for a mental and emotional break. She didn't want to set herself up for a fall. Spending time with Kevin proved to be an exciting ride that she didn't want to end. And even though she had only known him a few short months, she believed more great things were to come.

As the party began to wrap up, Ava, Toni, and Rene cleaned up empty trays and the leftovers, while other staff members from the counseling center emptied the trash bags and loaded up Ava's rental van. Kevin did his part as well. Concentrating on the task at hand was difficult for Ava to achieve as she stayed aware of his movements about the place.

Ava disappeared into the kitchen to see what else could be done instead of being concerned with Kevin's whereabouts. The Lord needed to be called in on this one. Having a friend of the opposite sex hadn't always worked out for Ava. Even if a friendship had been established at the beginning as the purpose of their relationship, it usually didn't take long for her and the significant other to dabble in "more than just a friend" behavior. She wasn't sure how to act.

Washing the empty reusable trays in the sink, her imagination ran wild of "friend turned to lover" stories she had heard of. Ava snapped out of it when Toni brought in a couple more trays. Ava observed Toni holding her head down with a big grin, like a child who had just stolen a cookie out of the cookie jar.

"What is it, Toni?"

"I have a confession to make."

What had Toni done now? It must have been something embarrassing for her to come and tell on herself.

"I invited Kevin to the renewal ceremony reception." She presented her information hands out as if to say "ta-dah!"

Ava giggled and shook her head. "Well, it's your reception, Toni."

Toni, bewildered, asked, "You're not mad?"

"Not at all. It's your party." Then she sang, "Invite whoever you want to, whoever you want to."

They snickered and squeezed each other in a hug. Ever since Toni and Eric became separated, she had put her meddling aside. But now that they were back on again, her meddling skills must've been back on again too.

"I'm glad you're not mad. It'll be fun. You'll see."

"Yeah, we'll see." Ava wanted to see. But if only the result was a good one. If it was going to be anything but a positive experience, she could skip it.

"Well, I'm about to head out, girlfriend. I had a good time, but gotta burn off. I'm meeting Eric so we can plan the perfect honeymoon trip."

"I understand. Tell him I said hello. And I appreciate all your help." Ava appreciated Toni requesting Kevin's presence at her nuptials, but didn't want to say it out loud. That might make it seem like she looked forward to him attending, and she didn't want to get her hopes up.

When everything was finished and the guests had pretty much headed out, Ava made one more round to check if any of her equipment or supplies were left behind. Kevin and Dr. Moses stood in the front hallway talking. Kevin took the white envelope that Dr. Glory held in her hand. As Ava approached them, Glory walked off, waving good-bye to Ava and giggling.

Ava, confused, cruised over to him. "What was she up to?"

Kevin's deep voice penetrated her heart. "Oh, nothing. She wanted me to give you the check for your catering services." He handed her the envelope.

"Thank you."

"You're welcome." He slipped his hand into the inside pocket of his sport jacket. "And here's my business card in case you ever wanted to call me." He suavely took out his cell phone in one fluid motion. "Mind if get your number? I'd like to call you sometime. We don't have to wait until Thursdays to hang out."

Ava exhaled. She recited her number to him, standing there in disbelief. Had he really met Toni and Rene and still shown interest in her? There were several other more attractive women at the celebration as well. But he was asking for her number? Could he be one of those rare individuals who got to know a person and cared about who they were and what they believed? Did he notice she had character along with her "pretty face"?

After everything was loaded up and she said her good-byes, Ava drove home with thoughts running through her mind like a sprinter in the Olympics.

Would he call? Would he show up at Toni's ceremony? Could Ava consider him coming to the reception a date between the two of them even though Toni invited him? Worrying about the answers to these questions wasn't going to add another day to her life. So, she handed her anxieties over to God and jetted down I-45. "Jesus, take the wheel."

Toni met Eric at one of their favorite late-night hang-outs. IHOP was packed with folks inhaling pancakes and other breakfast favorites. The smell of warm syrup tempted her stomach, but she was full from all of Ava's creations at the party. Still, she couldn't sit in IHOP and not order a pancake.

Eric stood as soon as he saw her walk through the door. She rushed into his embrace and laid a peck on him before they sat down. He was such a handsome man. *GQ* ready all the time. Onlookers probably thought they were both a couple of models. His outside hadn't changed one iota, but inside, he was a different man.

Toni couldn't wait until Valentine's Day to walk down the aisle for the second and final time. She caressed the ring on her finger, and then rubbed his face.

"So, how'd everything go at Ava's event?"

"It went very well. Food was great as always, and I got to meet her new friend." If Kevin was as good of a man as he appeared to be, Ava may finally get the chance to have the relationship she desired since she was a young girl. Hopefully, he wouldn't turn out to be a new and improved version of the past fools she'd dated.

"Oh, that's nice. Who else did you meet?"

"What do you mean?"

"Like, who else was there? Anyone I need to know about?"

Toni's face puckered. "Anyone like who?" The re-kindling of the fire between them had gone almost too perfect. But the intensity level of his questions led her to believe that the honeymoon stage was over. "What are you implying?"

Eric's face turned stern. "Did anybody try to holla at you?"

"What?" Yep, honeymoon over. And before they even got to discuss the plans for their real honeymoon.

"I'm serious. I've been to a party before and I know what the men do there."

Was he really about to go down that road? "It was a party at the Christian Counseling Center. Not a club."

He shrugged his shoulders. "So, men are men. Christian or not, I'm sure they found you attractive."

"Eric, do you hear yourself right now?" How old was he again?

"Yes, and why can't you just answer the question?"

Annoyed, Toni scooted over in the booth. Here she was, couldn't wait to see him. Dang near flew from the CCC's celebration on the other side of town to the restaurant, and he wanted to pop the top on this can of jealousy. She hadn't stepped a toe on the white linen down the aisle yet. Was he trying to scare her into running out the back of the church? "I thought we were here to finalize our honeymoon spot, not argue over petty stuff."

"Me too." He lowered his brow, peering into her eyes. "I just want you to answer the question. You keep dancing around it. Answer the question and we can move on."

"No, dang it! Nobody tried to holla at me." Her neck lost control of itself. "Are you happy now?"

"Yes, I am. Thank you." He paused in the awkward silence. "Well, were you attracted to anybody?"

"Okay, enough is enough." Toni leapt out of the booth. Had her Eric transformed into Jekyll or Hyde? She needed to flee from his vicinity quickly before she said something she regretted. "Why don't you holla at me when you decide to grow up?"

She stormed out of the IHOP, whisking by spectators. Her cheeks burned. Wanting to go back in and share more of her thoughts on maturity, Toni jumped into her ride. Along with the maturity talk, a possible curse word or two might slip out and she didn't want to ruin her newfound attempts to cut bad language out of her vocabulary. No, best scenario for her would be to head home.

The solution her mind put together was to call Ava. She didn't necessarily want to bother her, especially with something so childish, but hearing from a sane person would help in her time of distress. And it would keep her from calling Eric and turning the car around. The phone rang and rang. No answer.

With the renewal ceremony only a month away, Toni drove down the road in disbelief, replaying the scene that just took place in the restaurant. Her feet suddenly felt a little cooler.

Chapter 36

When the Sunday for Ava to get baptized rolled around, the service seemed more crowded than usual. Seeing the full house made Ava nervous. Her parents, best friends, and Kevin were all planning to attend.

She walked to the back of the children's church area where the baptismal pool was located. Checking in and dropping her stuff off, she ran into Pastor Monroe. Literally.

"Sorry, Pastor."

"That's quite all right, Ava." He smiled. "Are you ready for today?"

"I believe so."

"This is an awesome step in your spiritual journey, and God couldn't be more proud of you."

"I'm glad to get the opportunity to do this again. As a kid, I really didn't understand what I was doing. I got baptized in my grandmother's church at the age of six, maybe seven. All I remember was trying not to drown and stay away from the roach floating in the corner." She shared a laugh with Pastor. "But the class on baptism I took helped a great deal and I am expecting to come up out of that water a different woman."

"Amen!" Pastor Monroe placed his hand on her shoulder. "Well, everything else going all right with you?"

"For the most part." She folded her arms. "Counseling has helped my depression tremendously. I am wondering when God is going to bring that certain somebody in my life though. I'm tired of being single."

"Let me give you a bit of advice. Get busy doing the things that God is concerned about and He'll get busy doing the things you're concerned about." He cleared his throat. "In 1 Corinthians 7:32, God's Word says for you to be without care. The unmarried cares for the things of the Lord. How he"—Pastor grinned—"or she, may please the Lord."

"I get it." Ava would remember the verse and promptly write it down when she got her hands on some paper.

"Good. Instead of looking for a man, look for ways you can serve the Lord. And let God worry about the whens, wheres, and whos."

She side-hugged him. He definitely spoke a word in due season. "Thank you so much, Pastor. You are such a blessing to your flock."

"You're welcome, Ava. I must hustle on to prepare for service, but I'll meet you back here a little later."

Ava looked forward to rising out of the water. All of her issues and insecurities she planned to leave in the pool. God was perfect in His timing. He knew she needed to hear those words from Pastor Monroe. The Lord also knew she'd be feeling this way, ready to move to the next level spiritually, at this point in her life.

Trusting God for everything had been difficult in the past, but day by day, it became easier to give all of her problems and situations over to him. Her next move after getting baptized would be to explore areas in the church to serve. She loved talking to God and interceding in prayer for others. Being a prayer warrior would be a good fit for her. Ava would pray about being a prayer partner.

When she walked into the sanctuary, her self-assigned row was full. She didn't want to sit in the back anymore anyway. Ava strolled to the front of the church and noticed a row of open seats. There were enough spots for each person in her group.

"Good morning, Ava." Rene stood behind her, grinning. "Well, today's the day."

"Yep, today's the day. I'm excited."

"Excited about what? All the weight you've lost?" Toni walked up and gave Ava a hug and they all sat down.

"Thank you. I'm trying." Ava's outside was catching up with her inside. She had come a long way in a few short months mentally, physically, and spiritually. God got all the credit for who she was: a completely new woman.

Ava turned around to keep an eye out for her parents. Well, for Kevin. She kept her hopes in check, but seeing him would be a nice bonus. Through the multitude of folks, her parents appeared. She waved her hand and they came straight over.

Hugging her mother and father, they exchanged pleasantries. Ava's arms tensed up in her mother's embrace and relaxed in her father's. Why did she let her mother get to her? She was in the right place to give that over to God. Silently praying for her mother and their relationship, she touched her mother's hand and smiled when she was finished.

The only one missing from her invited guests was Kevin. Over their Thursday night coffee, Ava mentioned something to him in general about their church and her getting baptized for the second time. He threw in the fact that he'd like to come visit sometime and this Sunday seemed like a perfect time. So where was he?

As service started, Ava reached into her purse, which she now enjoyed carrying, to take out a spiral tablet and pen for notes. She decided to start carrying a handbag when she increased her makeup quantities. The newly purchased Guess bag also worked well to hold her wallet, shades, and car keys. Who would've thought? She still had to get used to holding the purse over her shoulder, but it was a welcome change. Ava felt more like a lady.

Next on her agenda were high heels. Well, maybe quarter heels. Baby steps.

Pastor Monroe preached a fiery sermon that spoke directly to Ava's soul. The message, "Matters of the Heart," tugged at her inner woman and opened her eyes. Whatever she believed in her heart was what would come to pass in her life.

"In Proverbs 4:23 the Word says, 'Keep your heart with all diligence, for out of it spring the issues of life.'" He sipped from his water cup next to the podium. "Protect your heart, church. Be diligent, watching over what you allow to come in your heart. Word in, Word out. Can I have an amen?"

The sanctuary shouted back in unison. "Amen!"

Someone in the back added a "Preach, Pastor!"

He wiped his brow. "Let me leave you with one more scripture. Turn to Psalm 37:4. When you have it say hallelujah!"

Hallelujahs popped up all over the room like kids in a bounce house. Ava used her cell phone to locate the scripture in her YouVersion eBible, proud she could easily find Psalms. There was a time Ava didn't know what book was in what section of the Bible, and why some words were in red in some Bibles and not in others. Diving into God's Word had been the best product to come out of her tragic events over the past year. All things really did work together for the good for those who loved the Lord.

"I like how the Amplified Bible puts it. The scripture reads, 'Delight yourself also in the Lord, and He will give you the desires and secret petitions of your heart.'"

God was speaking through a bullhorn. Ava couldn't write fast enough. Toni, who was also taking notes, reacted to every other word in the message. Rene, less demonstrative, looked on with an intent expression. *Lord, how you've turned us around. Thank you.*

"Church, today I want you to delight yourself in Him and His ways. Be honest with God. He knows how you feel anyway. He will give you the desires of your heart. In His will and in His timing. Be encouraged. Believe. And never lose faith. He cares about what you care about. Talk to Him, and live and act accordingly."

Ava was ready to go jump into the baptismal pool herself. She put the questions about Kevin to the side and focused on her spiritual well-being. How could she not? The message she heard that day, she suspected, would resonate with her for the rest of her life.

The associate pastor performed the altar call. Numerous people went up to the front for prayer or to ask Jesus into their heart. The scene was a beautiful thing. Tears filled Ava's eyes. Recalling the day she got saved took her back to her longest relationship. There were trust issues, money woes, infidelity, and physical abuse. The Lord met her right in her circumstances. And although she strayed, He'd never left her to fend for herself. She was grateful and ready to publicly show the world by getting baptized.

Everyone gathered in the children's church area to cheer on their family members and friends. As Ava changed her attire for her spiritual dip in the water, thinking about Kevin snuck back into her mind. Not wanting to focus on anything but God, she caught herself and said a brief prayer.

She filed into the baptism line, smiling at the encouraging words and cheers shouted toward the pool as each person rose out of the water. Anticipating a decent amount of noise coming from her family and friends added to her excitement level. Her brother and his wife walked in just as Ava entered the water. He would make sure Ava was embarrassed at the volume of his yells and whistles.

The water, warm and clear, waved with every move of her body. Her outfit, she was sure, made her look like a synchronized swimmer, tight head-fitting swim cap and nose plugs included.

Pastor Monroe took Ava's hand and led her to the center of the pool. "Church, welcome Ava Alexander."

Clapping and cheering filled the room. Ava's brother yelled, "Go, Ava! Go, Ava!"

Pastor went on. "Tell the church what getting baptized means to you."

"To me, it means I am turning my back on the world and am wholeheartedly living for God. I will be a new woman headed toward the Lord."

"Amen!" He placed one hand on her back and the other he raised to the sky. "By the confessions of your sin, I baptize you in the name of the Son, the Father, and the Holy Ghost." Pastor Monroe dipped Ava back into the water.

When she ascended out of the water, she had to have weighed a hundred pounds less. Every problem she'd had prior to the baptism now seemed smaller. God was all around her and peace rested inside of her.

As her applause died down and the next candidate entered the water, Ava waded over to the side and stepped out of the pool. She returned to the kids' restroom to change into dry clothes. As she turned her cell phone off silent, it beeped the text message tone.

Kevin's message read: Sorry I missed ur special day. My sponsee needed my help. I know God shined His light on u. Call u later. Take Care Kevin ☺

It figured. An important time in her life could never be done perfectly. He probably just didn't want to see her. *Wait a minute. Are you really going to give this spiritual step forward a negative slant?* The Holy Spirit went to work on Ava's thoughts.

All of her family and best friends were at church together, getting a timely word from the pastor. She took a huge stride forward in God's plan for her life. And now her family and friends were treating her to dinner at her favorite Mexican restaurant. Ishmael was in prison where he belonged. She and Rene were close again, and Toni and Eric bypassed the divorce and were headed down the aisle with an even stronger bond this time around.

An absent Kevin wasn't going to put a damper on all of the positive things going on in her life. And at least he sent a message letting her know his circumstances. That was more than any of her glorious exes had ever done. Nope, she was going to continue walking in the affirmations of the moment. Nothing could make her put a negative spin on her flawless day.

"Ava!" Her mother hustled to catch up with her in the parking lot. "I told your father I'd ride to the restaurant with you so we can talk."

Spoke too soon.

Chapter 37

Remaining silent in the car, Ava wanted her mother to speak first. Her mom's desire to ride and talk was an awkward one since the less they swapped words, the better their relationship.

"I know I may seem judgmental at times, Ava, but I don't mean any harm." Her mother reached to turn the radio off. "I've been praying for the Lord to help me with my speech toward you. It truly comes from a place of love. I've always wanted the best for you."

"Thank you, Momma. I want the best for me too. But your best, and what I think is best, or better yet, God's best, may not be the same thing."

"All I've ever asked is that you take better care of yourself. Eat right, do some sort of exercise, wear makeup every day. You'll never get a man the way you go through life. And I don't want you to end up alone."

Ava's fingertips pierced the wheel. "First off, having a man doesn't automatically equal what's best for me, or mean that I won't end up alone. You need to—" Ava's cell phone buzzed companied with the upbeat ringtone. *Thank God.*

Her brother's voice, hurried and excited, tore through the phone. "Ava, you and Momma need to bus' a U-ey and get to the hospital. Elaine's going into labor."

"Now?"

"Yes!" he yelled with uncertain enthusiasm. "Right now."

"Okay, okay, Alex. Do you need me to go by the house and grab you guys anything?"

"No. We had a 'ready for the hospital' bag in the trunk. Got everything we need. You and Momma just get there."

"We'll meet you there."

Ava couldn't even set her cell phone down. Her mother shook her head and hands. "What's going on?"

"Elaine's gone into labor. They're headed to the hospital now."

Clapping, her mother said, "All righty then, turn around." Beaming, she cupped her hands together. "My first grandbaby. Lord, I pray that everything goes smoothly. I can't wait to hold her in my arms."

Ava couldn't wait to hold her niece as well. They found out a few weeks before the sex of the baby, and how glad she was that she was finally here. Ava loved her sight unseen, and the little one already had her auntie's back. Her perfect timing in entering the world kept Ava from saying something to her mother she might have regretted later.

By the time they arrived at the hospital, her brother had paced a path outside the delivery room. She knew he had a weak stomach, but hoped he could take watching the delivery of his own child and not be one of those men who passed out until all the work was done.

Ava's family, Elaine's only relatives nearby, showed up with great anticipation. Elaine's parents died when she was a little girl and she was an only child. Her grandmother lived in New Mexico, but couldn't make the trip. So the Alexander family was her only family present. Excitement filled the room. Alex's best friend, Paul, rushed in with pink balloons and cigars that read IT'S A GIRL!

He passed out a cigar to everyone, including the ladies. Rene and Toni took theirs and traded it for a smile. When Ava reached out to grab hers, she was determined not to look down. Paul, a handsome six feet one inch build with smooth skin and a dazzling smile, sauntered about the room with a certain refinement.

"Ava, it's great to see you." His embrace was solid and alluring.

She caught herself before she batted an eyelash. "Wonderful to see you too."

"Are you ready to be an auntie?"

Don't you look at the ground. Raising her head and peering into his eyes, she nodded with confidence. "Yes, I am. I can't wait to spoil that little girl." Looking him in the eye wasn't so intimidating. What had she been scared of? Rejection? God would never reject her and that's really all that mattered.

Ava's father walked up and gave Paul a hug. "Thank you for coming, son."

"Ah, you know I wouldn't miss this for the world." Paul flashed a handsome smile.

"Alex could probably use you over there." He patted Paul on the back. "He looks like he's about to melt into a puddle right on the floor. You know how he is."

"Yeah, I know." Paul strode over to her brother and put his hands on Alex's shoulders. He began to pray. Paul was lovable like that.

Out of all of her brother's friends, Paul seemed to have his stuff together the most. Ava had always been interested in him, but never expressed that to Alex because she didn't want to make him feel weird as a middleman. And of course, if it didn't work out, she didn't want to be the one who messed up her brother's friendship with his best friend, or their brother-sister relationship. So, suppressing that desire and keeping quiet was best.

Ava's mother strolled up and handed her father a cup of coffee. "Henry, let me talk to Ava for a minute in private."

"Okay, honey." He kissed Ava's forehead. "Y'all be nice."

Wanting to be nice and staying nice were two completely different things. Her mother had the ability to control both. Ava hoped her mother had forgotten about their conversation in the car with all the baby excitement.

"Ava, come on. Let's go over here." She grabbed her by the elbow and pulled her to a corner of the waiting room. "I know the conversation on the ride over here didn't go so well. That's not how I heard my apology in my mind."

"It's okay, Momma."

"No, it's not. I'm not blaming your grandmother, but she used to make me feel as bad as I probably make you feel. And it's not okay." She interlocked her arm in Ava's. "I truly apologize for all the hurtful things I've said to you."

Finally. Was this really happening? God was working overtime. "Well, thank you, Momma. Your apology means a lot."

"I love you so much, and the things I say come from a place of love. They are just jacked up by the time they leave my mouth."

Ava giggled. Yes, they were. But she was glad her mother recognized that fact.

"I want to know you're happy, and you'll have that husband support and protection when your father and I are gone."

She kissed her mother on the cheek. "Thank you for caring so much about me, but I have the best Protector and Supporter in the world. Shoot, in the universe. You don't have to worry about me, Momma. God's got me in His hands."

"Amen."

"I've learned a whole lot from my mistakes these past several months. But the main thing is that God loves me no matter what. He meets you right where you are and pulls you up from there. He cares about me and for me.

He also cares about what I care about. Including a godly husband. And when He thinks I'm ready, He'll send him." Kevin crossed her mind even though she didn't want him to.

Her mother gazed into her eyes with a sense of peace.

"And the man God has picked out for me will love me for me."

"I see you have learned quite a bit. I'm proud of you, Ava. And I'm proud of the woman you've become. I love you, sweetie."

"I love you too, Momma." Ava's round cheeks rose, revealing a vibrant smile. "Very much."

"Well, since you've learned so much, what else can you teach me?"

They shared a laugh and then rejoined her father, who lingered close by. He seemed to be watching for any fireworks. Elated that she didn't need her father's assistance, Ava was pleased with how the conversation turned out.

As she took a seat on the couch next to Toni and Rene, her ringtone went off. She fumbled in her new purse and pulled out her cell. Kevin's name appeared on the screen. A nervous wave shot through her heart as she got up to take the call in a more secluded area.

"Hello, Ava. I wanted to apologize for missing your baptism. I had an emergency this morning with one of the men I sponsor and couldn't leave."

"Don't worry about it." He stuck to his word about calling her. Forgiving him for helping someone was the easiest part of the chat. "How is he?"

"He's okay now. He relapsed and was rushed to the hospital this morning. His parents and I are here now waiting to see if the doctors are going to send him home."

"At what hospital?"

"Methodist."

The Lord was showing out. "Believe this or not, I'm at Methodist. My sister-in-law just went into labor."

He chuckled. "Well, look at that. What floor are you on?"

Why did he want to know that? If he was going to come and see her, would that really be something she'd want him to do? Her mother's questions would go on forever and Ava would probably end up embarrassed more than anything. Kevin coming to see her would open all kind of doors to her family's curiosity. She'd just have to take that chance. "We're on the third floor. In the waiting room."

"Do you mind if I come by and see you? I have something for you. And since I couldn't come to church, I'd love to give it to you now."

God was orchestrating. Ava would fall in line with whatever He wanted to do. "Yep, come on. We'll be here."

Should she tell her family? Let Kevin's presence be a surprise? This was more than a simple coincidence. Keeping her exhilaration in check would be hard to do. Not only did Kevin have an awesome reason for missing her baptism, he called like he said he would, and had gotten her a gift. Ava liked him more and more by the minute. She didn't plan to step on God's toes, or try to move things forward on her own. Sitting back and enjoying Kevin's lead would be best. And no matter if all they ever grew to be was really good friends, she would cherish the journey.

Chapter 38

Ava's smile grew larger with every step Kevin took toward her while carrying a letter-sized purple gift bag. She cut her eyes toward her parents and brother to see if they noticed the new waiting room guest. Toni and Rene stood to exchange pleasantries with Kevin, and each of them gave him a friendly hug.

"Well, who might this be?" Ava's mother swooped into the small reunion.

"Momma, I'd like you to meet my friend, Kevin." Hopefully, by giving him the title "friend" her mother could relax some of her questions.

"Hello, Mrs. Alexander. It's nice to meet you." The dimple in his left cheek emerged.

Her mother's animated smile glowed. "Nice to meet you too." She then turned her attention to Ava. "Where'd you meet him at, Ava?" She spoke softly and out of the side of her mouth as if the only person who could understand her was Ava. "And why is this the first I'm hearing of him?"

Settle down, Momma. "If you must know. I met him at the counseling center. And we've only been hanging out a short while."

Kevin raised the bag. "Yes, and since I wasn't able to make the baptism today, I got you a small gift." Kevin had gone out to his car and grabbed the gift prior to meeting up with Ava.

Ava grabbed the token of his friendship, feeling special to be given a gift in front of her family and friends. "That was so sweet of you. You didn't have to do that."

"I know, but I wanted to."

Opening the bag, eagerness crept up inside her. She pulled out a purple Bible with a large cross made out of rhinestones on the cover. Oohs and ahhs slipped out of everyone's lips.

"This is lovely, Kevin. Thank you."

He proudly rubbed his hand over the cross. "Besides your favorite color being purple, I figured you'd like the sparkly cross. And most importantly, this new Bible represents the new person you are after being baptized."

No, he didn't. "I truly appreciate it."

"There's a scripture in Philippians 3, I'm sure you know it, but Paul says, 'One thing I do is forget what is behind and press forward to what is ahead.'" He tapped the front of the Bible. "I hope this Bible can help you to do that. Forget your past and press on to the prize God has for you in your future."

And then he added a scripture, too? Lord, what are you doing to me here? Ava didn't want to let her imagination run free, picturing walking down the aisle to Kevin and his groomsmen one day, but he was making it hard not to. She needed to focus on him as her friend. Yes, he was a boy who was a friend, but not a boyfriend. Not yet anyway.

After the gushing fest was over between her mother and her girlfriends, and Kevin said his good-byes to the men folk, Ava walked him to the elevator.

"Thanks again for my new blinged-out Bible. I'll get started reading it tonight."

"You're very welcome. That's what I wanted to hear."

"Also, I appreciate you coming up here. I know you probably hated to leave your friend in his time of need. Anything change with his condition?"

He reached out to push the down button for the elevator. "No, not too much has changed. But honestly, I don't know how much I'm helping him."

"What do you mean? What if you didn't go over there this morning? The situation could've been a lot worse."

"I know you're right, but he tends to slip back into his old ways when his personal life isn't going so well. His ex-wife got awarded full custody of the kids just when he was making changes to do better." Kevin rubbed his chin. "He overdosed after being clean for six months. What's to say he won't do that again when his ex-wife does something else he doesn't like?"

"You'll be there for him whenever he needs you." Ava silently asked the Holy Spirit to deliver the right words, so she wouldn't sound generic.

"I don't know if I can do anything to stop him if he doesn't reach out to me before."

She touched his arm as the elevator opened. "God has you in his life for a reason. He's blessed to have someone who cares about him as much as you do. All you can do is be there and help guide him the best you can." *Thanks, Lord.*

He stepped a foot in the elevator. "You're right. And use my best weapon. Prayer."

"Amen."

"Thank you for listening, Ava."

"Anytime." *Hope that didn't sound too eager.*

Kevin rested his hand on the sliding door, so it wouldn't close. "So, I'll see you Thursday at the CCC?"

"Not this week. We're taking Toni out for a finalizing of all the plans for her renewal ceremony. She ran her fingers through her wavy ebony locks. "You are planning to come to the reception, right?"

"I'll be there." He brought his arm inside the elevator.

"Great."Ava waved her fingers as the doors closed. For once, she got to encourage and uplift him. She had always been on the receiving end of his advice and encouragement. Delighted to seemingly have helped him, she looked forward to seeing him again.

She'd have to swallow her hatred for shopping and be sure to find the perfect outfit that mixed comfort with style for Toni's ceremony. The only requirement Toni gave was the color. She could be flexible with the style. Ava's mission the rest of that week was simple: find the ideal outfit that she not only looked attractive in, but felt attractive in.

When Ava returned to the waiting room, everyone was gathered around the entry to her sister-in-law's room. Alex was missing from the group.

Her father rapidly moved his hand back and forth. "Hurry, Ava. Your brother just went back in the room." His eyes lit up like a neon sign. "She's coming. Li'l momma's coming. Alex came out a few seconds ago and said Elaine is fully dilated."

Within a half hour, Alex popped his head out of the room, wiping tears out of his eyes. "She's beautiful. Complete with ten little fingers and ten little toes. The nurse is cleaning her up now and you all can come see her in a few."

Hugs and cheers were exchanged between everyone. Ava's daddy threw the unlit cigar in his mouth. "Glory!" Ava looked forward to the day her parents would celebrate her child coming into the world.

After getting the clearance to enter the room, Grandma and Grandpa held the little angel first. Alex kissed her forehead every time she was passed to someone new. Elaine, whipped and exhausted, radiated love.

Alex handed the baby to Ava. "Her name is Mariah."

Ava made goo-goo sounds and smelled her full head of jet-black hair. "Hi, li'l Mariah. I'm your Aunt Ava. I'm the one who gets to spoil you all I want."

"Hey, hey, hey. Don't be setting her up already, Ava." Her brother laughed.

"She's my niece. I can do what I want." She continued to gawk over the tiny caramel-colored newborn. Ava couldn't help but think what giving birth to her own child would've been like and holding him or her in her arms. A certain sadness rested in her soul for the child she lost. But she was confident she would get the chance to experience motherhood in her future. The right way.

As Ava returned God's precious little gift to her sister-in-law's arms, Toni saw an opportune time to make an exit. She said her good-byes to everyone in the room and motioned for Ava to follow her out the door.

"What's going on, Toni? You look a little worried."

Toni didn't want to put a damper on the baby festivities, but she needed to talk to someone. And Ava would get upset with her if Toni was in trouble and kept quiet. "Last night, Eric and I ran into a bump in the road."

"Oh, no. What happened?"

"Well, everything was fine and then when I left your party at the counseling center and met him at IHOP, he started letting that ugly jealousy streak he had creep back in." She folded her arms, embarrassed that a few weeks before her renewal ceremony was to take place she had issues. "I know a full change takes time, but I've never given him any reason to behave that way."

"I'm sorry he decided to show you that side of him, and especially in public. But maybe it's a good thing. Keep you grounded and not going into this with too high of expectations. I mean, yes, he's changed, but nobody's perfect."

"What if he's getting cold feet?" Was it possible to get cold feet the second time around?

"I'm not sure that's it. He loves you and, I believe, truly wants you back."

Toni lowered her shoulders and nodded, as she confessed her position. "Okay, what if I'm getting cold feet? I think my toes are starting to feel a little frostbitten."

Ava laughed. "Girl, you're fine. There's nothing wrong with a little nerves. I'm sure it happens to everyone."

"But the second time around?"

"Especially the second time around. Since you've been there and done that, you just want to make sure you're doing it for good this time."

"Maybe we're rushing this vow renewal thing and need to take a step back." Toni might be embarrassed to cancel the ceremony, but that would be nothing compared to the embarrassment if she ended up filing for a divorce after the renewal ceremony.

"Why don't you contact Pastor Sandra? I think she'll be able to help you clear your head and see God in this. I'm sure this is just a small hiccup that you and Eric will overcome."

Counsel from her pastor sounded better than anything Toni could come up with. "Okay, well I'm going to leave you to your new little niece. Eric texted me earlier. I told him I was here at the hospital with you and would call him later. I guess I will keep my word and see what he says about an emergency counseling session ASAP."

"Sounds like a plan, girlfriend." Ava hugged her friend. "Let me know how everything turns out."

Toni inched onto the elevator. Going home and relaxing with her thoughts and a glass of wine could help her until she got in a room with Pastor Sandra. Maybe instead of the wine, she could sit down with her Bible. All the answers were in the Good Book. She picked that fact up since she'd been attending church on a regular basis.

What she needed was for Eric to get his stuff together. Her love for him wouldn't be enough this time. He needed to make peace with his inner man and be the man he had shown her the past few months. Walking down that aisle toward his handsome face was something she looked forward to, but not so much that she'd put her sanity on the sideline.

The elevator bounced when it reached ground level and jarred Toni a bit. The stunning, picture-perfect day raised her spirits. Although she knew it would be hot and humid when she hit the parking lot, the vivid sun seemed to brighten her mood.

Hustling to the car and its air conditioner, she searched her purse for her Gucci shades. After she hooked the glasses over her ears, Toni located her car across the lot. As she approached her ride, a giddy demeanor overtook her mannerisms. Shaking her head, she froze in her spot.

Eric, cheesing from ear to ear, sat with open arms on the hood of her car.

Chapter 39

Toni tried to ignore her cold feet for two weeks, then a week before the ceremony, she found herself in Pastor Monroe's office, sitting next to Eric, sharing the details of their argument at IHOP with Pastor and his wife. This meeting was needed; however, her hope level was low. Sure, Eric's apology seemed sincere and she believed every word, but looking to a renewed future with him, she didn't want to have the jealousy animal rear its ugly head every so often.

Pastor Monroe rubbed the tip of his chin. "Can I be frank, Eric?"

"Please do, Pastor." Eric nervously ran his hands on his lap.

Yes, Pastor. Please do.

"After hearing both sides of your story, I must say, Eric, this is something you're going to have to get in check."

Eric sat back in his seat and leaned on the armrest. Toni liked the turn the discussion was taking with Pastor's one sentence.

Pastor cleared his throat and went on. "Toni hasn't done anything for you to lose your trust in her. Your jealousy streak or trait, whatever you want to call it, stems from your own infidelity."

Toni could see Eric's body language change as she read unhappiness in his face. He looked like he wanted to chime in, but instead just listened.

"If you continue to accuse her of things, you will eventually push her away. Is that what you want?"

"No, of course not."

"Well, I suggest you pray when those feelings rise up in you, and ask the Holy Spirit to help you work through it." Pastor Monroe turned to Toni. "And, Toni, you'll need to understand that he will be working through. It's a process and will get better with time. Are you willing to put in the time and work through those moments with him?"

Why did it require work on her part? Eric was in the wrong. *Let's be mature here.* "Yes, Pastor."

"Good." Pastor took hold of his wife's hand. "Got anything to add, dear?"

Pastor Sandra smiled. "My suggestion is that you both continue couples counseling after the ceremony for at least six months. The enemy is real and he will throw everything at you to break this union created under God's eyes. You need to stay strong and stay together. And continuing to do healthy acts for your marriage will only enhance your relationship. Can you both commit to that?"

Toni glanced at Eric. As the man, he was the head of their relationship. She'd follow his lead. They nodded together. After Toni and Eric thanked the clergy couple, they talked specifics for the renewal ceremony and Pastor Monroe prayed a blessing over them as individuals and as a couple. He prayed that God's will would be done in their lives together as a strong couple serving the Lord.

Before they left the office, Toni and Eric practiced reading the couples prayer for the ceremony. The words were imprinted on Toni's heart and gave her spirit hope again. God was all in their relationship and she couldn't be more grateful.

Thursday evening rolled around and Ava sat at the Olive Garden restaurant waiting for Toni and Rene to show up for Toni's celebratory dinner. Ava was glad that Toni and Eric kissed and made up. With the ceremony one day away, everything was set and ready, and Ava had been preparing food two weeks prior. And no renewal between the couple equaled a whole lot of food without a whole lot of mouths to consume the scrumptious feast.

The unselfish reason the ceremony needed to take place was Toni seemed happiest with Eric in her life. She didn't want a divorce, no matter the circumstances. Toni had conveyed many times over she believed God brought her and Eric together and the time they spent apart ate away at her soul. Ava wanted Toni to be happy and living as close to a righteous life as she could. They all needed to do that.

Toni trotted up to the table as if she moved to an upbeat tempo song. Her smile only reconfirmed that she and Eric had made up and Toni's feet had warmed up.

Ava stood to give her friend a hug. "Hey, Ms. Bride-to-be-again!"

"I said that was only funny the first time."

"I know, but it seems so creative." Ava thought that phrase up all by herself and wanted to milk it at least until the ceremony was over.

"It's cute." Rene rolled up and took a seat.

Toni shook her head and shrugged her shoulders as if to give in. "Well, I appreciate you two coming out with me before my big day. And I thank you for all you have done to put this ceremony together."

"We wouldn't have it any other way. You will always have our support." Ava was not only talking about for physical things, but emotionally as well. Toni, the liaison when Rene and Ava were not speaking to each other, kept their bond strong in that difficult time. Ava owed her a great deal.

"And you guys will always have mine." Toni reached into her suitcase that masqueraded as a purse and fished out two long, rectangular velvet-covered boxes. She handed one to Ava and the other to Rene. "This is a token of appreciation. Not only for standing up for me a second time, but for taking the time to put everything together, and for sticking by Eric and me through all of our issues."

Ava couldn't open the box fast enough. "Oh, Toni, you didn't have to do this."

"Yeah, we're supposed to give you something." Rene winked at her and opened the box.

Both ladies stared at the sparkling tennis bracelets that shone brilliantly off the black cases. After Ava closed her mouth, she placed the exquisite jewelry over her arm. *Hope it fits.* "Toni, this bracelet is beautiful. Thank you so much."

Rene held hers up in the light. "Girl, thank you. You know my cheap behind never had anything like this."

Hooking the bracelet on her wrist, Ava planned to wear it to complete the perfect dress, shoes, and handbag she'd bought the day before to stand by Toni's side at the altar. *Whew! It fits.* Kevin would probably notice it first thing, and the bracelet could serve as a good conversation starter.

"Well, since we're giving gifts now." Ava took her purse off of the back of her chair and dug out a greeting card and handed it to Toni. "This is from me and Rene."

"Ahh, you guys really didn't have to. You gave me a gift the first time around." She laughed nervously.

"Stop saying stuff like that, Toni. This is just as special as the first time. Enjoy what God is doing in your relationship."

Toni smiled and slid the card out. As she opened it, a gift card fell out on the table. Ava picked it up and handed it to her. "This is a one hundred dollar gift card to Victoria's Secret. So when y'all go on your second honeymoon, you can buy some new lingerie. You and Eric have a new cause, which calls for some new drawers!"

Each of them burst out in laughter. Toni was almost in tears. They toasted Toni's new beginning, while going over the timeline for the event the next day. As they ate and conversed, Ava couldn't believe how much everything in her life had turned around for the better. God's better.

Ava rode the emotional rollercoaster for most of the year. But she was healthier for it. Healthier inside and out. Her relationships had been restored, she found inner peace with who she was in Christ, and whether she had a man or not, she was a complete woman in God. He lifted her out of her own hell and placed her feet on solid ground. From that point on, no matter the circumstances around her, Ava would hold on to Him and never let go.

Chapter 40

In the ladies' lounge just behind the sanctuary, Ava and Rene assisted Toni with getting ready for her ceremony. Eric's sister, Dana, helped by setting up the electric fan to cool her down. Toni raised her arms as the three of them lifted her dress over her head and carefully laid it over her body in a flowing-like manner.

Ava pictured what her wedding day would be like. She knew the where, the when, and the how. Her issue was the who. The colors would be similar to Toni's, with purple being the main attraction, and she would let someone else cook for her. All the details had been planned out to the letter during the course of her twenty-nine years. God just never let her in on the most important detail. Who would be standing there waiting to receive her as his wife, as her father passed her along with his blessing?

The one thing Ava was not envious of was Toni's thin frame. That was even difficult for her to believe. With her eating better, working out, and losing some weight, her goal changed to be the best she could be, instead of being a version of someone else's best. God made her in His image. And if she allowed the funny looks of others and their snide comments determine her value, or continued to down herself, she was downing God's handiwork. And who was she to put her two cents in on what God created?

Toni and Eric's guests packed the church. As Ava walked down the aisle, she acted like the nuptials were her own. Smiling and stepping, each stride was timed appropriately. *Left, right. Left, right.* She enjoyed the procession, consumed by the moment and the attention. Pastor Monroe nodded toward her as she arrived at her destination and took her spot. When she turned to face the onlookers, the beauty of the cream and purple flowers, candles, and soft music increased the want for her day in the wedding dress to be sooner rather than later.

Eric seemed on the brink of tears as Toni glided to him. His smile seemed to grow larger with each step she took toward him. Pastor prayed a prayer for the service and the union, and then asked the guests to have a seat.

The soloist from the church crooned a love song, while Toni and Eric stared into one another's eyes. After they exchanged vows and new wedding bands, the lovebirds lit a unity candle. Pastor Monroe then explained the importance of the couples prayer and what it meant for their union. Pastor Sandra got up from her seat in the front row and handed Eric a framed copy of the prayer as Pastor handed them a microphone.

Eric and Toni read the heartfelt words in unison:

"Dear Lord, we come before You in agreement asking that You would cover our relationship and marriage. We vow to love and respect one another as your Word says. We know You have a plan and a purpose for bringing us together. May we see it through until its completion. We thank You for the grace You've shown us as individuals and as a couple. And when we have an issue with one another, please help us to forgive quickly, as You forgive, and move past it. May we be in your will and honor You with our lives, as we strive to be a blessing to those around us. We love You and thank You for loving us. In Jesus' name, Amen."

Sniffles scattered around the room, along with a few amens. Pastor prayed over them as a renewed couple in the eyes of the Lord and then gave Eric permission to salute his bride. As they shared a passionate lip lock, cheers rang all over the sanctuary. Toni and Eric marched back down the aisle hand in hand while everyone stood and clapped them down the walkway.

It was now time to celebrate the night away. Ava needed to gather her belongings as quickly as possible, so she could go oversee the crew hired to serve the food. She changed into more comfortable shoes, turned her phone off silent, and headed for the door. Before she could make it into the banquet hall in the next building over, her phone's ringtone went off.

When Ava viewed Kevin's name on the screen of her cell phone, butterflies fluttered about in her stomach. He'd probably gotten lost on his way to the church and needed directions instead of following the GPS lady's voice. The church sat back off of a main street and many people had gotten turned around. She'd help him find his way to the church. And to her.

"Hi, Ava." His voice sounded dry and monotonous.

"Is everything okay? Are you lost?"

"Actually, I'm not going to make it."

Ava's heart sank into the pit of her stomach and knocked the butterflies right out of the way. "Not coming?"

"Yeah, I apologize. It's Curtis. The guy I was with at the hospital a few weeks ago."

"Mmh?"

"He's going through some things and asked me to come by. He's been clean for five days and is going through some sort of withdrawals." The breaking in his voice made his words give the impression he was regretfully sincere.

"I understand." *No, I don't.* Ava had looked forward to this all week. Shoot, the past few weeks. "Take care of him, and I'll keep you both in prayer."

"I appreciate you being so understanding. I'll give you a call and we can hang out sometime this week."

Yeah, that's better. Not! "Okay, good luck with everything."

She tossed the phone back in her purse. *Figures.* Her flesh took over. Being understanding and wanting what you wanted when you wanted it was hard to balance. The past couple of months of engaging in a friendship with Kevin, she had raised her hopes too high. This was how things always turned out. Why should this day be any different? Yes, he was a godly man. And yes, he was helping someone. But to Ava it appeared to be the same story on a different day.

Chapter 41

Lavender and white roses floating in clear water created the centerpieces for each table. Guests devoured Ava's appetizers, which she was thrilled about. But even more thrilling was seeing the glow on Toni's face as she gazed into Eric's eyes. The couple walked around arm in arm, greeting partygoers and stopping to share a kiss every time their eyes met or someone in the reception tapped an eating utensil on their glass.

Ava kept an eye on the food, making sure plenty was available, while she periodically checked her phone, hoping Kevin would call back and say he was on his way. The call on Kevin's life to help those struggling with addiction was honorable and important to him, but her desire to have a date for the reception trumped everything. She didn't want to be selfish, but couldn't help how she felt. Being with him in a social setting would help her navigate through their relationship.

Wanting to remain positive and enjoy Toni's day, Ava went about her catering and mingled with the guests. However, on occasion, her eyes traveled to the banquet hall doors, hoping they'd burst open and Kevin would traipse through them, run to her, and hold her in his arms. He didn't even have to run. He could slowly walk. Or even crawl. As long as it was in her direction.

Dr. Moses, sitting at a table adjacent to the dance floor, shared an intense conversation with the man next to her. Ava wasn't sure if she wanted to roll up on their discussion, but before she could turn around, her and Dr. Glory's eyes met and she motioned for Ava to come over.

Ava scooted over to them, smiling. "Hello, Dr. Moses."

"Hey, Ava. I told you not to be so formal. You're not my patient anymore, you're my friend."

"Sorry. I meant Glory. I'll have to get used to that." Ava smiled.

"You do that." She nodded toward the gentleman beside her. "This is my husband, Gregory."

He was a nice-looking man, slender built with almond-shaped eyes and curly eyelashes that went on for days, but his body language didn't read so pleasant. "Hello, Ava."

"Nice to meet you." Ava pointed to them. "That's cute. Gregory and Glory. It must've been meant to be."

Dr. Moses gave an uncomfortable giggle. While Ava made small talk, Gregory slumped in his chair, looking like he'd rather be anywhere else than that reception. Ava remembered his struggle with his job search and figured whatever issue they were currently having probably stemmed from his frustration. As far as Ava could tell, Glory seemed to have it together. Meeting her husband gave her a different perception of what Dr. Moses' life situation might be outside the office.

Ava, grateful single ladies were called to the dance floor for the toss of the bouquet, shot forward to claim her spot on the floor. Toni waited for all interested women to take their places. She faced the stage, back to the ladies, and counted to three. Her first toss, a fake throw, grew the excitement and received a few boos from the geared-up group of women.

The second count to three sent the bouquet flying in the air in an arch-shaped line, and women began pushing and shoving with their hands fully extended. Ava pulled an old block-out technique from her basketball days as if she were getting a rebound. A couple women hit the floor in amusement as she swiped the bouquet out the air.

Laughter filled the reception hall and a few bystanders fell out almost in tears. Ava fixed her clothes, putting everything back in place, and wiped her dress down. She smiled, held up the bouquet, and received cheers in her honor. After she and Toni took a picture with the prize, they scooted over to the wedding party table where Rene was already sitting.

Taking a seat between Rene and Toni, Ava sipped her water and searched for the right words to say. One friend was high on the mountaintop while the other was down in the valley. "Why didn't you hop out there and go for the bouquet, Rene?"

"I'm not ready. I don't need any bouquet." She grinned. "I'm happy you caught it though."

Toni leaned over to see Rene straight on. "Girl, you'll need it one day. You know, I can always introduce you to my cousin Cletus Jr. He's been looking for a holy hookup."

"Yeah, Rene, there he goes now." Ava smirked.

Cletus Jr., complete with powder blue tuxedo and eighties box haircut, busted his moves on the dance floor.

Rene waved her hands in the air. "No, I'm good."

Ava swayed in her seat back and forth. So much in her life had changed, it was almost unreal. But one key issue that had been resolved inside of her was the fact that she did not have to focus on if she would get asked to dance. If she wanted to, she had no problem jumping out on the dance floor herself. Cletus even made it look fun, like it used to be when she was younger, before she started thinking too much.

Nor would she focus on how many purses may or may not be under her care that night. Ava's mindset had changed. She was living and breathing proof of Romans 12:2. Her mind was transformed, renewed, and searching God's will for her life. Not only had she been given a revelation about her catering business, now called Manna Catering, but she knew that serving as a prayer partner in her church was a part of her calling. Ava was doing exactly what she was supposed to be doing at this time in her life.

"We've come a long way this past year. Aren't you guys just thankful?" Ava wanted to check in with Rene and Toni and see if they were on her page as well.

Toni popped in first, as usual. "Lord knows I am. God restored my marriage and I know He did it and not me, because y'all know I wasn't feeling Eric anymore. But my love for him was always there, and the Lord reconciled that and so much more between us. I pray you guys experience this love whenever God believes you're ready."

"Well, I am thankful too." Rene slapped the table when she spoke the word "too." "I am going to step out on faith. I'm going to put in my resignation at the state prosecutor's office and open my own practice. I've been too scared to do it being hitched on to Ishmael because I wanted to make sure one of us had a steady income. But it has always been a dream of mine to go into business for myself. And I'm going to do it." She hit the table again. "And I believe I dodged a very big bullet not marrying Ishmael. And through all the pain and struggle, I have my best friend back."

Ava placed her hand over Rene's. God was in that situation for sure. Only He could turn Rene's heart back toward Ava's in forgiveness. And now they could join Toni on the mountaintop.

"I feel like this is Thanksgiving. You know, before you eat, everyone goes around the table and shares what they're thankful for." They all giggled as tears filled the corners of Ava's eyes. "But I certainly am thankful to have my best friend back as well. And I'm also thankful I've learned to not only love, but like who I am in Christ. I see myself through the eyes of the Lord now and I must say, I like what I see. God is good!"

"All the time!" Rene and Toni spoke together.

Ava smiled. "And all the time!"

"God is good!"

Picking up her fork to cut a sliver of the last of her cake, Ava took in every good thing in the room. When her eyes reached the banquet hall doors, her heart danced the twist. There Kevin stood, all six feet two inches of him, broad-chested, in a fitted suit, magnetic to Ava's heart.

Their eyes met and he cruised over to her table. "Good evening, beautiful. I made it after all."

Yes, you did. "I see. What a surprise." Giddiness controlled her actions. "I thought you got caught up with your sponsee?"

"I let another sponsor take him to a meeting. I wanted to be here." He nodded. "With you."

Ava's soul double-dutched. "I'm glad you came."

He placed a violet corsage on her wrist. His old-school ways were endearing. "Have you been sitting here long?"

"No, we just sat down after I caught the bouquet."

"Oh, you caught the bouquet, huh?" Kevin snickered.

"Yes." *Hopefully, for our wedding-to-be one day.* Ava couldn't help herself.

"Well, how about you leave the flowers here for just a minute? I wanted to know . . ." He paused. "Would you like to dance?"

Would I like to dance? Heck, yeah! Was this really happening? She wanted to pinch herself, but if it was a dream, she wasn't ready to wake up. Toni and Rene were sitting right there and he wanted to be there. With her. Ava needed to like herself first before anyone else could. And she, with God's help, had accomplished that.

Something good came out of all her mess. Actually, three positives accompanied her out of her pit. She gained a better self-image, a deeper relationship with God, and of course, there was Kevin. The Lord had squeezed, poked, and prodded her lemons into lemonade.

Ava stood, clutching the strap of her lavender purse. She froze and turned to put the designer handbag on the table. Smiling at Rene and Toni, she asked them, "Will you watch my purse?" before being led on the dance floor, where she gladly danced the night away.

About The Author

Keisha Bass has a bachelor's degree in kinesiology with a minor in English and holds teaching certificates in English, speech, and physical education. She has been a teacher and coach for fourteen years, and currently teaches middle school physical education and coaches girls' volleyball and softball. She grew up in Houston, Texas, but now resides in Arlington, Texas. Keisha is also vice president of the DFW Ready Writers, a local chapter of American Christian Fiction Writers, and a member of North Texas Christian Writers.

Permanent Resident at the Purse Table is Keisha's first novel. She has published nonfiction articles in magazines and two online publications, TheChristianPulse.com and sober24.com. Her article "Heart Problems" was published in *Chicken Soup for the Soul: A Book of Miracles.*

Readers' Guide Questions

1. Ava's prayer at the beginning seems sincere. Do you think she truly believes she can overcome her past behavior where men are concerned? Have you ever prayed a prayer that you weren't totally confident in? What was the result?

2. In chapter 1, Ava compares herself to Rene and Toni physically. What do you think drives us to compare ourselves to others?

3. Xavier has had a mental hold over Ava. Do you feel if she had a better self-image, she would've been able to let him go sooner? Have you ever been in this position? How did you respond?

4. In chapter 8, Ava's mother calls and compares Ava to her brother. Have you ever been a part of a sibling rivalry? Was it one you created, or was it parent-driven? How has this judgmental behavior of her mother affected their relationship?

5. After Ava and Ishmael sleep together in chapter 8, Ava immediately feels regret. Have you ever done anything you knew was wrong, but went ahead with it because you felt important, special, or loved? What was the result?

6. In chapter 12, Ava prepares to tell Rene what happened between her and Ishmael. Do you think you'd be able to fess up to your friend? Why or why not?

7. In chapter 19, after Ava learns she's pregnant, she has suicidal thoughts. Sometimes we have to hit our

rock bottom for our eyes to truly be opened to the self-destruction we are committing. Have you ever gone through this? How'd you handle it? How did this scene affect you?

8. When Dr. Moses prays over Ava, she says that Ava is "fearfully and wonderfully made." Do you feel that way about yourself? If not, what has kept you from thinking this about yourself?

9. Sometimes it takes a tragedy to bring people together. After Ava is struck by a car and put in the hospital, Rene comes to visit her even though they haven't spoken in months. Have you ever overcome a struggle with a close friend? Did the relationship go back to normal or did you treat each other differently than before?

10. In the last chapter, Ava says that she must like herself before anyone else can. How do you feel about that statement?

11. The last line of the novel, Ava gets to ask her friends to watch her purse, something she's had to do all her adult life. How do you think this monumental moment added to her confidence to move forward in who she is at the end of the novel?

UC HIS GLORY BOOK CLUB!

www.uchisglorybookclub.net

UC His Glory Book Club is the spirit-inspired brain-child of Joylynn Ross, Author and Acquisitions Editor of Urban Christian, and Kendra Norman-Bellamy, Author for Urban Christian. This is an online book club that hosts authors of Urban Christian. We welcome as members all men and women who have a passion for reading Christian-based fiction.

UC His Glory Book Club pledges our commitment to provide support, positive feedback, encouragement, and a forum whereby members can openly discuss and review the literary works of Urban Christian authors.

There is no membership fee associated with UC His Glory Book Club; however, we do ask that you support the authors through purchasing, encouraging, providing book reviews, and of course, your prayers. We also ask that you respect our beliefs and follow the guidelines of the book club. We hope to receive your valuable input, opinions, and reviews that build up, rather than tear down our authors.

What We Believe:

—We believe that Jesus is the Christ, Son of the Living God.

—We believe the Bible is the true, living Word of God.

—We believe all Urban Christian authors should use their God-given writing abilities to honor God and share the message of the written word God has given to each of them uniquely.

—We believe in supporting Urban Christian authors in their literary endeavors by reading, purchasing and sharing their titles with our online community.

—We believe that in everything we do in our literary arena should be done in a manner that will lead to God being glorified and honored.

We look forward to the online fellowship with you. Please visit us often at *www.uchisglorybookclub.net.*

Many Blessings to You!

Shelia E. Lipsey,
President, UC His Glory Book Club